FILTHY CREATION

FILTHY CREATION

Caroline Hagood

MADHAT PRESS
CHESHIRE, MASSACHUSETTS

MadHat Press
MadHat Incorporated
PO Box 422, Cheshire, MA 01225

The Library of Congress has assigned
this edition a Control Number of
2023931929

ISBN 978-1-952335-56-3 (paperback)

Words by Caroline Hagood
Photo by Alice Teeple
Cover design by Marc Vincenz

www.MadHat-Press.com

First Printing
Printed in the United States of America

For Adriel, Max, and Layla

For all my beloved art monsters

A thinking woman sleeps with monsters
—Adrienne Rich

Chapter One

Here's what I know so far. My father had a birthmark on his neck that looked like Europe, and I have a group of freckles on my arm that resembles a constellation. He once joked that he was a continent, and I might secretly be a group of stars. I loved the idea that my humble freckles were undercover astronomical matter, that I might actually be something larger than a girl. I got that sense when I made my sculptures—like when I created, I was doing something astronomical, spewing energy into outer space.

Here's something else I know. All good things come to an end, even continents and stars. Only in art can they live forever. Listen and I'll tell you the tale of how my life split open at eighteen, in my senior year of high school. It all started the night my parents called that family meeting.

We sat at the dining room table. Mom smoothed her hair repeatedly. Dad looked smaller, dug for something in his pocket for too long, smiled too wide, the sides of his mouth moving down without his permission, renegades.

"Ray?" Mom said.

He covered his face. "Jane, I can't."

"Okay," she said. Mom had always been braver than Dad. Her eyes were glassy. "Dylan," she continued, "Dad's cancer. It's not getting better. We need to just try to enjoy one another right now." It took me a minute to react because the words were so odd. *Enjoy one another?* This wasn't how she talked. It was something she'd read on a grief website.

We all sat there in perfect stillness, as though we'd passed into another dimension. Maybe we were all floating in that same celestial sphere as my constellation freckles. Or at least that's where my mind went as it tried to run away.

I'd been quiet too long. "Dylan, don't you even care?" Mom snapped. Her tone so sharp I pictured an all-shielding birdcage around my big, leaky heart.

"Of course I do. Immensely. You know that. I'm sorry but it's just a lot to take in. Dad you get it, right?" I asked.

He nodded, but, as usual, didn't stand up for me. He survived by tiptoeing around her moods, same as I did. I wished just this once he'd stop being a doormat, rise up and say, "Never speak to our precious daughter like that ever again, you pernicious harpy." Although I meant no offense to harpies.

Instead, he looked out the window, said, "Nice weather we're having, eh, ladies?" The comedic timing perfect, thunder booming just as he'd finished his sentence.

To distract myself, I fixed my eyes on Mom's sculpture of Medusa beyond the dining room table. Mom had made Medusa her last year of art school, before she'd gotten pregnant with me, dropped out, and given up what Dad said was quite the promising art career. Mom had applied a multicolored finish to the aluminum. But as a child I'd pictured her painting actual rainbows onto Medusa's metallic skin. Instead of Perseus holding Medusa's decapitated head, she held his. Medusa's eyes were unexpectedly warm, emitting the otherworldly glow you often see in mothers looking at their children, which would make Perseus's head her bizarre baby.

Medusa's snakes in particular were exquisite. Mom had welded them into a labyrinth I'd been trying to decode since I was little. They had always communicated to me that being a woman was to be a chimera, part this, part that, marvelous, powerful, and always bound to evade definition, just like Mom. But the snakes were also a warning. Look what happens to potent women: they end up with cobras for hair. Look what happens to women artists who become pregnant like Mom did: she was now a secretary at my artsy high school instead of a professional artist herself.

I found myself rising from the table to go to Medusa, as I had so many times when feeling down over the years. I traced her snaked head gently, looking out the window, hoping to see Shay.

And there she was. After school, she could often be found making her ornate chalk drawings of fantastical creatures on the sidewalk in front of Brooklyn Arts. I couldn't help but feel an affinity for this strange girl who seemed as obsessed as I was with myth, magic, and monsters. I could still remember Shay's first day of school freshman year like it was the moon landing, a celestial event that would change everything, fitting for the likes of continents and stars.

I knew this was how everyone felt about their first love, but I swore it was different with me, that I'd gone so far around the amorous moon I could no longer be compared with those earthlings and their wishy-washy high school sentiments. Shay's mom, Ms. Burgess, also happened to be my favorite teacher at Brooklyn Arts, and they lived in the faculty housing complex across from ours.

My parents bickered in the background but it only registered as static as I watched Shay loosening her hair from a post-shower towel turban, her weapon of a body hidden under another striped towel. As she unwound her hair, I hallucinated Medusa snakes falling out of there. That hair was the kind of black you could imagine snaking all the light from the room if it happened to, say, fall over your face in bed. Not that I imagined that obsessively. No siree.

Shay walked over to the bed and for an instant stood, glistening and naked, in the garish radiance of her red lava lamp. Playing all over her body were the stars of her planetarium projector.

But even Shay wasn't enough to distract me. Mom was now rubbing Dad's back a little too hard so that his body moved beneath her hand like a marionette. He was unable to make eye contact. Mom was making too much eye contact, trying too hard as always to make me feel seen. I felt less seen and more, like, eyeball-fucked, but I appreciated the gesture anyhow. How was it possible to feel so many incongruous emotions at one time about a single person? As Mom stared at me across the table until her eyes bugged out, I basked in her gigantic, irritating, anxious, messy, ferocious love. I fed on it, in fact.

There always seemed to be some shared dark energy between Mom and me. Maybe that was even why we fought: because we saw each other too well. Like the time I stayed up all night trying to craft the perfect papier-mâché piñata for my tenth birthday because I'd just found out Grandma died. Mom got it. She plied me with tissue paper and other provisions while Dad just made some joke about my morning breath. But she'd still yelled at me afterward for staying up all night. She was scared, maybe, that I'd end up like her.

Mom was still moving her hand over Dad's back. Absurdly, I prayed that I could make my art into something supernatural that could cure him and then proceeded to ugly-cry, my face becoming fluid, rocking back and forth. I hoped I was doing this grief thing right. In the most awkward maneuver ever, Mom ran around the table, yanked me out of the chair, plonked herself down, and then pulled me onto her lap, which was not easy given how much smaller she was.

There was something about being close to her body that reminded me how I'd come out of there, how it had been my first house. Even though they'd let my father cut it at the hospital, I could still see the invisible umbilical cord that connected me to my mother. Eleanor Roosevelt hung her first baby in a cage outside the window of her Manhattan apartment until a neighbor threatened to call child services. The cage was the brainchild of Emma Reade of Spokane, Washington, who patented the idea in 1922, and distributed the first cages to members of London's Chelsea Baby Club in 1937. The coops were meant to give city kids a hanging backyard of sorts, an outside still connected to an inside, much like, I figured, motherhood. Where Mom's skin touched mine, it tingled with memory, because, as I saw it, that's what happens when someone comes out of your body—they sort of stay a part of it.

I sank my head into her neck, leaving snail paths of snot. She smelled salty and sharp as I sobbed into her skin. I gathered her long hair in my hands and scrunched it as I'd done since I was small.

That feeling was everything. She smoothed my short hair and did her rub-rub-pat-pat thing on my back, too hard as always, but it felt wonderful.

It hit me for the first time that this was not only happening to me. This was Mom's person too, the one she'd made a life with, who was "terminally ill." I sobbed then as much for Mom and Dad as for myself. I got off her lap, sat on the chair next to her, put a hand on either side of her face, and said, "I got you."

She looked touched and nodded, saying, "I know, kiddo. But you don't always have to take care of me. It's my job to take care of you, you know. I'm sorry I screw that up sometimes." Her self-awareness made things both better and worse somehow. When she was lucid like this, I always felt, incorrectly, that she'd never be snippy with me again.

Dad came over and sat on the other side of me, holding Mom's hand across my lap and squeezing. It was our family's Morse Code. You had to squeeze back the number of times you were squeezed, or basically the other person would think you were mad at them. This time I could feel Dad continuously squeezing Mom's hand, as though if he stopped, everything would stop. From the way Mom flinched, I could see her hand was starting to hurt. But I also saw the determination on her face. She would have sat there and let him squeeze as long as he needed to, even until her flesh turned to mush, because that's what he bloody needed and she bloody loved him.

Sitting there like that felt complete. It occurred to me that, all sitting in a row, equally grim, we probably looked batshit crazy. Then I wondered if other people saw themselves from the outside all the time, like they were always in a movie. Why does it always feel like someone's watching, even when I'm alone? Is this a modern sensibility? An urban sensibility? A feminine sensibility? Or do men always feel this pair of outside eyes, too?

I used Dad's shirt to mop my face because I knew it would make him giggle, and it did. He then put me in a gentle headlock, impish as always, despite the topic of the night. I must have still looked pretty serious because he did the thing where he tickled me under the chin like I was a small dog and said, "Whatever you do, don't smile. I mean it. Under no circumstances. Absolutely, positively no smiling." And of course, that's right when I finally smiled, a crescent moon.

Mom didn't approve of the roughhousing, and I braced for her to order us to stop. But instead, she leaned close and whispered in my ear too wetly, hotly, loudly, "Want to make a piñata?" And I did. Very much.

Chapter Two

For the papier-mâché, Mom poured in the flour and Dad added the water to make a sort of gelatinous snow. All our hands in the bucket to squish the lumps away, the feeling of our fingers sliding into the white abyss was calming.

As I tore the newspaper into strips, Mom asked, "What shape are we doing?"

As I thought of losing the one cheerful member of the family, I madly leafed through the remaining newspapers, ripped out only the obituary sections, and created a black and white epitaph, long strips of torn obituaries glued together into an incoherent message that made total sense to me: My one-of-a-kind father was dying.

"It's not bad, actually," Dad said, leaning back with his hands clasped behind his head, looking somber, then gently pulling a strip of newspaper out of my hair.

Mom put her hands around my shoulder, looking proudly at my work.

That night Dad fell asleep on the living room couch, and I smooshed myself in beside him. It was the sort of intimacy I hadn't had with him in years, since that age when things become weird between you and your dad's body. But it didn't seem to matter anymore. I decided I had to explore him so I could remember every detail. I would archive him.

His hair was gray and white now, but the chest hair that peeped out of his pajama top was still a deep dark hue and seemed to cover all of him like a fur coat. I went in to look closer.

From that viewpoint, each individual hair had little roots. I realized I was surveying a mighty hair forest. I took a whiff. It smelled like dark fruit. There was a hint of plum. There were even small drops of sweat, streams in the forest.

I buried my head in his chest, inhaling what might have been the most concentrated essence of Dad I'd ever encountered. Like I could eat his spirit. It smelled musty and also like a pinecone. This was the only way I knew how to love something, by wanting to taste every part of it, and this was too much. I was too much.

Dad was a deep sleeper, so I knew he wouldn't wake up, even when I mushed my face directly against his, nose-to-nose, cheek-to-cheek, forehead to forehead. We were one face. Wetness developing where he breathed against my skin and where my tears rolled down his stubbly cheeks. No end or beginning.

I said, probably too loudly since I was my mother's daughter, "Stay with me forever. Don't leave me, Papa." The sadness was so complete. What would it even be like not to exist anymore? For my father? For me? Would I still exist if my father didn't? Before I could go any further down this rabbit hole, Dad stirred. It felt like he had risen from the dead.

His features did a twitchy dance. He made a snuffling sound, opened his eyes, and then quickly jerked his head back, unable to place what was directly in front of him. He was understandably not used to waking to his daughter suction-cupped to his face. His now-open eyes upset me because I could imagine how I'd have felt if they'd never opened again. Somehow, I didn't know what else to do but rehearse losing him repeatedly.

"Aw, don't be sad, Bear," he said, pulling me back close to him.

"Okay," I said, like this would work.

"Listen, my girl. I must tell you something before it's too late. And this is very important to get out. You see, I'm not exactly who Mom and I have said I am."

He looked ready to launch into some confession but then pulled back after I gave him a *what the hell?* look. For a moment it seemed like he wasn't sure what to do, but then he launched into a fit of giggles. I mean, my dad laughed a lot, usually at his own jokes, but he didn't typically *giggle*. There was a false note in his voice.

"I'm just messing with you, kid," he said.

"Wait, no you're not. I can tell," I said.

Then, in a misguided attempt to lighten the mood, he told a joke, as usual. "Here's one I haven't told you yet, I swear. Pixar finally made a movie for people with cancer. It's called 'Finding Chemo.'" He attempted a weak laugh, but I just glared at him.

"We said no more cancer jokes." We'd had to make this rule right after he got the diagnosis, about a year ago. For a few days there, as we all tried to figure out a treatment plan and convince ourselves everything would be okay, it was just nonstop jokes, a marathon comedy special all about tumors.

"You should get to bed," he said, not meeting my eyes. "So should I. It's late. No rest for the malignant, eh?"

I sighed and let whatever near-confession slip away for now. He was right; it was late, and I couldn't handle any more bad news tonight.

When I got to my own bed, I crawled under the covers, into that childhood land of safety. As the fabric fluttered down, it almost felt like the outside world might go away. Now you see it, now you don't. Like I could start fresh, maybe build a new world out of all this one's messed-up pieces.

I had this bear with one missing eye that I still slept with even though I was too old, and I hugged him tightly as I lay awake replaying Dad's words: "I'm not exactly who Mom and I have said I am." What did that even mean? Was Dad a mole for the CIA? Did he have a secret second family in Schenectady? I regretted not having been brave enough to receive his confession but with all the bad news lately, I was afraid to break him—or me—if I asked anything further.

As I got up to go to the bathroom, I caught sight of the haunting obituary-cum-piñata I'd made. It wasn't half bad. I usually hated my own art, but this … this was the kind of thing I could imagine submitting as part of a portfolio. Dad had always been the biggest proponent of my applying for the Clay art scholarship, so I felt inspired, in honor of him, to finish the application I'd been too chickenshit to complete before.

As I woke my computer, I basked in its comforting glow that assured me I was still there. I tried not to read the grandiose language on the Clay website too closely. Who comes up with this stuff, anyway? The scholarship was, "Designed to give one the freedom to pursue one's greatest passion, deepen one's creative practice, and develop one's oeuvre alongside fellow artists in the burgeoning metropolis of New York." What a mouthful.

In truth, I felt as drawn to the glittering art scene's decadence as I was repelled by it. It was the opposite of my father's unpretentious gift for fixing cars and making furniture. Sometimes I went to museums with Mom and marveled at those artless canvases that sold for a boatload. Yet, if you'd seen Dad fix a truck in his shop or build a table out of car parts in the basement, you'd understand art. He'd take me to the junkyard after work to show me the things you could make out of what seemed like garbage. In my eyes, he was a visionary. He once showed me how to make a chair out of a totaled truck. It was exquisite. The way Mom hurried us home from the junkyard that night, I think she was jealous.

I'd recently become obsessed with a type of art known as assemblage, or the creation of multidimensional collages, with ancient origins, no doubt, but I prefer the version of the story in which this dude Jean Dubuffet constructed a series of collages made from butterfly wings in the 1950s. He was not the first but, I mean, butterfly wings. To watch Dad take a car apart and then make from it the city of Oz was to witness assemblage at its best. I get that the art world wouldn't acknowledge him, but screw them; he was a true artist.

Still, I must have been wide open to all that art-world BS on some level, since I did spend a whole hour filling out that dreary paperwork. I probably wasn't going to get it anyway. These things just didn't happen to people like me who were just normal-level talented, but it didn't stop me from wishing to be a meteorite.

It was the same scholarship Mom had gotten all those years ago, the one that sent her to NYIA—until she got pregnant and dropped out. Admittedly, I hoped it might go a little differently for me. To finish the application, all I had to do was create the artwork that could impress the committee members, crack open all that came before, dissolve every image that had previously defined the field. You would recognize it as that dark, precious thing inside you never dare talk about. But was I capable of such a thing? By age fourteen Picasso had already painted that evocative portrait of his sister Lola in *The First Communion* and even his *Portrait of Aunt Pepa,* which one art critic called, "without a doubt one of the greatest in the whole history of Spanish painting."

As I passed the full-length mirror, I caught a glimpse of something monstrous that, on second inspection, was just myself without my contacts in. But I felt I'd seen my own art monster beckoning to me from the shores of creative lands I couldn't yet reach. Or could I? But how?

Like Dr. Frankenstein from my favorite book, I longed to *pioneer a new way, explore unknown powers, and unfold to the world the deepest mysteries of creation.* But with Dad sick, grief seemed to shrivel my artistic faculties. I was terrified I'd have to follow in Mom's footsteps. I often heard her crying at night in her bedroom. I didn't want to embarrass her, but I wanted to comfort her, so I'd press my hand against the wall between our rooms, just hoping she could feel it.

I opened the closet in my room where I kept art materials. Ever since I was little, Mom had showed me how to trawl the streets for other people's garbage and haul it home to make my creations. Tonight's makeshift plan was to use the hot glue gun she'd given me to secure a unicorn horn, actually a Prospect Park pinecone, to the ghost horse that I imagined to be Dad, actually a child's discarded My Little Pony. Then I'd place this hybrid Dadly monster in some newly constructed land, made entirely from the car parts Dad and I had collected over the years, where it would be safe from the angry villagers and, of course, from loss or illness of any kind.

After spreading out supplies like an artistic *mise en place,* I glanced out the window and caught sight of Shay again. She suddenly ran over to her chalkboard wall and started scrawling what appeared to be a heartbroken angel—the heart shattering into blue bits. I feared this was somehow autobiographical and had to stop myself from running over there and comforting her. The angel's mind was illustrated as a cartoon thought-bubble, three times the size of the angel herself. Inside the bubble were little scenes of suffering, like Shay was some medieval miniaturist reincarnated in modern-day Brooklyn. There were ghosts and ghouls in various scenes of pursuit, and at the center of the angel's mind cowered a crying girl I feared was Shay. With the news I'd just received, maybe I feared that sad girl was also somehow me.

Shay orchestrated off-the-chain contradictory impulses in me, stuff you can't even write in a locked diary: her genius was something I wanted to autopsy but keep alive, to both protect and eat, gather all its pixels and swallow so I could feel them inside me, understand what made them virtuosic, feel Shay Burgess swimming inside my veins like a minnow. Loving Shay was a commitment.

Shay was now drawing furiously, her hair troubling her eyes until she blew it up and away. She paused for a moment, and then her face crumpled, and she appeared to be screaming so hard it shook her whole body and made me tremble. I felt that tickle in my nose like I might cry too. I liked to feel things along with her because that's being in love. I wanted to run across the way and hold her like a baby, but we weren't even friends. As I saw it, my mystery to solve was this: what could possibly make the magnificent Shay cry like that? Maybe it was the fact that her father had died not too long ago. As I made the connection, I felt Shay was feeling for me all the emotions I hadn't yet let in. Which placed Shay and her angel right at the center of my own interior museum of pain.

I pictured Shay in some absurd actual museum inside me, covered with my guts and stuff, and Medusa's snakes laughing with their own lipsticked cartoon mouths at the whole batshit proposition.

But then I brought my attention back to my work. My room became a mystical kingdom lit by the accidental shimmer of the X-Acto blade as it knifed through cardboard to create the floor of my ghost horse's future dwelling.

But I only made it as far as hot-gluing the pinecone to a broken My Little Pony before deciding I had no talent and hated everything about the stupid ghost horse.

I told myself I wouldn't do it. I willed myself to cease and desist. But there I was, in a trance, taking what I'd made, a lighter, and some lighter fluid, and heading toward the building's courtyard.

Mom had made me see the first of many shrinks at the age of five, when I set my first fire. What can I say? I was a pyro right from the start. I knew I was supposed to feel ashamed of it, but I didn't. I'd spent my life stalking that blue part of the flame. Have you ever truly watched fire's color progression? Seen an origami bird catch fire, then turn to ash?

I had no real way of describing why I made fires, outside of saying it felt like a creative compulsion, but emphasis on the *creative*, and all these shrinks wanted to talk about was the *compulsion* part. I always pictured them catching fire like Roman candles themselves as they finger-wagged for forty-five minutes. Then I'd leave, sparking up a cigarette on my way out.

On this night, I yearned to set something ablaze, so I took my middling art out to the grill in the courtyard. I figured if I was safe about it, setting fires where they were meant to be set should be okay.

I felt better as I saw that shock of flame, the fingers of smoke, smelled the burning rubber of the toy pony, the woodsy tang of the pinecone. But I also felt extra shitty for burning this one, since this was supposed to be the artwork that could secure Dad's miracle salvation.

When I turned to go back inside, Mom was standing there. The red light of the flames played on her face, making her appear spectral, giving me a little chill.

"How long have you been there? I'm sorry. Are you mad?" I asked, a knot in my stomach.

"You just remind me of someone, that's all," she said, as though from a distance.

"Who? Dad?"

"Yes, well, no. Never mind. It's not important. Why do you do it, Dylan? Why do you destroy things? Why do you destroy what you take all that time to make?"

"I—I honestly don't know. I feel like I freak you out with the fires and it—it makes me feel bad."

"I'm sorry you feel that way."

"Well, do I?"

"What?"

"Freak you out?"

"To be honest, Dylan, you do a little. What teenage girl needs to set things on fire like this?"

"What does my being a girl have to do with it?"

She sighed and rephrased. "What *person* needs to?"

"Now you're really making me feel bad."

"Sorry," she said.

"Sorry," I echoed, hanging my head.

She came up behind me, put a sweatshirt over my shoulders and wrapped an arm around me.

But then she gave me an eerie look as she picked up the lighter fluid and poured some more on the grill fire. It rose as if in surprise, crackling. We jumped back in shock.

"Mom, what are you doing? You're not supposed to put lighter fluid on a live fire."

She didn't look apologetic. For an instant she looked wild, elated, a smirk on her face like the whole thing was comical. Then she seemed to rein it in, becoming my mother again.

"You're right, Dyl, that wasn't very safe of me. Let's go back inside and have some tea, okay?"

I let her lead me in, wondering about this different Mom I had just seen. Feeling confused and excited by this other mother who'd fanned the flames.

After she fell asleep, I still wasn't feeling sleepy, so I sat by the window in my room and twirled my rolling papers into the most perfectly formed joint I'd ever made. I wished I could submit it as my art object for the scholarship. I liked to smoke "old school" style, as Dad had called it when he'd taught me how to roll. Since then, odd as it may seem, smoking always made me feel close to Dad. It also made me feel like a movie star from an old French movie, Anna Karina's face superimposed on mine, my own mediocre face lit from within.

I only ended up taking a few puffs before I stopped, holding the joint in front of me and watching its slow demise into smoldering nothingness. Now you see it, now you don't—impermanent, like all living things.

Chapter Three

In Dad's last week home with us before hospice, I cut his hair. Little pieces of curly gray fuzz fell to his shoulders, grazing the new frailty of his body, the crepe-paper skin, the crooked back of my once-handsome father.

I'd seen plenty of old pictures of him in the family albums. In each one he was gigantically tall, with a full head of curly brown hair, deep brown eyes, and always that playful grin. There was one shot Mom had taken of him boxing in an amateur match the night they'd met. His face was coated in sweat, and he was punching out into oblivion, his opponent not visible in the frame. Dad hadn't boxed seriously in years but apparently he used to be pretty good. Although he boxed with me frequently as a kid, this official Boxer Dad was like this alternate persona that only lived for me in photographs. I always half expected to find photographic evidence that he was Rocky.

In those faded photographs he'd seemed indestructible, and now here he was disintegrating.

When Mom wasn't strong enough to help him shower, he asked me, sheepish, ashamed, to help, and I said yes. He was a large man, but I was quite tall myself. Mom was miniature, and he feared taking her down with him. He had a home health aide who was supposed to do this with him, but he felt even more embarrassed around her. He also didn't know how to relate to her because she had no sense of humor and talked incessantly about a TV lady detective, and how that same actress had played a teapot in a Disney movie. He found it hard to keep a straight face and didn't want to offend her.

Dad was a proper Southern gentleman and insisted on wearing his swim trunks throughout the washing process, which I found to be a relief. Even after all the caring for his body toward the end, I still felt a wave of discomfort at the thought of catching a glimpse of his private part—shower-irrigated, gnomic, and no doubt all-knowing. I feared it would have an all-seeing eye that would peer back at me with contempt, knowing all my shortcomings, demanding why I hadn't created a brilliant masterwork that could save Dad yet, and wanting to know what it meant that I had a crush on a girl when I thought I'd liked boys before. "What fundamental piece did they leave out in the factory when they made you?" I imagined it asking me. I also for some reason imagined it wearing a bonnet. I put that on a mental list to discuss with my psychologist.

At some point, though, my embarrassment about Dad's body, along with any thoughts at all, seemed to pass, and there was just my love for my dad, which I tried to channel in the gentle way I used the washcloth to remove soap from his back.

Toward the end of the shower, Dad pivoted his careening body away from me so he could gingerly wash inside his bathing suit. I held him up with all my strength to ensure he didn't slip, while averting my eyes to give him privacy. I don't know if he had that same surreal sense of what lay down there as I did, but he shared my desire to keep it a secret. As I rinsed him off, he sang an old country song softly under his breath, *The moon just went behind the clouds to hide its face and cry.*

I had to think of baseball, a game I understood not at all, so as not to weep over how I was about to lose the person I loved best. Years ago, when I wasn't tall enough to reach the shelf where he kept my markers, paints, and craft stuff, he built me a small crane to lift the desired items off the shelf. It was hilarious but it also made me feel like someone worth building a crane for. How do you come back from losing someone like that?

Seeing that I'd taken a turn for the melancholy, Dad pivoted his large body slowly. He turned to me, clad in wet swim trunks, both of us embarrassed, but I could see he needed to tell me something. I craned toward him, sure that he was about to reveal whatever secret he'd broached before. This time I was ready. The muscles in his throat worked, and I tried to look encouraging, but I saw the moment he swallowed whatever words needed to come out. Instead, he asked, "Why do ghosts ride elevators?"

"I don't know why they would ever do that, Dad," I said, sick of his jokes when he obviously had something more important to say.

"To lift their spirits," he said, roaring with laughter. He moved his arms, which were already around me for support, to form one of his signature bear-hugs. "Just make sure my funeral is not a grave affair, my girl," he said, still laughing. But I didn't find it funny at all.

He must have noticed that his morbid humor was not cheering me up because he pivoted the subject.

"You going to invite Shay to the funeral?" he asked, with a mischievous smile.

"Dad, how many times do I have to tell you? I don't want to talk about your funeral."

But he did coax a little smile from me. Whether I liked it or not, there was Shay in my fantasy, squeezing my hand on that dreaded day. In the vision, she passed me a slip of paper. When I opened my hand slowly, there was a tiny doodle of two monsters embracing and a little note that said, "You are not alone." When they started putting dirt on the coffin, I fell to my knees and she gathered me in her arms, whispering, "I got you." The feeling of safety and wellbeing was all-encompassing. Too bad it wasn't real.

"Not to worry," Dad was saying back in the real world, "I'm opting out of the whole funeral thing. Too much of a downer."

"Of course you are," I said, gently poking him until he made a little cooing sound. "What does that even mean?"

"Just that the whole thing's depressing and you know my whole phobia about being buried alive. So, I've asked for cremation and then you two can scatter my ashes in the junkyard, cool?"

"Not cool, Dad. This is too much. Thank you for the info but this is just. It's too much. I can't right now," I said.

"I hear you, kiddo. Mom's taking care of all of it anyway. So, we going to work tonight?" he asked.

"Yup, of course," I said.

I got him hoisted onto the toilet seat to dry himself off, and then went to start looking through the closet in my room for art stuff. I didn't think Dad would want to brave the stairs to the basement. We'd gotten a lot of use out of Dad's trips to the junkyard, back when he still had the energy to make them. Since he'd lost steam, his best friend Wally—who worked in the auto shop with Dad and made junkyard furniture with him on the weekends—had been bringing stuff by. The treasures had eventually overtaken the storage space of the basement until our whole apartment had become a veritable car graveyard, adorned with old hubcaps, carburetors, and steering wheels galore.

Tonight, Dad was too weak to do much, but he still insisted on sitting beside me at the desk in my room and fiddling with the scrap metal I was sorting through to add to our Frankenstein monster. Each metal scrap I touched felt like some part of him, some key to understanding the riddle of my father, some key to loving him and—most inconceivably of all—to letting him go.

He watched me doing my thing, bobbing his head up and down when I was on the right track, patting my back lightly, repositioning my hand when something wasn't working.

"Dad?"

"Bear?"

"Can I ask you something?"

"Shoot."

"What does it feel like to be—"

"On the way out?"

"Um, yeah." I looked away from him.

"I guess it's like there was all this noise, and now there isn't, and the smallest things are the big ones. Like yesterday. I watched a fly for half an hour like I was Emily freaking Dickinson. Not something I'd have done before. But it's still sort of nice. Meditative. I like to think it's all a circle and I'm just going back to the old womb. Either way, every day this week I've been to the lake in Prospect Park to feed the ducks. They have some kind of killer algae there now, so the whole thing feels pretty perfect since I'm, you know, about to kick the bucket."

"Oh, please don't say that. You know it makes me sad when you say stuff like that."

Silence.

"Dad?" I asked.

"Yass?"

"What did you mean when you said you weren't who I thought you were?"

His eyes widened before he tried to look casual. "Oh, that, just messing around as always, you know me. Zany."

"Seriously, Dad. You weren't."

His knee was hammering up and down now, as it did whenever he was nervous.

"Look, kid. I've done a lot today and I'm tuckered out. I need to rest," he said.

"Okay. You want me to help you to your room?" I felt disappointed and, frankly, more than a little pissed at his holding out on me. He must have known I wouldn't force anything out of him in this state.

He shook his head. I kept working and he did start to drift off. His mouth hung open, his body stooped forward, his large hands hanging in front of him as though they'd forgotten what hands were. It was the loneliest sight in the world.

I let him doze for a few minutes before it got to be too much. Then I reached out and roughly shook him awake, calling him something I hadn't since I was small for the second time: "Papa," I said. His eyes opened, and I could tell it took him a while to remember where he was, who I was. I put my face close to his, our cheeks almost touching. I wondered if this would be the last time. The doctors said he probably had a few weeks left, but he still seemed pretty feisty. I didn't know how long he would still be himself.

He looked solemn. "Dylan, you're right. I wasn't messing around with you. It's just. So hard to say."

My head shot up. "What is?"

"You know I love you more than anything."

"Of course, Dad. Oh my God, what is it?"

"And nothing can change that. I love you more than if you were mine."

"*Yours?* Of course I'm yours. What the hell does that mean?" I thought the cancer might have started eating away at his brain. He was making no sense. Or was he? "Wait. Do you mean? Are you saying? That I'm not. That you're not my actual—"

"Your father. Not by blood, kiddo. But in ways that are more important. You know what I mean. And who cares about blood and labels anyway?"

"What? But if you're not—then—who is?"

"That's not my place to say. But, kiddo, I've been here your whole life, loving you with all I got. I think that pretty much makes me your actual father."

"Not your place? Are you kidding me? You drop a bomb like that and now you're done?"

"You'll have to ask your mother."

I'd been holding my breath. Could I hold it forever? This revelation changed everything—my whole history rewritten. I visualized myself with a baseball bat, fighting back a gang of warring feelings: shock, curiosity as to who this *real father* might be, guilt over this curiosity when the person who felt like my real father was sick and sitting right across from me, anger at my parents for not telling me all these years. I'd have to restructure my brain to survive the mystery this disclosure had blown open. I needed to rebuild networks of thought, dendrites, and neurons, but I wasn't really sure how since I'd never paid attention in science class. I'd need to become a detective.

"Kiddo, can you walk me to my room? This has all been exhausting, and I'm not feeling so well. You better get me to bed before I make a joke about paternity and jism. I'm working one out right now as we speak."

I cringed. "Uh, yeah, of course. We definitely don't want that."

After I put him to bed, I could hear the beep of Mom holding the fridge open too long. I entered the kitchen out for blood, ready to redirect all my anger toward her since she wasn't dying. Oh no, she was all too

22

alive, illuminated by the neon refrigerator light, framed by vegetables.

"Do you know what Dad just fucking told me?" I asked as I walked in.

She looked surprised. "Dylan. *Language*. What's going on?"

"He just said he wasn't my father. So, who on earth is?" I demanded.

She turned ghost-pale and looked like I'd hit her.

When she spoke, she sounded panicky: "Dylan, it's all very complicated. You see, your biological father is—you can't see him," she said.

"What is he, invisible?" I was too angry to guard her feelings.

"He's—he's dead," she said. Something about the way she said it was off, though, like she was lying. But why would she lie about a thing like that? Actually, I could think of many reasons. All of them awful.

So, I had one father who may be dead and one who was dying? Or just a lying mother covering something up? I couldn't process this. Mom looked like she maybe wanted to say more, offer up some platitudes, but I couldn't hear it. I walked into the bathroom and lay down in the waterless bathtub and wished for death—not because I wanted to die, but so I could be with both my fathers forever.

As I lay in the tub, trying to picture Dad going to join my biological father in the land of the dead, I fished my phone out of my sweatpants pocket, dialed *67 and then Shay's number. She'd given it to me when we'd been assigned to work on a project together for English class. I often called just to hear her voice, let it steady me, but then hung up. She picked up.

"Hello?" she said.

My heart jumped. I had never, not once, managed to force words out on the phone with Shay, but maybe this time I would. I prepared to declare my love. I wanted to say, "my family is falling apart and you're the only thing that feels real anymore." I wanted to say, "your face is the archive of every emotion I've ever had." But I couldn't make my mouth work, so I hung up like an idiot. I felt ashamed of myself, and vowed that the next time she picked up, I would speak.

Since I didn't have the guts to talk to Shay, I decided the thing that would make me feel better was to walk along the Brooklyn waterfront, which I often did in the mornings before class. I liked to start my day by gazing at Manhattan, but I confess I only picked up the habit after seeing Shay there one morning. I only saw her there once more after that, but I retained hope. Maybe Shay was there right now. Maybe she had put her phone back in her pocket, shaking her head at the mystery caller, and now she was staring out at the river wishing for company. I could get up, put on shoes, go try to find her. But then I was too down to get out of the tub, so I ended up just sleeping there.

As I headed into English class a month later, I was still in dark mode. Shay looked concerned and before class asked: "Dylan, what's wrong?"

"Just having a bad day," I managed to say.

She looked worried, then she rummaged in her bag and came out with a blank sketchbook.

"Whatever it is, put it here," she said.

I spent half the class sketching dead fathers, until I couldn't think about them anymore. I turned the page and started a portrait of Shay, capturing every detail of her face with the attention of a lover. After class, I ripped out the drawing of her and left it in her locker, unsigned. I should have signed it.

I was called out of art class later that day because Dad had taken a turn for the worse. I rushed to the hospice care facility on what I didn't yet know was his last day.

When I saw him in the hospital bed, looking so fragile, I was plagued by memory. There he was, lying helpless in a strange-smelling new bed, but there he also was as he'd been in key instants from my childhood. These memories superimposed themselves until he became numerous, a time-lapse photo of pure Dadness.

I remembered swimming with him in the ocean as a child. Mom didn't like to swim much, so the water had been our place. Even as a little girl I would ride the big waves with my dad, feeling totally safe from sea froth and beast things. I'd dive deep and purposefully let the saltwater flood my nostrils, a mock drowning, a mermaid's painful yet pleasurable return to the sea. Then I'd burst out of the water to find Dad's curly head rising from a recently ridden wave. I could still feel the sensation of wrapping my arms around his strong neck and floating near the dark curlicues of his chest. That was what I felt whenever I said the word, father. Now I wondered if I'd have to conjure a different image every time I said that word. Or never say it again.

I had daydreams about busting him out of that depressing hospice facility. He'd be played by Tom Hanks, and I'd be the unknown quirky female lead: introducing Dylan Cyllene. It would be our moment of glory, rising above life's sorrowful edges on the sheer power of our film-screen-sized charisma that could conquer all, speeding his wheelchair through the hospital halls, accompanied by unidentifiable indie music. We'd go to a beach somewhere we could both be free. We'd watch seabirds, collect shells, knowing full-well they were the husks of creatures already gone. We'd make a graveyard for life and all its dying creations, read a heartfelt eulogy for each. My father could be king of all dead sea things. But I never took him out of there. Instead, I watched as his face grew less his, day after day, in a place that smelled like pee, which even the ocean had forgotten.

On this final day, I was pleased to be whipped out of my dark daydream when Dad's friend Wally came walking in, with his customary calm and good cheer.

"Hi folks, I come bearing chicken soup," he said, a smile further crinkling his already-wrinkled face.

"Thanks so much, Wal, but I'm not sure Ray is in an eating place," said Mom.

Wally sank down on the chair beside Dad's bed, looking defeated. His salt-and-pepper hair drooped into his eyes. But he stayed, and made small talk, patting Dad's hand occasionally. I could tell Dad appreciated it, even when he was in too much pain to say much.

After about a half hour, Wally said, "Okay, folks, I'll be back tomorrow, 6 p.m. again, like clockwork."

Mom gave him a long, hard hug. I wasn't sure I'd ever seen them hug. Wally was facing me as they embraced, and I thought I saw him sniff her hair, but I must have been imagining things since I was so exhausted.

Wally gave Dad a pat on the shoulder, me a quick hug, and shuffled out of the hospital room.

Mom started fussing with Dad's pillows. She always seemed to be doing that, since Dad was very particular about how he liked them. When the door pushed open again, we braced for one of the nurses or doctors in their endless parade. But our visitor was neither doctor nor nurse. I blinked, trying to convince myself she was actually there.

"Dylan? Um, hi. This is so random," she said.

And there stood Shay. I hadn't found my voice yet, so I just took her in.

Oh, Shay. Fingernails painted black, except for a longer one she'd pierced with a tiny safety pin—where did she even get such an idea? She was always doing stuff like that, the one thing you hadn't thought of.

She stared back at me in surprise. Her eyes were a startling green, her lips heart-shaped. She resembled an old painting, but with army boots and lots of eyeliner. She also looked like she could probably kick your ass if you tried anything.

"Hi, Ms. Cyllene," she said, turning toward Mom. "Should I come back another time?" she asked. We must have all looked startled when she entered.

"No, of course not, Shay. Please stay," said Mom, always fond of Shay and well-aware of how I felt about her.

Shay pushed in a cart full of art supplies so she could lean in close as she always did when someone spoke to her, listening as though it were the most groundbreaking thing ever—unless you were being sexist or a jerk, in which case she tuned you out.

"Great. Can I interest you in anything from my bag of tricks?" Shay asked, placing her hands over her heart, as she did whenever she said anything that mattered to her. She looked in particular at Dad. She always had a soft spot for the underdog in any given situation. Back at the beginning of the school year she'd even tried to make small talk with me, invite me to parties and stuff like she actually wanted to be my friend, but I'd gotten so tongue-tied every time, she'd probably started to worry she was doing more harm than good and backed off.

I knew Shay had started volunteering at the hospice after her dad died. Everybody at school knew as soon as it happened; death made for choice gossip. I had left a rose in her locker the day she'd returned to school. She was crying a lot that day, and right before I went into Spanish, I saw her take the rose out of her locker and crush it beneath her heel.

She started wearing only black after that and doodling not-so-cheerful scenes like the pop-art rendition of Mr. Bean getting beheaded. When our science teacher, Ms. Angelo, asked if it would kill her to wear a different color, she'd responded, "Funny you should mention death, since goth style came out of the Victorian cult of mourning," and everyone shut up.

She'd started photographing dead people at her aunt's funeral home and taping the photos to the school's bathroom stalls. What's more, in the middle of science class she'd taken out a lighter, sterilized a needle, dipped it in India ink, and poked it into her skin repeatedly. She announced that she was giving herself a tattoo of the Emily Dickinson quote, "Dying is a wild night and a new road," but only made it as far as, "Dying." Mr. Sanderson sent her to our famously eccentric headmaster Oscar Edison's office for that one. Mom was my spy in the office, so that afternoon I heard all about it. Mr. Edison had called Shay a "loose cannon," but declared the tattoo she'd given herself to be an "art object," and let her off easy, with the request that she "please refrain from future self-harm during school hours."

"Is this the girl you won't shut up about?" Dad asked me, and Shay blushed.

I thought I might die of shame.

Luckily, Mom was used to smoothing over Dad's gaffes. "Ah, yes, Dylan has mentioned that you're in her English class with Darby, er, Ms. Burgess. Right, Dylan? Aren't you guys about to read your favorite, *Frankenstein?*"

"Yeah," was all I could think to say.

To calm myself, I focused on the light dusting of freckles on Shay's cheeks that you had to look really close to see, which made me think of summer beach towns.

"Anyway," said Shay, "I do art with the patients if you want to do a project? Always cheers people up." She leaned down to grab something from her cart.

Her backless dress revealed her tattoo of a mermaid eating a ship. The exhilaration of this panoramic view threatened to propel me out of my own skin.

When she turned back to us, she was holding a couple of magazines, scissors, and a glue stick. Rumor had it she'd started making her own films in grade school. For the set pieces she would use anything from paper, wood, or cloth to broken glass, toilet bowls and other found objects. These days, she worked with the film teacher Ms. Gambito to splice together movie clips into haunting tunnels of image. She also dabbled in performance art, such as the time she stood in the cafeteria under a sign inviting students to paint her with an assortment of condiments. It was a free-for-all.

So it felt odd, her standing here offering to make some kind of simple cut-and-paste collage with Dad. Like she'd flattened down her weird for the hospice patients.

"Or maybe you just want to rest right now?" she asked, since we were all just staring at her without speaking.

"It's okay," Dad struggled to say. "We can make something."

She looked thrilled, and rushed over to throw her arms around his neck in a hug that knocked his IV tube out.

"Oh my god, I'm so sorry," she said, beet red, trying frantically to insert it back in herself.

"No worries," Dad forced himself to whisper, pushing the button for the nurse.

Mom rushed over and tried to help, but she was only making things worse. Shay looked mortified. I saw that I had to speak to make her feel better, which was all the motivation I needed.

"Thanks, Shay. For all of this. It means a lot," I said.

She leaned in close to my face to answer, too close, and said,

"Thanks, Dylan. I'm so glad." She smelled like cherry Chapstick.

She had one of those nose rings like a bull. It was tiny and delicate, so it made her look somehow softer around the edges, but still like a bull. I wondered if she was the mermaid who ate the ship.

"I know it's nothing fancy, but families often enjoy making collages?" she said.

"That would be great. Thanks, Shay," I said, taking the materials from her, my hands shaking, proud of my heroic act of actually responding to something she said.

"Great. I'll be back in a bit to check in on you," she said, wheeling her cart out of the room—after making sure the nurse had successfully re-fastened all of Dad's tubes.

Not surprisingly, the mood was pretty dark, and we weren't in a big hurry to get started on arts and crafts. Mom went to use the bathroom, and Dad squeezed my hand with a peculiar urgency.

"Kiddo," he said with a lot of effort, almost too quiet to hear, "Tell Shay how you feel, get the Clay, make me a big old masterpiece, okay?"

He didn't normally talk like this. He was not big on the discourse of destiny. He was more of a NASCAR guy, with an *everything's better after a beer* attitude. I knew he was trying to make sure I didn't give up on love, on art, on him, but it still felt like a lot of pressure.

"Dylan." His eyes got strange suddenly, as he said it, his lashes fluttering. "Ask Mom to tell you the story. Let her explain."

"What story?"

Just then, something in the hospital room started beeping and the doctor came rushing in. Dad's eyes glazed over in a way that might have been beautiful in a different situation. And he was gone.

Chapter Four

When Mom returned from the bathroom and took in the scene, she dissolved, falling on her knees on the hospital floor. I knelt and held her, as she'd done for me so many times. Wisps of her flaming red hair were plastered to her forehead. Her eyes seemed bluer. Her parting lips revealed her small teeth. She looked up at me, her sharp features blurred into a softness I wasn't used to seeing, but I could still make out the petite, perfectly chiseled beak of her nose.

Her bird-like features reminded me of Icarus, the myth that makes me cry every time: the father warning his son about flying too close to the sun and then watching his child burn. But in this case, it was me, the child, who had to stand by and watch the fire take my father.

I started sobbing in that way where everything disappears. I cried for my daddy to come back, to enfold me in his borderless love.

When I tried to open my eyes, I started seeing some other place that wasn't quite the hospital and wasn't quite wherever my father had gone. An in-between land that floated amid living and dying, where I could view every memory of my father, a cruel inner cinema that showed me every second I would never get back.

Then the sound of Shay laughing in the room next door snapped me out of it. If my father were still here, I realized, he'd want me to find something to laugh about too. So I said to Mom, "You know what Dad said he wanted us to do with his remains?"

She looked up at me in shock. "How could you talk about that at a time like this?"

"He said, 'Cremation is my last hope for a smoking body,'" I said.

She looked furious for a second, then her face scrunched up, and she started laughing hysterically. It was as if my father's humor had come back from the grave to comfort us in our time of need, to give us one last laugh.

"Did he really say that? You just can't make this stuff up," she said.

The joke had broken the spell of sadness for the moment. My mother drew herself off the ground, almost robotically, tucked a strand of red hair behind her ear, and walked over to her dead husband.

"Nurse!" she called out. When the poor guy came running, she said, "Would you please get this man a blanket? It's freezing in here. What kind of service is this?"

The nurse looked confused. "But isn't he ... isn't he ..."

"Just get it already," my mother said. I stood, as I always did when she got like this, perfectly still, just letting her have her feelings. The nurse dutifully left to find bedding.

"Now help me prop him up with these pillows," Mom said to me. "You know how he loves his pillows. Chop-chop." It was true. He did love his pillows. We went to work.

And then she did it. She climbed into the small hospital bed next to him, saying, "Well, are you going to leave your father hanging in his time of need?" I scrambled onto his other side. His body felt just as it had during life, but he was not alive. It was uncanny but also a tease. Only the ghost of cuddling still available to me.

"If it just ends like this, why do we do any of it?" I asked Mom. She looked at me. Her eyes shaped so much like mine I felt I should be able to see through them.

"Because at one point when you were three you tried, with utter love, confidence, and conviction, to shove a piece of broccoli behind my ear like a flower," she said.

"You're so weird," I said.

"I just mean it all comes down to love in the end, to what we love, who we love. Like this moment. Like right now."

"Ah," I said, not totally sure I got it. "But isn't this like the worst moment ever?"

"Yeah, but we're making lemonade out of the lemons. We're holding each other close. Quite literally. It's about love, but also knowing when to release. As Mary Oliver says, 'To live in this world you must be able to do three things: to love what is mortal; to hold it against your bones knowing your own life depends on it; and, when the time comes to let it go, to let it go,'" she said.

"Ah," I said, still not really buying it.

"The little things, like how as a kid you'd order me, in the booming voice of a sea captain, to turn over so you could lie on my back."

"Yeah, Mom, you've told me this," I said, but it was like she hadn't heard me.

She squeezed my hand harder and kept talking like she was looking back in time, seeing the exact moment she was describing. "You would dart and scratch nervously around my back like a stray cat trying to find a home. It left me sore the next day, but there was so much love there." Then her eyes got strange, as they often did, as though looking through me at some other person far away.

"Uh-huh, I love you too, Mom," I said, drawing a strand of sweaty hair out of her eye.

"But can you blame me for still longing for more?" she asked.

"Like what?"

"Like greatness. Is that so wrong? I feared someone up there would penalize me for wanting to be bigger than I was."

"No, Mom. I don't think it's wrong. Everyone wants to be great. But what makes you think you're not?"

"Art-wise, I mean."

"Oh. And you feel I had something to do with that?"

"No, Dyl, of course not."

I was relieved when the nurse returned with the blankets. With my father gone, I wasn't sure I could shoulder Mom on my own. He'd always had a way of diffusing things, throwing a dose of humor on that overactive mind of hers that I'd inherited. I wasn't sure it was fair to ask that Mom shoulder me alone either. I had been a difficult kid from the start, roaring and refusing to be touched all through infancy and then transitioning into some older form of that.

The nurse paled when he saw us snuggled up to Dad. He deposited the blankets and hurried out of the room. There we were, all crammed into one bed, dazed, starting to smell of the supposed sterility of the hospital. Our little family now eternally altered. Mom and I hugged my father's body as tightly as we could from both sides. Afterward, we stared up at that high ceiling where our feelings about losing Dad had so much room to rise.

But the thing was, *I still saw him*. What seemed to be my father's ghost was floating over us. He was hazy and ambient. His features seemed to drift, his hair moving gently around his face. His motions more jellyfish than man.

He looked nothing like the version of him lying on the bed next to me. He looked as he had when he was young in our photo albums. A bear of a man, full of life. It made me expect Dad's body to jolt up beside me in the bed, yell, "Psych, I fooled you; last one home is a rotten egg," and then dart out of the room with Mom and me jogging behind him. I wondered if this apparition was a final gift sent by dad, a reminder to laugh in the face of gloom.

But then ghost-Dad's expression went serious. "Don't forget to ask your mother," he said. His mouth was moving as it normally did, but his voice had a croaky echo, a bullfrog singing through his throat. The haunting sound came from a place at once inside and outside me. His face was a riddle. What was it trying to tell me? I reached out for him, my hands shaky. I was about to grasp his hands, joy flooding my systems, but he dissolved before I could make contact.

Now, it should be said that at the time I was high, as always. I had ducked out of the room earlier to smoke in the bathroom, not feeling I could face the whole thing without my magical marijuana—or at least the terrible approximation this dick in my class, Cash, stole from his dad and sold for cheap. When she was grieving, Shay turned to tattoos; I turned to pot. I'd always smoked, but it became a daily thing around the time Dad got sick.

But could weed really explain a paranormal event? I wasn't so sure.

I knew what I'd seen floating over the hospital bed wasn't actually Dad's ghost because I didn't believe in such things. At most, I understood this specter to be a manifestation of my own melancholy.

Before I could explore this further, the door swung open. I expected the disgruntled nurse again, but instead it was Shay.

My mouth hung open. Mom, though, was too deep in her feelings to really register Shay.

"Oh, sorry. Should I come back when he's not sleeping?" Shay asked.

My mother and I were mute.

"I'll come back when he's awake," Shay said with a warm smile, turning to go.

"Wait," I surprised myself by saying. "He's not sleeping."

"Oh, I guess it's just been a long night for him then, because it looks like he's out like a light." As she said it, I could see her really starting to take in the tableau—the quiet monitors, the expressions on our faces, the incongruity of it all.

"Shay, he's not sleeping. He's—" I couldn't finish, hot tears streaming down my face. I glanced over at Mom, who looked catatonic.

Shay left her cart, ran over, and crouched down beside the hospital bed. She wiped a tear from my cheek, which made me cry harder, so she just hugged me tightly and rocked us both a little.

Then she surprised me by drawing herself up and saying, "Come on, let's do an art project. This is the time for it. I wish someone had done this for me."

"Now? You've got to be joking," I said.

"Now," she said, more forcefully, shoving a stack of magazines into my hands and saying, "Rip."

Mom still stared blankly ahead while I took up the child-safe scissors and tried to make my hands work.

Shay pulled up a chair beside me, and asked, "What are we going for here?" lifting a magazine and taking the scissors out of my trembling hand.

"Cut out anything that looks like a dad," I said.

We all sat quietly as Shay dutifully snipped fatherly images out of the magazines and placed them down on the tray next to Dad's uneaten pudding cup. While Shay cut, I grabbed up the pudding and ate it in gulps, not really sure why. As soon as I choked it down, I felt sick.

When Shay had created a pile of people peering up at me from the tray, she said, "Ready?" She handed me a glue stick and I rubbed it over the paper like a zombie, then started pasting the torn people to the paper, until the very end when I became suddenly so goddam furious with Dad for leaving us that I took the last of those hellish smiling faces, crumpled them into a ball and threw them against the white hospital wall as hard as I could.

"Well, I think my work here is done. You do feel just a little bit better, though, don't you?" Shay asked, squeezing my shoulder.

"I actually do," I said. And I did. A little.

"See you around. Oh, and Dylan, keep your head up. It gets better."

"Promise?"

"Yeah."

"Shay?"

"Yeah?"

"Thank you."

"Of course. Any time. I'm here. Goodnight, Ms. Cyllene."

"Such a nice girl," Mom said mechanically, her eyes fluttering closed in exhaustion.

Mom fell asleep there, and I listened to her nocturnal sounds to calm myself. Her bird body curled up, she snored like a lawnmower, sounding like she might choke. Sleep apnea? Swallowed a roaring bear? I never knew what the trouble was. I was so exhausted that I started to feel delirious. I pictured Mom and me as two raw, beating organs that had no way out. We glowed in the harsh hospital light together, froze in the overly conditioned air. I think neither of us knew how to leave that hospital. How to go home without him there? Who would tell us jokes?

Unable to sleep, I sat cross-legged on the hard hospital chair and tried to read *Hamlet* for Ms. Burgess's class, but I couldn't concentrate on a single word. I kept picturing myself as Hamlet and Shay as Ophelia, except I worried this meant she would end up killing herself in the end.

Mom finally woke up. She looked confused at first. Part of me hoped she'd never fully wake up to what she'd lost, but she did of course. She ran her hand through my hair and said, "Bear, let's go." She hadn't called me "Bear" in years—usually that was Dad's special name for me. She placed the softest kiss on Dad's lips, said, "Love you forever, Ray-Ray." I gave him a last hug, and then she gathered me up from the bed, and marched me out of the hospital room before I could try to stay there forever.

As we walked out, I took her hand and squeezed three times. She squeezed three times back, letting me know she was still in there.

That night I hurt so badly I thought I might go insane. First, I cried alone on the toilet while eating Doritos. Not that it took too much to make me cry alone on the toilet while eating Doritos, and that part of the whole picture was something I really needed to examine. Then, I curled in a ball on the floor of my room and screamed into a pillow. Next, I let my head rest on the ground, face juices wetting the hardwood, imagining life as the mad woman in the attic until I had an urge to call Shay.

With Dad gone, I suddenly didn't care anymore if she rejected me. I also felt some sort of uprising in me, the specter of the "nice girl" exhausted from being nice. Plus, I was hurting too much to even register fear as I dialed her number.

From where I was standing, I could see her in her room holding the phone. She was wearing red pajamas. She picked up, and I think my heart might have stopped. This was always when I hung up. But not tonight.

I was preparing to say something, anything, when she spoke first: "Dylan? Is that you? I can hear your mom calling you in the background."

She was looking at me across the way. I freaked out and turned off the lights in my room, and then slammed my door closed in the hopes that Mom would stop calling, which she did. But then I regained courage. I switched the light back on.

"My dad's dead." I dumbly blurted out this fact Shay already knew. "I'm sorry, we're not friends and I don't know why I called you, except you were there when it happened and that has to mean something."

"It's totally okay. And I'd say we're friends now that we shared an intense moment like that. Oh God, Dylan, I'm so sorry. I know. It's like your heart was ripped out, right?"

"Yeah."

"It gets better."

"Promise?"

"Promise."

"Can I confess something?" I was all ready to tell her I loved her.

But then I could see her mom coming into her room, looking mad about something, and Shay said quickly, "Dylan? I gotta go, but keep your chin up, okay? This too shall pass."

"Oh, okay, sure."

I hung up. I felt embarrassed but also aglow with what I'd done. I had acted, actually spoken when she picked up, and told her something important, even if she already knew it.

Uncertain how to sleep on my own, I finally got up and crawled into bed with Mom, who wrapped me into her body so immediately I think she might have been waiting for me to come. I remembered how she'd said I'd always crawled on her back when I was little, and tonight I considered doing so again, before remembering I was legally an adult. I would have crawled back into her womb if I could.

At one point, when she thought I was asleep, Mom unwound her body from mine, crept over to her purse, took out the collage I'd made with Shay, took a little key from her underwear drawer, reached behind the mattress, used the little key to open a closet I'd never noticed, and deposited the collage there.

As I tried to fall asleep, I tried to imagine what touching Shay's body would be like. One time in the cafeteria I'd seen down her shirt when she bent to tie her shoes. The sight of the snow-white silhouette of her breasts had been too much for me, and I'd dropped my tray of ziti. But tonight I entertained a different scenario where I actually made contact. The sensation was the same as one of my favorite memories: the first time I went apple picking. As I let myself get lost in the imagery, the whole room filled with the smell of apple blossoms.

Chapter Five

It definitely helped to get back to school, or back to the streets, as Ms. Burgess would say. She often took her Senior English students out into Brooklyn to get writing inspiration. In addition to the royal title of being Shay's mother, she was the kind of teacher most students never got. She was John Keating from *Dead Poets Society*: inspired, inspiring, caring and massively cared for by her students. She had even jumped on the desk one time in class, shouting for us to "seize the day," and inviting us to tear pages out of a stuffy old English textbook, just as John Keating had done in the movie. Yes, Ms. Burgess often went overboard. Her teaching strategies would fly only at a school like Brooklyn Arts, where the rules were flexible.

Actually, I'm not sure Brooklyn Arts had any rules at all. On any given day you could find students painting all over the sidewalk (Oh, Shay). The daughter of a famous artist had once spray-painted the school bathroom and, being the kooky headmaster he was, Mr. Edison had left it. He'd said that if this guy's daughter did it, it must be a work of art. Mr. Edison's mustache was curled like Salvador Dalí's, and he had a pet parrot who sat on his shoulder as he fussed with paperwork in his office. He had been known to barge into classrooms and unleash confetti and other such antics, all in the interest of "switching it up to enable creativity" or the "mandatory nature of performance art," or something like that.

Mr. Edison was as eccentric and antiquated as Brooklyn Arts itself. The historic building was a work of craftsmanship itself with a distinguished and somewhat unsettling history. This stately, red brick building that reached out of the pavement of Joralemon Street was the brainchild of what some deemed Brooklyn's top architect. The construction of the building had been described as seemingly simple but actually quite complex and not without its Gothic qualities. From what Ms. Burgess herself had taught us, these might include such elements as a tale that takes place in a spooky old building, possesses an atmosphere of enigma and foreboding, and contains a woman in trouble. Was that me? Shay? Ms. Burgess? My mother?

Strange things often happened in Brooklyn Arts. On Monday wind had blown through the classroom, causing all the papers in the room to rise, right after Ms. Burgess had said the name of the play one was never supposed to say, *Macbeth*.

The building had been listed in campy articles as one of the most haunted in Brooklyn. Hard to say if anyone truly believed it, but there was always an uncanny feel to that building in the Richardsonian Romanesque style with elements of Italian Renaissance, Beaux Arts and Colonial Revival. And now I was worried about seeing my dad's ghost there.

Aside from getting the inside track on the Gothic, I was lucky I had Ms. Burgess for English, because the other English teacher, Ms. Woods, called the students "Sir" and "Miss," and had at first called me "Sir." Sure, Mom had cut my hair a little too short, but I really didn't appreciate that one. I wanted to be able to do what guys were allowed to do in life, but it didn't mean I wanted to be mistaken for one of them. So many of them were dicks anyway.

Ms. Burgess too, like her daughter, was strikingly beautiful, messy all over and old enough to be my mother—though younger by a decade than the other kids' moms—but striking nonetheless. Like her daughter's, her hair was so black it was almost blue, and she wore it every day in a messy bun. When I saw it, I visualized a ballerina with a tight coil who'd run until it unfurled into chaos. She wore no makeup save for the same deep red lipstick every day, which during her lessons always smudged till it looked like her mouth was bleeding. Her teeth were very white, and she was always quick to smile. There was, as they used to say of Saint Nick, a lingering twinkle in her eye that indicated she was merry.

Ms. Burgess often told us that real stories don't live on the page but rather on the streets. "Look at these shards of broken windshield glass. What tale do they tell? What happened here?" she would ask, picking up the glittering shards, risking being cut, cupping them in her palms like they were precious. Then, making her hands into a megaphone, she'd call out in a Dracula voice, "take all these pieces and make for me a beautiful monster." I was riveted by her style of teaching. Sometimes the other students got it and sometimes they looked at her like she was nuts. But I knew she lived for our moment of learning, when our eyes, once humble organs of the visual system, transformed into what they were always meant to be: portals to another world.

Today she'd taken us under the Brooklyn Bridge to forage for scraps. Cars rushed over us as we searched for "inspirational objects" to write poems about. I liked to look up at the bridge structure as the vehicles sped over, all whirr and rumble in the city morning.

Then as we sorted through the ruins of downtown Brooklyn, Ms. Burgess moved from student to student, surveying our findings, squinting her eyes to imagine how each piece might be translated onto paper. Shay screamed with joy when she found an old Bible with half the pages torn out.

"Look at this," she said, turning to display her prize to the class. She quickly drew back whenever anyone tried to touch it—but smoothly enough that nobody else seemed to notice. As she started tearing out the pages, she got this naughty glint in her eye like she was capable of anything.

My least favorite person on the planet, Cash—whose only value was the weed he dealt—had found a green sliver of beer bottle, battered by the city into something like sea glass. "Ooh, maybe I'll use this in the project I'm working on for the Clay Scholarship," he said.

I wanted to punch him. Even though, as he put it, he did have "mad skills," he also "summered in Nice," while kids like Shay and I actually needed that scholarship to go to art school at all. Shay, though, had opted out early, saying she wasn't planning on applying for the Clay because she wasn't going to college; as she put it, she was not a sheep. Her plan was to get an RV and travel the U.S. photographing its ghost towns.

When I looked over at Cash, he mimed cutting his throat with the piece of glass in a menacing way. I walked up to him and shook the cracked tambourine I'd found in his face with what I hoped was menace but feared was mere foolishness. Back when I learned the word "nemesis," I decided Cash was mine because he basically bullied me and also had a thing for Shay. Not that she'd ever be into him, judging by the DYKE tattoo on her knuckles, but Cash had always liked a good challenge, so maybe he thought he could "convert" her. How gross. Of course, he never mocked Shay for being queer because he'd probably already planned out their wedding. But at some point Cash had figured out how I felt about Shay (not that it was difficult) and started teasing me about it relentlessly. As I was walking in late to science class the other day, I'd heard him saying, "I'll bet she's late because she was jerking off to Shay." He was probably correct, but still.

I didn't constitute any real romantic competition for Cash. There's probably a divine kingdom allotted to all good-looking people at birth that I missed out on. Don't get me wrong, I have my own brand of appeal, but only if you have a thing for Edward Scissorhands. Cash, on the other hand, resembled a Greek god and knew it. I mean, I found his looks boring as hell, but others seemed to enjoy them immensely. He had brown eyes and hair, chiseled face, straight teeth all in a row. He'd tried to give himself some edge by getting gauges in his ears sophomore year, which you could tell he thought made him look tough. He told anyone who'd listen that his "specialization" was graffiti art, which gave him "street cred." Just what the world needed: another graffiti artist with a house in the Hamptons.

As much as I hated to admit it, Cash's graffiti art was unique. He didn't get a free ride to Brooklyn Arts, as Shay and I did since our moms worked there, but what bothered me is that he could have gotten a scholarship there. He was that good. He would case out a spot, making sure the "po-po" wouldn't interrupt, then whip out his spray cans and cover whatever subway car or roll-up storefront door he could find. He was obsessed with history, particularly the 1960s, and would turn a shop door into a moment out of time by creating a stunning mural of, say, the historic March on Washington.

In our senior class, judging by the number of times our work had been on display in the student work museum, Shay, Cash, and I were considered the natural competitors for that year's Clay Scholarship, which sent one student each year to the New York Institute of the Arts with a full ride. Almost every artist I worshipped—including my mother—had gone to NYIA.

But Cash was the worst, personality-wise. Case in point, he'd described Frida Kahlo last semester as a "unibrow lesbian type Dylan might like to hang out with," right after asking me if I got my haircut in prison. He'd been sent to Mr. Edison's office for that and come out with the assignment to read about the lesbian experience in America. This, as you might imagine, was embarrassing. I get that Mr. Edison, gay himself, was trying to be pro-queerness, but I hated having any attention called to me at all, especially to a sexuality I was still trying to figure out.

I pretended not to care what Cash had said, but in truth I wished I'd been made less sensitive. I felt everything too much. I wanted everything too much. Somehow, I was born without skin, while everyone else was so well-protected. Due to the whole skinless situation, I have had to be tougher than others in many ways. It's the only way to be when you've been kicked around by life. When I was younger, people probably assured themselves that my whole hopeful, wide-eyed, half in love with the world thing would pass. They fantasized, perhaps, that the world would beat it out of me. They didn't know it had already tried. It was a kind of stubbornness, a means of survival. I didn't have that outlook because I didn't know how ugly things could get, but because I did. Instead of naïveté, I saw it as a form of wisdom: the knowledge that even in the ugliest thing there's something to value–even if it's just that you're strong enough to survive it, that I was an artist and could therefore make something out of it. These pages are my smoke signals. They tell you I'm still here.

Often, I pictured a creature from another planet without such limited views on gender and sexuality roles visiting earth. Its brain would just explode. That was me: an alien stranded on an inhospitable and gravely simplistic planet. My dad had understood; he knew that some things live beyond definition. When I was about twelve, he took me to my first figure drawing class, and I stared with wonder at the naked female model standing before me. I was totally paralyzed. He didn't directly say anything about my sad little twelve-year-old libido, just leaned in close, brushed my hair behind my ear, and took his eraser to my paper, saying, "You know, you can show just as much using negative space, try this," as he demonstrated his technique.

"What's negative space?" I asked.

"Mom taught me about it. I guess you could say it's the space around and between the thing you're supposed to be drawing." I didn't really get it at the time, but I know now that he was communicating in code something neither of us had words for about what it meant to be a woman, and how limiting it was.

Under the bridge, Ms. Burgess broke into my reverie, seizing a teachable moment. She said, "Okay, so we've been talking about how to let the found object tell the story and look at this little treasure I just found. What story does it tell you?" She leaned down to pick up a stained teddy bear as though she'd found a thing of great value. We all gathered around. She cleared the dirt from the animal to reveal still more stains. The bear did have striking green glass eyes, though, that matched Ms. Burgess's own.

"Twinsies!" Cash said, too loudly, and Ms. Burgess jumped a little. Cash looked at Shay to see if he'd gotten her attention, but she was oblivious, totally absorbed in leaning on her mother's shoulder to see what she'd found.

Shay raised her hand and said, "I guess the story I'm thinking here is how even this once-domesticated children's toy has found its own wild life."

Ms. Burgess nodded. "Interesting. So, Shay, you can try writing on that for the homework tonight. Oh, and I also wanted to give you guys a heads-up about a great opportunity coming your way. Mr. Edison has gotten a world-famous photographer, Simon Ambrogio, to come to Brooklyn Arts. He's a bit macho and arrogant if you ask me. I also don't know if I agree with his whole thing where he buys up famous art and then photographs himself burning it, but he's undoubtedly brilliant and I know Shay's looking forward to his coming. He'll be teaching your Special Seminar. If you're not already familiar with it, I'd like you all to research his work beforehand."

Shay was looking off into the distance in a way that made me want to see through her eyes. I could always tell when she needed a hug. Her shoulders slumped a little and her arms would rise for a moment, as though she were a baby wanting to be picked up, before she jammed her hands into her pockets. I wanted nothing more than to put her in my kangaroo pouch.

"How you holding up?" she asked, touching my arm as I walked over to her, which thrilled me.

"Hanging in there. Thanks for being there for me the other day. Are you okay? You looked a little upset when I came over."

"Oh, I was just looking at the bridge and thinking about something. Anyway, did you hear? Simon Ambrogio is going to come teach at our school?" she said.

She seemed to think this was a good thing. I'd have to do some deep research then, as Ms. Burgess had suggested.

That evening, I decided to ask Mom about it, since she'd heard of every artist ever. "So what do you know about this Ambrogio guy who's coming to teach the Special Seminar?" I asked, while shoveling Mom's spaghetti into my mouth.

She froze while eating, a fork full of noodles midway to her mouth, sauce on her upper lip. Her voice was icy when she finally started speaking and moving again. "Why do you ask?" She chewed the spaghetti quickly, looking at me like I was planning a heist. I wanted to laugh since she still had tomato on her lip, but there was something very unfunny about her expression.

"Um, because I heard he was coming to teach and wanted to know about his work, crazypants. Why are you being so weird?"

"I'm not. I'm just not hungry anymore," she said, getting up from the table.

She was big on table manners, so leaving in the middle of dinner was odd. But I had no idea what it meant.

I started to Google this Ambrogio guy. I got as far as the fact that he was most famous for a photograph called *Art Monster*, and beyond that for the photos of other artists' burning work, as Ms. Burgess had said, as well as a series of recent paintings he'd created by dipping his gloves in paint and boxing the canvas. Apparently, he'd summoned others from the art world to engage in publicized art battles using this same boxing technique, resulting in many evocative action paintings. Maybe that was why Mom didn't want to talk about this Ambrogio guy: because she didn't want me getting any more pyromaniac ideas. I was just about to search for images of his work when Mom yelled from the next room that she was going to bed. I was still in a delicate place where I didn't feel I could sleep without her, and so I went running to her room.

Mr. Edison regularly brought in stars in the field to teach Special Seminars. This was nothing new. It usually created a bit of friction between the regular teachers and the temporary hotshots. Mr. Edison claimed, though, that a little healthy competition was "all the rage," and good for the teachers, forcing them to "innovate and really bring their 'A games,' so to speak."

The only thing different with Simon Ambrogio, apparently, was the size of the star. It seemed the other teachers were jealous. I heard Ms. Bennett, who taught puppetry, talking shit about him in the teacher's lounge. The lounge was right next to the red stairs, where I often hung out, so I was always up on the faculty gossip.

The stairs were in the center of the lobby where assemblies were held. They were covered in velvety red carpeting. The irony being that it was mostly the losers—or those who didn't have anyone to sit with in the lunchroom or go out to eat with on Montague Street, who sat there—who got to "walk the red carpet." But I attributed a different valence to my velvety stair headquarters, associating it with my favorite director, David Lynch—a nod to both his *Blue Velvet* and the red room in my beloved *Twin Peaks*. The image of this room came to Lynch while leaning against a car still hot from a hard drive. In the spirit of the red room, I hoped the red stairs might also be an extradimensional, apparently infinite space, which defied the laws of gravity, and could therefore, by the mere act of sitting on them, totally remake me. They never did.

Ms. Bennett had an infamously big mouth, and was talking to Mr. Moody, who taught poetry craft and was usually not one for gossip. "Why do we need this Simon Ambrogio to come in and teach art to our students when they already adore Mr. Pheder?" she asked. "This guy's big thing is photographing burning works of art? You've got to be kidding me. I hear he's a total asshat."

"Florid language aside, Barbara, I take your point," Mr. Moody had said, nodding his gray head wearily. "But, as you well know, it all comes down to the question of fame, our Mr. Edison's drug of choice."

Shay cornered me by my locker before Mr. Ambrogio's first class.

"You ready for the Ambrogio seminar? It's always cool when famous artists come here. It's like meeting The Wizard of Oz or something."

"Just an old guy behind a curtain," I said, wishing I could be her wizard.

"But like who the Wizard was supposed to be," she said, not allowing me to rain on her parade.

"Now that you put it that way," I said.

But she was not in a place where she could hear sarcasm.

Chapter Six

As I shuffled in behind her, there this famous Mr. Ambrogio was, sitting back in his chair, arms crossed and boots up on the desk. Probably around 60, but still handsome, a bit of a silver fox. He had a full head of dark hair with some white around the temples, and the air of a guy who had been a badass back in the day but had mellowed—if James Dean had lived and taken side gigs at a prep school.

There was a silence in the classroom that didn't appear to make him uncomfortable, and that nobody seemed to want to disturb. Though I'd tried to play it cool with Shay before class, I felt enthralled by Mr. Ambrogio too, excited to be close to his great talent.

He sat there, eyes roving over everyone's faces like he was studying a painting at a museum. Then he looked right at me, narrowing his eyes as though contemplating a certain problematic color choice.

"You there, what's your name?" he asked me.

I was dumbfounded. "Um, it's Dylan?"

"Are you sure? Sounds like there was a question mark somewhere in there," he said.

I just nodded.

"Say it loud and proud," he said.

I nodded again, wishing to disappear entirely.

Luckily, Hilda interrupted the awkward exchange: "Um, Mr. Ambrogio, do you prefer notebooks or trapper keepers?"

Hilda had very blonde hair, did everything in a retro way, was on the shy side, and had been one of the few people I'd attempted to have a playdate with back in the day. She had seen Mom's *Medusa* and fled.

"You can call me Simon. Trapper what?"

"No worries, I have both," said Hilda, pulling out a notebook with the Eiffel Tower on it and a trapper keeper with a poodle wearing a beret.

"I wasn't worried. Anyway, let's get this show on the road," said the famous artist who had just invited us to call him Simon. "I know you guys are about to read *Frankenstein* in your English class with the smoking-hot Ms. Burgess, and that's an amazing work, so I thought I'd do a little tie-in. Today I'm going to have you access your own creative violence."

Eyebrows went up.

Shay had a disgusted look on her face. "Hey, that's my mom you're talking about," she said.

"You're not so bad yourself," Mr. Ambrogio said. And then, "Just joshing with you, trying to get you all to lighten up a little. You're all so serious, sitting in your seats like you're at a funeral. You're young. Put a little pep in your step."

We all looked from Mr. Ambrogio to Shay. Shay was blushing furiously. I shot her an *I'm mad too* look, but she couldn't seem to read it.

"Not cool, not cool at all," said Shay, seemingly no longer in awe of Mr. Ambrogio.

Hilda raised her hand and, as though she'd missed the whole Shay and Mr. Ambrogio exchange, asked, "I just wanted to be sure I heard you correctly for the notes. Did you say we'd be accessing our, uh, *violence?*" A few eye rolls from the class.

"That I did. Okay, everybody up."

Most everyone looked at each other, wondering what to do. Cash, though, shot up out of his seat like he couldn't wait for the promised violence.

"And your name is?" Mr. Ambrogio demanded. I still couldn't think of him as "Simon."

"Uh, it's Cash."

"Cash, huh? Your parents really screwed you with that one, huh? Or maybe they just love money that much. I know your dad actually, and I think it might be the latter."

A few titters from the class, some widened eyes at the prospect of Cash being teased, and by a teacher no less. If I'm being honest, I enjoyed it a little myself. Cash looked like a piece of the sky had fallen.

"Okay, everyone follow Cash's lead and get those keisters off the seats. You can't make art while sitting on your ass. Let's get ready to fuck shit up."

The whole class was now standing, but they looked confused. Also scared.

Mr. Ambrogio reached down into a huge sack and started handing out hammers. We all continued to stand in silence. I stared at my hands. There was something that felt shameful about an adult acting so out of the ordinary.

"Okay, it looks like you all need a bit more context. Fine. I'd like you all to meditate on the ontology of creative, and I mean *metaphorical*, violence. Violence as a form of thought rather than merely action. Think more serial killer than butcher. We're going to get cerebral about this whole thing—no actual deaths in this classroom please, ha-ha."

Nervous, frightened laughter from the class. And did Mr. Ambrogio look at me when he said the thing about actual deaths? I was probably being paranoid.

Mr. Ambrogio continued, "If you want a bloody carcass, go to your local grocery aisle. I'm talking about the kind of art that will emerge from these powerful exercises, and the exotic new form of thinking needed to get you there, which I can, it has been proven, teach, so pay close attention, kids. This is not your grandma's art course.

"Now, as an initial thought exercise—and you don't have to actually answer this aloud—ask yourself what kind of serial killer you'd be. It's crucial to know this about yourself. Are you organized, disorganized, visionary, mission-oriented, hedonistic, power/control driven? For example, would you be mission-oriented like Ted Kaczynski, the Unabomber, who preyed on agents of industry and wrote a pretty good manifesto about the evils of technology? You can then extend this inquiry to ask yourself how someone like, say, Ted Bundy, a famously organized killer, can bludgeon someone and then go home to a family. How can these killers' minds work in two distinct ways at once? And, by extension, how can you make your mind work in two ways at once without actually killing anyone, mwa-haha?"

We were all shooting each other looks like, *oh wow, is this guy a serial killer?* But we were also, it had to be said, in awe. Even Shay was back to looking agog.

I'd watched *Fight Club* with Dad. Celebration and provocation of toxic masculinity aside, I'd found it to be an eye-opening piece of work. I, like its passive protagonist, had longed for the vitality I found in Shay that I couldn't seem to locate in myself, most especially as a girl, the most neutered of all animals. That the hero had secretly been the raucous ringleader all along, that he'd carried him inside the whole time, a Hyde to his Jekyll, drove me toward a question that lingered with me long after I'd made my way home from the movie theater to finish my homework and that resurfaced now, as Mr. Ambrogio made his bizarre speech: What sort of creative violence did I have waiting to be unleashed in my PG life? And what would be my catalyst? Shay? Mr. Ambrogio? Little old me?

"You there, Dylan." In what felt like slow motion, Mr. Ambrogio pointed right at me.

"Me?" I stammered.

"Yes, what kind of serial killer would *you* be?" he asked.

"I wouldn't be a serial killer," I forced myself to say, feeling shellshocked by this line of questioning.

"I think you'd be surprised. In the right situation, all of us could be killers. But, without literally doing any harm—and I want to be clear on that so I don't get fired—you now need to get in touch with your own creative violence, and I'm especially directing this at the women in the room whose violence has been even more repressed because: society. Then I want you to record what you find in these exercises, in blood if necessary.

"Go out into the world and do whatever you have to do but bring me back that bloody beating heart of experience. Get it down on your canvas, take a photo of it, build it a monument, whatever. Just make me some genius art. I'll make sure they give you all the prizes for it. Ah, I see now. That's all I had to say to get your attention, eh? Dangle an award in front of your faces. Interesting. But I guess not surprising. Okay, let's take this to the field, folks.

"We'll be using a mixture of techniques to get you in touch with your inner monster—yes, yes, there's your *Frankenstein* tie-in— smashing stuff, martial arts, axe throwing, etc. But, for this morning, let's get away from metaphor, shall we? Let's get back in touch with our bodies, with their desires, their fetishes, their furies."

Finally, Hilda raised her hand, and thus also her hammer. Her face looked more pinched than ever. "I'm sorry, do you mean we're going to be literally hitting each other in class?" she asked.

"Yup, literally hitting each other, but first a warm-up," Mr. Ambrogio said.

We all exchanged looks. What on earth were we getting ourselves into? Was pursuing artistic excellence even worth it with nuts like this in charge?

"I see," Hilda replied.

The rest of us, sheep that we were, went along with it. Mr. Ambrogio pulled what looked like little wooden toys out of the sack and started handing them out. "I order you to smash the shit out of these, please," he said.

We all looked lost until Shay, with a look that meant trouble, raised her hammer above her head and then brought it down with all her might. Her colorful little toy shattered into shards all over the gray carpeting. It was a study in contrasts.

The room was noiseless. Shay stared at her hands like she'd just murdered someone. Then a smile I'd never seen before edged its way onto her face. The other students promptly began shattering their own toys, whooping, hollering, ushering in doom like the horsemen of the apocalypse.

In the middle of this mayhem came a knock at the door, which creaked open to reveal Mr. Edison. We all tensed, freezing, hammers in hand. He entered, an unlit pipe poking out of the corner of his mouth, circled around, and then exclaimed, "But this is marvelous. Bravo, Simon. What a pedagogical extravaganza," and then he started applauding. "I'll have to fetch Jane, who has the honor of being both our esteemed Secretary and young Dylan's mother, to record this with her nifty new camera for our donors," he said, trotting out.

A few minutes later Mom was sticking her head in, but I noticed she had a peculiar look on her face, didn't bring her camera, and didn't say a word. Mr. Ambrogio looked up when the door opened, caught her eye, and went still. The chaos of hammers slowed as people seemed to realize there was drama afoot. Finally, Mr. Ambrogio lurched toward Mom, face blank, and scurried out into the hall.

As soon as the door shut behind him, we could see them start arguing. It was hard to hear, though, since Mr. Edison had soundproofed the classrooms to rid us of "noise pollution," his catty way of referring to the less-talented students in the music classes.

I'd never seen Mom like this before. Sure, she screamed at me all the time, but not like she might actually take my head off. Even when I had set fire to things, she'd yelled at me, sure, then given me her dreaded silent treatment, pursing her lips in this way that made my heart sink, but she hadn't turned into an actual beast. And the last time she'd even played along, adding to the fire. Now her cheeks flushed hot from screaming right in Mr. Ambrogio's face. He was hollering back at her at first, but then he started backing away, seeming to make excuses or apologies, like he was guilty of something.

In a flash, she drew her hand back, making it into what I can only describe as a claw. She resembled her Medusa sculpture, capable of wielding Mr. Ambrogio's bloody stump of a head, gazing at it with a mother's love.

I was scared but also thrilled to find my mother to be suddenly less secretary and more she-wolf. Shay, who was sitting next to me and also able to see the whole scene, briefly touched my back, steadying me. Mom brought that new claw of hers forward with astounding velocity and scratched the face of this famous photographer.

His hand flew up to touch where she'd pierced his flesh. Then she turned on her heels and stalked away. I felt like maybe I didn't really know my own mother. What on earth was going on here? How did she know Mr. Ambrogio? Was Mom a secret agent? Would she be fired for physically assaulting our new hotshot teacher?

Shay and I exchanged glances. The class sat silently, avoiding eye contact as Mr. Ambrogio came back with a scratch mark on his cheek. This was fucking bizarre.

Far from his former princely countenance, he now resembled a dog who'd just been kicked. But then he seemed to pump himself up again as he said, "Excuse me, just a little misunderstanding. Okay, let's take this up a notch and into the ring. I'm feeling ready for a fight. How about you?"

"The ring? Awesome," said Cash, though his hands were shaking.

"The ring," said Mr. Ambrogio, marching to the back of the classroom where he banged around in a closet. I took a couple deep breaths, trying to get back into the spirit of things, but part of my mind was still with Mom, wondering what could've possibly gotten her so worked up, and if she was okay.

Mr. Ambrogio came back after a minute, drew a huge square on the carpet with chalk as our "boxing ring," and handed out headgear, mouth guards, gloves, hand wraps, and groin and chest protectors as though it were the most normal thing. We put on everything the way he showed us, ritualistically, like knights donning sacred armor that could somehow link us to Arthurian legend. Putting the stuff on grounded me a little more. Though I was nervous, as a kid I used to go to the boxing ring and playfully spar with Dad, so this all felt a little like going home.

Most of my classmates started laughing, batting at each other impishly, our wrists having suddenly sprouted huge gloves. I felt removed from any conventional notion of reality and it was exhilarating. I couldn't have told you what we were learning exactly, but the whole thing did feel strangely edifying.

"No, no, take this seriously, everyone," Mr. Ambrogio said. "Here, look." And then he was right before me, his ruggedly handsome face now veiled but not diminished by the unearthly headgear.

"Look into my eyes, Dylan," he said.

I wondered why he kept singling me out.

"Now, as we do this, I want you to hold two things in your mind simultaneously and let them play against one another. Remember every way you've ever felt wronged and fight back. At the same time, let the images flow in—the ones that can come only when you open these particular floodgates. Then, aggressively chase your inner naysayers away. Access your old trauma and let it rip. Turn it into creativity. Shit into gold. Become the monster," Mr. Ambrogio said.

I nodded. Mr. Ambrogio wanted me to access my trauma? Fine. My dad had told me he wasn't my biological father. And then he had died. I had plenty of trauma to go around. Become the monster. Crazy. It was as though the words switched something on in me, and I was alight. I pulled my arm back, pivoted my hips and tried to hit him. But he was prepared and blocked my punch with an easy gesture. Then he pulled me into a sort of hug. "Next," he said.

"No, let me try again," I said.

Cash, looking annoyed, saying, "Give the rest of us a turn, Cyllene. I'll bet I can sock you."

Mr. Ambrogio spun around. "What makes you think the aim of boxing is to hit someone? Why, you're nothing but a schoolyard bully," he said.

Cash was humiliated.

"You want another try? Let's go," said Mr. Ambrogio to me, spittle at the corners of his mouth, removing his mouthguard and then reinserting it as though resetting something inside himself. He no longer looked like he was messing around.

This time I put the full force of my body into it, trying to punch him in the gut, where a baby might live if he were a woman. But he deftly parried and then lightly punched me in my own stomach.

"You just have to use your opponent's energy against them, and then you got it made," he said.

We were both sweating, and I felt a new door opening around my stomach region, right where he'd struck me with his glove. Was it my womb? Was something being made in there? Art of some kind?

"Do you feel transformed?" he asked, with a crooked smile.

Without missing a beat, I said, "I really do."

Mr. Ambrogio nodded, looking thrilled. He took out his mouthguard and raised his voice to address the whole class. "For homework for next class, I'd like you to make, or at least take a crack at beginning, an artwork that channels some of the fierce themes we've covered in class today."

As I was gathering my things, Mr. Ambrogio said, "Uh, hey, Dylan, can you stick around for a sec?"

I felt like I'd been chosen by a god. Cash gave me a dirty look before filing out.

"Sure. What's up?" I approached his desk, my feet feeling heavy as I tried to lift one in front of the other.

"Did you like the boxing?" he asked.

"I really did," I said.

"I thought so. Does it make you want to go home and make something awesome?" he asked.

"It kind of does," I said.

He looked delighted. "Great. Go get 'em, sport. Try to do something totally different, break out of the old ruts. As Rilke said, 'You must change your life!'"

Somehow, for no reason at all, it felt like he'd already changed mine.

Chapter Seven

I got home that day all set to make something awesome, as Mr. Ambrogio had urged, and to confront Mom about what on earth had gone down earlier and whether she would be fired or what. But then another issue surfaced that threw me even further off course.

As I came in, Mom was talking to Aunt Gemma, whom Mom called a "cold fish." I could tell by the way Mom held the phone away from her ear as Gemma crowed into it. Mom was rolling her eyes and faux yawning, as she always did when Gemma called about once a year, but then her voice changed.

She said, "Hold on, hold on," and ran into her room with the phone, shutting the door behind her.

It had already been a weird day for Mom behavior, and it definitely felt fishy that she suddenly didn't want to talk to Aunt Gemma in front of me. Who was this woman I called Mom?

I gave her a minute and then picked up on the landline, which Mom insisted on having like she was a hundred years old, to listen in. My reality had been altered so many times at this point that my paranoia was on the loose. Also, reading *Hamlet* in English hadn't helped. I now wondered if Mom was going to tell Gemma how her new lover (who didn't exist) had done away with my father by way of poison in the ear to bed her and take over the kingdom, à la *Hamlet*, but instead I encountered a different mystery altogether. As I hovered near the receiver, Gemma was saying, "But when are you going to tell Dylan who her real father is? You owe her that much. And what if he tells her first?" So my real father was *alive*? I knew it.

When Mom finished her call, she opened the door to find me standing there, waiting to confront her. Her eyes widened and her mouth hung slightly open.

"Mom, you told me he was dead," I said, straight to the point.

I expected her to get defensive, piping mad even, but instead her face went blank as though there were no Mom behind it. Then she said, "You must have misheard."

I knew exactly what had been said. In fact, I'd memorized the exact sonics, my aunt's precise vocal notes as she'd delivered the news that would change my life yet again.

"How could you? First you lie to me for my whole fucking life and now you lie again? Who is it?"

"Look, what I meant is that he's dead *to me*," she said.

"That's rich, and so not what you said. How can I trust a word that comes out of your mouth anymore? Did you even think how it would break my heart to think I had two dead dads? Like maybe there was a common denominator there. Like having me as a daughter was deadly or something? How could you say it? And up and hitting my teacher today? Who even are you? Mr. Edison could have fired you."

She smoothed her hair, then started to twist the ends.

"Edison won't fire me. He's on my side," she said, her eyes flinty, chin up, ready for battle.

"On your side? What side is that? I'm not even sure anymore. Are you like a double agent all of a sudden? I can't even with all these lies right now. Are you even my real mother? Or do I have another one of those too? Or is she dead?"

"Dylan, of course I'm your mom. You've seen photos of a doctor pulling you from between my legs. There's nothing more real to me than my connection to you, even if I have fucked it up time and again," she said, trying to hold my hand before I jerked it away. "I know how all this must look, and I regret that I can't tell you everything. I am sorry about telling you your father was dead. There's no excuse for what I did, but I panicked. For a number of reasons, I didn't want you seeking him out. Anyway, I'm not going to discuss this with you right now," she said.

"You're not going to talk about it? Great. Just shut me out like always. I wish Dad were here so there was someone to tell me the truth, someone to love me." As I said it, I knew it would sting. But she seemed more hurt than I had foreseen.

In her eyes anger, then sadness. She did the little breaths that calmed her, clapped her hands over her face. "How could you think I don't love you? I love you so much it tears me apart. Everything I do is for you. Can't you see that?"

I relented, just a little. "I know, Mom. I know. I shouldn't have said that. But it doesn't change the rest of what I said. I can't believe you're still not telling me now that it's clearly tearing me apart. Don't I deserve to know?"

She brought her face uncomfortably close to mine, her eyes beseeching. I focused on the hypnotic presence of newly discovered minuscule hairs in her nostrils.

"Bear," she said, her voice very soft now, "it's more complicated than you think. There are things about being a mother you won't understand until you do it yourself. I will tell you. I promise you that. Just give me a little more time to make a plan. I also don't know if I'm ready to relive it all so soon after losing your dad."

She'd done it—invoked losing my father. Now I couldn't in good faith push it. So I backed off, but we didn't have anything to say to each other after that, and for the first time all week I didn't try to come sleep in her bed. I lay in my own room for a long time trying to go to sleep, but I couldn't stop imagining who my biological father might be. Was it Wally, then? He was the only adult man I'd seen my mom spend much time with. Well, and Mr. Edison, but I couldn't imagine Mr. Edison ever sleeping with a woman.

I cycled through all my favorite male artists and even a few female ones before I snapped myself out of it.

I crept out of bed and out into the hallway, trying not to wake Mom. I'd agreed to a ceasefire tonight as far as demanding answers from her, but that didn't mean I couldn't try to figure this out on my own. As she slept, I grabbed Mom's phone from her bedside table—her passcode was my birthday, super predictable—and scrolled through her contacts, looking for leads. I called the few man names I didn't recognize to investigate. Doing this in the middle of the night was a bad idea; the first three numbers went straight to voicemail, and the next seemed to be disconnected. But finally one guy picked up, Alex Cooper, who sounded so kind, so open, that I dropped all attempt at working up to it and just blurted out, "Are you my father?"

Silence on the other end. Then a hang up.

Was that him?

The next morning, breakfast with Mom was awkward to say the least, since she'd effectively barred me from discussing the one thing I wanted to talk about.

"Can you pass me the milk?" I asked, seething.

Without lifting her face from her paper, she pushed the carton toward me.

I felt stranded at the center of a mystery I wasn't equipped to solve. But then I figured I couldn't ask about my mystery father, but I could ask about this other guy.

"Hey, by the way, who's Alex Cooper?" I asked her as she pretended to be unusually fascinated by the *New York Times*.

I was hoping to read her face as to whether this guy was my father, but she looked more puzzled than anything else.

"Alex Cooper? Uh, Alex was this sweet gay guy I went to art school with. Where on earth did you come up with that name? Haven't thought about him in years."

"The past," I said, eating my cereal but tasting nothing, not knowing whether I could believe her about anything anymore.

Finally, I left my bowl there and went to my room. I'd lost the dad who'd taught me about the birds and the bees, but he hadn't been the one who planted me. Someone else put a baby in my mom. That baby was me. Half of me belonged to someone I'd never met, someone I knew nothing about. It seemed almost sordid.

And my dad had known it. He'd known he was raising someone else's kid, and he'd never treated me like someone else's kid, but then again, maybe he had. Maybe he'd possessed untapped depths of love that could've been unleashed on his real kid, and he'd just had to settle for me. Maybe the love I received was just a fraction of what he possessed. If Alex Cooper wasn't my father, then who was?

That night I couldn't sleep again. For the second night in a row, I eased myself out of bed. But this time I didn't even have the comfort of my own lame detective work. I hadn't really expected to find a contact in Mom's phone conveniently labeled "Dylan's biological father." But the best I'd come up with was some random gay classmate, and now I didn't know where else to look.

I padded around the apartment, replaying in my head all the pieces of information I had on my mysterious birth father. It wasn't much. My birthday was in November, so Mom must've conceived me around March—and my mind immediately filled with an image of Mom tangled together with some faceless stranger, creating life.

I took a couple breaths and tried to focus. I knew she had been in school at NYIA, in her senior year, and dropped out not too long after she figured out she was pregnant. So someone she knew around March of that year—a one-night stand? But no, she knew his name, she just didn't want me to know his name.

I placed my hands on the urn where Mom kept Dad's ashes, wondering about this mysterious interloper whose very mention had soiled his memory. I felt angry at her, too, for the fact that she hadn't yet scattered the ashes in the junkyard as he had wanted. She'd kept them for herself instead, ignoring Dad's wishes.

Mom had quickly squirreled away most of Dad's stuff after we got home from the hospital. She thought she was helping me but, on some level, I hated her for it. She had left some things out, though. Things she didn't have the heart to hide away. I pictured her sparing them, placing them back where they had been, refusing to sacrifice them to her grief.

What grit, what ingenuity had preserved these specific objects? There was the baseball Dad had painted with the evil queen from *Snow White* to try to interest me in the sport; the bawdy illustration he'd made with crayons on a takeout menu as part of his 'birds and the bees' talk; the clock whose numbers he'd removed, replacing each one with my name so it was always "Dylan o'clock."

In my rage, in my confusion, I found myself grabbing up the clock, taking it to the basement, locating Dad's tools and dismembering it. It was a spiteful way to treat a relic of my father, but the only way I could understand something was by taking it apart and putting it back together. At five I'd taken Mom's watch apart and re-assembled it into what I called a "Not-watch." Mom had been angry at me for destroying her timepiece, but Dad had been impressed. "This is marvelous," he'd said.

Then, when I was thirteen and a drunk driver totaled Dad's truck (luckily leaving him unscathed), Wally had helped me take out, deconstruct, and reconstruct the engine into what I called, again, a "Not-engine," inspired by the Batmobile.

Mom had been furious because she didn't want me handling hazardous car materials, or destroying anything else, after all the watches. But I'll never forget the look on Dad's and Wally's faces when they saw what I'd made. They beamed like I was Leonardo freaking da Vinci.

Dad submitted photos of my creation to an art contest run by a car company. I don't know where he'd even heard of such a thing. The idea was for a young artist to design a dream car or car part. Even though my Not-Engine didn't fit the bill, I won a cash prize and a tour of the manufacturing plant. Dad and Wally had gone as my proud escorts. Dad had kept the photo they'd taken of us at the plant on his bedside table. Luckily, Mom hadn't dared to move it after he passed.

It was hard for me to love or understand anything without studying its every piece, imagining what other things it could be. I almost wished I could have done it with my father's body. That's the bare truth of it. The only way I could ever possibly have wrapped my head around his death would have been to take his body apart and then build something new with it. Now, I am a sane, moral, law-abiding person, so I would never actually do this. Not to mention, faced with his actual body, I would have just cried. But picturing an actual Frankenstein creation from his organs, a not-Dad, helped me grieve, nonetheless.

All Dad's wonders started spinning around the room in my peripheral vision, and I dropped the partially dismembered clock to shatter on the floor, now destroyed.

Seeing Dad's stuff broke my heart; not seeing it broke my heart; my heart broke regardless. After so much pain, I pictured my heart growing into a Godzilla inside me, bursting out of my chest, and terrorizing the city.

I felt terrible about shattering Dad's special clock and attempted to put it back together. When that was unsuccessful, I decided to try to build something new with it, an attempted tribute to him, and a way of assuaging my guilt.

I was driven by what I can only describe as an inner roar. The same ear-splitting interior blare that overtook me every time I smeared a canvas with paint or built a labyrinth out of paper towel rolls. Since Dad died, the only thing keeping me going was the possibility of my own genius. It was an organism I fed liberally, willing it daily: grow. It was what I wished for every time I lost an eyelash, passed a wishing well, or found the time to be 11:11. My father had suggested its possibility to me in the first place, always leaving me paintbrushes, canvas, and paint in the basement with little *Alice in Wonderland* style notes: *use me.*

I figured making something would make me feel better, down there in the basement. That basement was full of memories of Dad; it was where he'd always used his punching bag, or made his little car-part cities, while I toiled away in the makeshift studio he'd made for me on the pool table.

I gathered the broken clock parts and the materials I'd recently scavenged from the street. From a neighbor who had decluttered her apartment, I'd found treasures such as a stack of old *New Yorkers*, and as I flipped through them I formed a fledgling plan to shred them into shards of text and image, and then paste them onto an old dollhouse I had been holding onto for a while now with the vague intention of deconstructing and rebuilding it.

But then as I started cutting up the *New Yorkers* and trying to figure out how I would bring them into my poorly conceived clock project, I caught a glimpse of something else Mom hadn't cleared out yet.

Right next to where I was working sat a Joseph Cornell-style shadow box we'd all been making together, with Dr. Frankenstein greeting the creature he'd given life. I marveled at its craftsmanship. We'd carefully arranged our creation so you could peer into the box like a wonder-filled tourist to see little sculptures of the doctor and his monster.

In the book, Dr. Frankenstein's mom has recently died, and this is part of what prompts him to study the creation and destruction of life, its mysteries, and to ultimately make his creature. But after it's finished, he wakes to see it and is horrified by what he's made. In our version, though, mine and Mom and Dad's, we reversed the scene. Rather than being repelled by the grinning monster, in our shadow box, the doctor embraces his greatest creation. Mom had drawn each stitch on the creature's face, each wrinkle of smile, of age, on the doctor's face. It reminded me of the man I thought was my creator who'd died, but also of the mysterious other creator who hadn't stuck around.

I found myself badly blocked yet again, threw the pile of New Yorkers to the floor, and then sank down myself. I considered quitting art entirely, which was a new low. My inner space of invention was empty. For the whole of my eighteen years, it had been overly full of images—surreal, malformed entities, beckoning from the far reaches of my experience. I thought of them as my beloved monsters. But as I crouched on the cold basement floor, fatherless, my mother distant as the moon, all my monsters deserted me.

I kept hearing my aunt's words: *When are you going to tell Dylan who her real father is?*

I couldn't stand it any longer. I tore up the stairs, located my phone, not even caring if my mom heard, and called my aunt, which took a lot of guts given the hour and what a screamer she was. I would demand the truth.

After yelling at me for waking her up, she merely said, "Listen, young lady, it's not my place to tell you who your father is, brilliant or no. Now I'm going back to bed. It's simply not an appropriate hour to be calling people." And with that she hung up.

Instantly I became a detective. *Brilliant?!* Who was this ingenious asshole who had abandoned me? Was I more like him or like Dad? My aunt and mother would be of no help. If I wanted to crack the case of my own origins, I'd have to do it myself.

The next day was a Saturday, and I was feeling punchy after two nights of very little sleep. Mom could sense my mood, but she couldn't ask me about it when we were both so busy avoiding talking about the one thing I wanted to know.

I waited until she went out grocery shopping, and then rifled through her room. I finally opened the closet lurking halfway behind the mattress that she was always super private about, which I'd seen her open recently when she thought I was asleep. I'd never looked inside. But now I was intoxicated by what might be in there: clues to who my biological father was, maybe even my biological father himself? Alive? Dead? Was my mother Bluebeard? Clearly, I'd read far too many scary stories.

I turned the key with shaking hands. There was the collage I'd made with Shay after Dad died. I had to quickly move it out of the way, so I didn't lose it. Then, as I forged on, I was disappointed when the whole closet seemed to just be a stash of Mom's art: some figure drawings of naked women and an impressive diorama of a scene from the Salem Witch Trials I had no time to admire.

But then, right when I was about to give up, I found a shoebox, painted with a wild thicket of flowers, a sort of secret garden at the bottom of the closet. I opened it.

At first, I thought it was another dead end. The only thing inside was a collage my mother had made. She'd written lines from what I knew to be her favorite poem, "The Summer Day" by Mary Oliver, beneath a disturbing photograph of a naked woman wearing a Frankenstein mask standing behind a burning dollhouse. Something about it made my hair stand on end.

Suddenly I heard a creaking sound, and I whirled to find Mom standing behind me.

I was ready to make a joke about being Sherlock Holmes, but her expression floored me. Her face was screwed up in rage. She raised her hand as if to strike me—something she'd never done before.

I cowered on the floor. We stayed like that for a frozen moment before Mom let her arm fall. I could tell by the way she looked at her hand that she was as shocked as I was by her behavior.

"Oh god, Dyl, sweetheart, I'm so sorry. I don't know what came over me. Please forgive me. There are just some things in here that are very, uh, private."

"Why do you always push me away?"

"I don't."

"In a way, you do."

"I guess sometimes you remind me of him."

"Of Dad, or the other—"

"The other. It's uncanny and, frankly, a little traumatic for me."

This was a revelation. I thought of how I burned my art, and of how Mom looked at me when she caught me at it, like she was seeing through me. I didn't really like that side of myself either, to be honest, but I hadn't known just how much it haunted Mom. I did like fire, but I didn't like the compulsion to burn my own art, to obliterate what little footprint I left on the world. It felt strange, unbalancing, to know that maybe this piece of myself came from someone else. "Mom," I said quietly. "Who is he?"

"I can't, Dylan," she said. "I can't talk about him. Not yet."

"I hear you, but I can't wait much longer."

"I know."

After seeing her wrath, I was too scared to ask about the photo I'd unearthed from her closet. But I considered taking it out of that box one day and burning it. I knew it was nothing but trouble.

I slept that night with Mom's arms wrapped so tightly around me it almost hurt. Smushed up against her body, breathing deeply the aromas of my first home, my ears pummeled by her snores, finally I was able to fall soundly asleep, pondering those poetry lines on Mom's secret collage: *Tell me, what is it you plan to do with your one wild and precious life?* Three words came to my mind in response: *Father, Art, Shay.*

In *Frankenstein*, after making his creature, Dr. Frankenstein has a dream about his dead mother's corpse and wakes to find the monster he's made standing over his bed. That night, I had just such a dream about my father's body. In it, I was back in that moment where I'd sniffed his chest while he was alive, but this time I drew back in dread as I realized I was inhaling the aroma of a cadaver.

I woke to see Dad's ghost knocking at the window. Maybe this was just a continuation of the dream, but it felt so real. I was scared that this specter was really there and at the same time worried that it wasn't. Ms. Burgess told us that all Keats' negative capability involved was accepting "uncertainties, mysteries, doubts, without any irritable reaching after fact and reason," and this was just what I was trying to do.

I glanced at the bedside clock: just after 1 a.m. Mom's grip on me had relaxed but she was still holding me tightly, so it took a minute to wriggle away without waking her. I went over to the bedroom window and opened it. My father flew into my arms. He was sobbing, long threads of snot forming a spiderweb beneath his nose, and his arms wrapped around me as tightly as my mother's had done earlier.

His voice had a roughness and echo it never had in life. He said, "I'll always be your *real father real father real father.*"

"I know, Dad. But can't you just give me a hint as to who the other guy is?"

"He's close," he said.

"What does that mean?" I asked, but he was already gone, and I was staring at a fatherless window.

You'd think it would be hard to get back to sleep after that, but I wasn't even totally convinced I was awake in the first place. I let myself drop back onto the bed and closed my eyes, let my mind go slack. When I opened them again, I had another ghostly visitor. It was a looming figure of a man I'd never seen before. I imagined it to be my real father, and I decided he was Alex Cooper—gay or not. In my fantasy, I reached out to embrace this unknown father with brown hair and brown eyes just like mine, but as I was hugging him, he morphed into Shay.

Then this Shay-Alex flickered and was gone. I felt emptier than ever, and totally awake. What if my real father was a ghost, or just not alive anymore as Mom had originally said? What if I was my real father? Or my Mom was? Or Shay? Or Ms. Burgess? I was clearly losing it. But what if I never had the reunion I longed for with him? Never had the union I longed for with Shay? What would Shay do if she were in my place? I decided she'd have stayed on the line with Alex Cooper until she had an answer instead of hanging up like a sissy, so I grabbed Mom's phone, not even really scared she would catch me anymore, went into the kitchen and dialed his number again.

I must have woken him up again because he sounded foggy. "Hello? Hello?" he said. I had become his ghost, a spectral silence on the other end of the line.

But I forced myself to speak. "Um, Mr. Cooper. This is very awkward, but you went to school with my mom, Jane Cyllene, or it was Rainey then, and I'm wondering if you know who my dad was?"

There was a long pause and then he said, "Ah, you must have been that strange late-night call I received. You must stop doing that, darling. I need my beauty sleep."

I wished he would say, "Oh honey, I'm not actually gay and I've been searching everywhere for you for years." But he only chuckled softly and said, "So you're Jane Rainey's little girl, eh? I'd love to help you out, my dear, but I have no idea. I do remember that she mentioned being very, uh, close with someone who taught her a lot about art. Maybe that will help you out? Good luck in your search and tell Janie I said 'hi.' Oh, and if you want to call again, maybe wait till like, noon, okay? I'm not loving the middle-of-the-night calls."

I walked back to Mom's room like a zombie, my head emptied of anything resembling sense. I rested my forehead against the windowpane, leaving face marks. But at least now I had a lead. Someone who taught her a lot about art? One of her teachers at NYIA, maybe?

Chapter Eight

The next morning, I tried following up on my new lead with Mom. "I really like Ms. Burgess. She's a great teacher," I began.

"Mm-hmm, I know. That's great, honey," said Mom, immersed in her stupid newspaper yet again.

"Did you have any teachers you were close with at art school?" I tried.

"No, not really. That's part of why I left." Alex Cooper had specifically said she was close to someone who taught her about art, and unlike Mom, Alex Cooper had no reason to lie to me.

"I really learned more about art from your dad and Wally than from anyone at that pretentious school," she added.

A regular snoop now, as Mom was getting dressed, I grabbed her phone and scrolled through her contacts again with all the clues orbiting my brain, trying to figure out my next move, knowing that, despite having read all Mom's old *Nancy Drew* books, I was a truly terrible detective.

And that's when I saw the text: "In Florida visiting my mother until Friday. Let me know if you need anything. Miss you," from Wally. Miss you? I stared at the words, paralyzed. I thought back to how I'd seen him sniff Mom's hair at the hospital.

Of course, this whole time I'd been trying to figure out who my father was when the answer had been right there, just as Dad's ghost had said: if anyone was close to the family, it was Wally. Wally dropping off his chicken soup and car parts. Wally who Mom herself said had taught her so much about art. *One of her teachers.* The way he looked at her, and talked about her work, the tender way he'd always been to me ... *like a father.*

I cracked the bathroom door and called out to Mom: "I'll actually just see you at school. I just remembered something I have to do before class."

I wasn't about to miss the first class where we covered Frankenstein, but I knew I had time to run the ten blocks to Wally's apartment before Ms. Burgess's class. His place was way too easy to break into, seeing as he always left his key under his doormat like the older, trusting guy he was. Clearly, he shouldn't have trusted me.

As I sprinted into his apartment, mopping sweat from my forehead, knocking over a can of quarters, I wondered if Wally was really my father. If so, how must it have felt for him to stand by and watch Dad raise me? Why would he do such a thing?

I wasn't totally sure what I was looking for. I walked around eyeballing all Wally's stuff like, "Is this my *father's* comb? My *father's* slippers?" I got more frenzied as I realized how little time I had before class and started jerking open cabinets and doors, searching everywhere for some symbol of my parentage, smelling Wally's particular smell—gasoline and fried food—and thinking how easy it would be just to sink into his paternity. He'd always been there, my whole life; when I was little I used to call him "Uncle Wally" and he would babysit when my parents wanted a night out. Honestly, I hoped it was him. That would make sense. But I was also completely unsure how I'd ever ask him, if it came to that.

Suddenly I heard footsteps behind me. I froze like stillness would make me invisible. Of course Wally's house would be robbed while I was there. I wondered if I'd have to fight an intruder.

But then I heard, "Dylan?" I turned. And there was Wally, in his own apartment, just where he should be. I was unfortunately holding a pair of his boxers like a pervert.

"This. This isn't what it looks like," I said, and dropped the boxers to the floor between us, where we both stared at them. "But—but I thought you were in Florida?"

He just stood there, looking at me with a raised eyebrow, rubbing engine grease off his hands with a dish towel.

"Came back early. I don't even know what this looks like. Whatchya doing here, eh?" he asked, looking just the slightest bit amused.

"We were out of eggs," was the absurd thing I thought to say.

He laughed and I laughed nervously along with him. "Okay," I continued shakily, "I don't know how to say this, so I'll just say it. I came here to try to figure out if you were—my father—but I suck as a detective, so I wasn't able to—"

"Your *father*?" He sounded incredulous, chuckling softly.

"Look, I know. I know Dad wasn't the one who—"

"Ah," he said. His face filled with understanding; obviously Wally knew this secret already. Was I the only one who didn't? "Let's take a seat, eh?" he said, motioning toward his patched couch.

We sat next to each other stiffly. I could smell beer on the couch fabric.

"Now, look," he said, "I love you like a daughter and all, but no, I am not your father."

"Oh," I said, feeling crushed, like I'd somehow lost another dad. I'd already gotten so attached to this gentle giant as the perfect guy to fill Dad's shoes. We could have gone to the junkyard together after school and made something wonderful.

"But, let me ask you something. What is a father, anyway?" he asked, holding the boxers he'd picked up off the floor.

"What do you mean?" I asked.

"Look, Dyl, it's like this. Who is more important, the guy who plants a seed in the garden and walks away or the guy who comes every single day to water it? Why do you need to know who planted the seed?"

"This feels like a conversation about God or something. I don't know. I just need to know," I said.

He nodded sagely. "I get that."

"But you didn't, um, plant the seed in the, uh, garden, huh?"

"Oh, sweet Jesus, no," he said, nervously tugging on the boxers now.

"Oh, okay. Well, I have to get to class," I said, staring at my feet.

"Dylan, stay for a coffee," he said, patting my back. I must have looked rough because he even pulled me in for a small, terribly awkward hug. I didn't know where to put my arms, so I held them rigidly straight over his shoulders like I was trying to fly.

"No, no, I should get to class. I just need to use the bathroom before I get on the subway, though, if that's okay?" He nodded.

I washed my hands and splashed a little water on my face. Of course Wally wasn't my father. What a stupid conclusion to jump to. What was I thinking—that he and Mom were close? Of course they were close. Wally was a family friend. Clearly my detective skills needed some honing. But then as I was looking for a towel, since there were none on the rack, I opened a drawer and saw a photograph of Mom. There she was, youthful, staring back at me from a nest of deodorant and toothpaste boxes in Wally's bathroom. I ran out of there without drying my hands.

"Let me know if you and your mom need anything, you hear?" he called as I dashed out the door.

"Yeah," I called back, not sure what to think about anything anymore.

On the subway to school, I felt unmoored. So was Wally my father after all? Had he just lied to me too? Was that all adults knew how to do? Lie and make bastard daughters? Why did he have that photo? Or was there another explanation? Did he just have a crush on Mom?

I stared at every man swaying with the train, grasping a subway pole, wondering if any of them might be my secret progenitor. Maybe they all were. Like each one was a piece of him, a piece of me, pixels in the larger mystery of my real father.

I thought about what Wally had said. *What even was a father?* There were tons of biological fathers who beat their kids, so what made their genetic contribution so sacred? And what did this person have to do with understanding my own origins? Maybe nothing. Maybe my own origin was up to me. I was the artist, after all, wasn't I? Hadn't I built myself, piece by piece, a female Frankenstein? Would that be my greatest creation?

Or had Wally really meant nothing by his comment but just said it to throw me off his trail? But if he were my father, why wouldn't he tell me? We could start having ice cream sundaes together and everything. I had to stop myself from planning our future attendance at a father-daughter dance.

The train car got packed as we approached Jay Street, people clustering together cheek-to-cheek. I felt so lonely that I was relieved to feel strangers breathing against my back. I relaxed when my head ended up cradled in a giant shoulder behind me. I could smell the man's aftershave. Right before I got off at Jay, I turned to look at him.

He was enormous. There was sweat trapped in the great elephant folds of his face. His eyes were small and hopeful, probably unused to any kind of female attention. I had the urge to put my hands on his cheeks, tell him what nobody had ever told him, "To me you're beautiful." I wanted to tell him I loved him. Like I loved Dad. Like I loved Wally. And, in that moment, I truly did.

He looked at me quizzically as I stared at him. I took a tiny step closer and whispered, "Father." But he just looked weirded out and put his earbuds back in. Fair enough. I walked off the train, re-entering that bubble of public solitude where all New Yorkers learn to live.

I slipped into Ms. Burgess's classroom right before the bell. I was still in a weird headspace after the whole Wally thing plus the strange subway interaction. I had to shake myself out of it, remind myself that we were starting *Frankenstein* that day, and despite everything going on at home, or maybe because of it, I was excited to get Ms. Burgess's take on my favorite book.

I blamed (credited?) her for intensifying my obsession with my one dead father and one absent one, and also with gothic elements such as ghosts and monsters. She'd had us study the hero's journey while reading *The Odyssey* (son seeks lost father amidst monsters) and *Hamlet* (son sees ghost of lost father) in the same semester we watched *Star Wars* (fatherless boy battles monstrous entities in space, one of whom turns out to be his missing father). This last one gave me a particular gnawing hope that I, too, would find my long-lost father. As if that weren't enough, now we were starting *Frankenstein*—the monster is the unwanted child, rejected by the scientist "father" who created him; needless to say, I identified. It bothered me that all these protagonists were boys, but I still hoped I secretly might be a hero like Odysseus, Hamlet, or Luke Skywalker, especially since one of the sources of their specialness seemed to be fatherlessness.

I grabbed a seat in the front row with my pencil case ready to go, waiting for all the wisdom of the world to come zooming into my veins, longing as always to be filled by some force I couldn't yet understand.

When everyone else had settled into their seats, after Malcolm had pulled out his fingernail clippers (why?) and Hilda had applied lip-gloss (again?), we started wondering where Ms. Burgess was.

Malcolm had white-blonde hair, with a sour face that only became sourer as he clipped nail after nail, as if nobody had ever told him this was an at-home activity.

Hilda had an anxious edge to her, and this waiting seemed to increase it. Finally, after putting the lip-gloss away, she pulled some knitting out of her bag, and started to look more placid as she worked on what appeared to be a tea cozy.

Jeffrey was biding his time by picking his teeth. He didn't even try to hide it. I suppose you had to admire his lack of self-consciousness. No polite way of putting this, but the most memorable thing about Jeffrey was how precisely he resembled a Saint Bernard—pronounced jowls, thick lips and a tongue that always protruded a bit. His eyes were droopy and he always had a look on his face partway between boredom and disdain.

Shay tapped out a text on her phone, checking if her mom was okay, I imagine. Then she let the phone fall into her bag and sat there, alternating between biting her nails and doodling stingrays in her notebook. I'd never realized what majestic animals they were until I saw them through Shay's eyes.

Meanwhile, I had to hide my paper because I was doodling Shay, trying to capture the exact angle created by her chin resting in her palm. I wished I could doodle moving images to capture the restless way she moved. Always in motion. Right hand shoved in her mouth as she gnawed at her nails. Then she grabbed up the pen again, saliva still glistening on those sheared nails as she went at the notebook like she was angry at it. Then finishing off the whole sequence by taking her gum out of her mouth, glaring at it, surreptitiously smelling it, mushing it into the center of her stingray drawing, crumpling the whole thing into a ball, and chucking it at the garbage can.

"Ooh, nice, three-pointer, Burgess," said Cash. He grinned at her, a predatory smile if I ever saw one.

I made a mental note to salvage the gummy, crumpled-up stingrays after everyone had left the classroom.

We sat there awkwardly, a group whose only commonality was being in this class together. Cash and Malcolm were chattering away about basketball, but the rest of us just stared at the ceiling. Where was our teacher? As the time wore on, I took out my phone and Googled Simon Ambrogio again to get some more intel.

As I scrolled through Google images of his work, I quickly caught my breath when I saw what Google was telling me was Simon's most famous photograph, entitled Art Monster. The one I'd read about last time I researched him. But here was the image now. It was just like the one Mom kept locked away in her closet except, instead of standing next to the burning dollhouse, the naked woman in the Frankenstein mask appeared to be running away from it, looking backward in that strange mask.

Next, I Google imaged "Simon Ambrogio art monster Frankenstein mask photos" and scrolled through image after image, but the one that Mom had never appeared.

Unless there was some huge glitch in Google, Mom had a photo of Mr. Ambrogio's that wasn't public? A secret photo?

I Googled his bio and found that he had taught at New York Institute of the Arts right around the time Mom went there. So he had been *one of her teachers.* And he also taught there, of course, right around the time ... I was conceived.

I sat, paralyzed, trying to take all this new information in. Talk about someone who was right in front of me, close. Here he was teaching in my school. I didn't want to jump to conclusions, but the evidence was piling up here. Not to mention the weird fight Mr. Ambrogio and Mom had had after his first class.

Cash was starting to pack his stuff up, and I was in the process of freaking out, wondering if this famous artist Ambrogio could possibly be my father, when the lights went out. A few students screamed. One was me.

Chapter Nine

Then the lights came back on and a Frankenstein monster, no, a person wearing a monster mask, was standing where our teacher should have been. With its green skin, bloody gashes, visible stitches, and bolts, the monster's face was fake and hellish. But what almost stopped my heart was how much it resembled the mask on the woman in Mr. Ambrogio's photographs. The other eerie thing about it was the pair of human eyes glaring out, and the delicate female body beneath.

"I'm calling 911 on this freak," called Cash, yanking out his phone.

"Holy shit," screamed Shay, looking thrilled and not scared at all. She took her huge, old-school camera out of her bag and started snapping photos. I admired her ability to turn this moment into art; meanwhile I was about to soil myself. Shay was one of those people who would have captured the last arresting photographs of any tragedy she experienced. She was at the frontlines of life while I was ever the supporting character. I wished to gather the girls in the room and be like that feminist *Ghostbusters* movie, but when I tried to stand up, nothing happened. My legs didn't work.

"I'll get Mr. Edison," said Hilda, dropping her lip-gloss and hyperventilating. She had gathered her ancient satchel and was preparing to flee with a rustling of her old-timey skirts, complete with what looked to be petticoats. I imagined an episode like this could kill someone like Hilda, who was afraid of her own shadow and desperate for the trains to run on time. But the monster gestured forcefully for Cash and Hilda to cease and desist. And so they did.

I sat still, familiar by now with things falling apart, not fighting it, just letting the figurative boat of the classroom fill with water, preparing to go down with it, hoping for rare treasures at the bottom of it all. I had a sweet glimpse of all my possible fathers saving me. In my imagining, first they assembled, holding up numbers as in a police lineup, and then they teamed up to deliver me from this monster who had suddenly taken over our classroom.

Then the monster was laughing, removing its mask, and shaking out its long black hair. It was Ms. Burgess.

Once removed, I could see she was holding a cheap Halloween mask.

"Gotcha," she said, and the whole room quickly sculpted itself into one big carefree smile, heads thrown back, laughter, "you got us"—as though a moment ago we hadn't all been about to wet our chairs.

Everybody seemed to get the joke except me. I stared at my teacher's bared face, then I stood up. "I have to go," I said, not waiting for a response before rushing out into the hallway, knocking my notebook onto the floor, not even taking my bookbag with me.

Ms. Burgess followed me out. I wasn't sure if this was what I wanted or not.

"Dylan?" she said.

"That wasn't cool," I said, not turning to look at her.

"Did I scare you for real? I'm so sorry. That was not my intention," she said.

"You did. I've been imagining things lately and this didn't help with the, um, confusion I'm having between reality and, well, fantasy?" was all I could think to say.

"I hear you, Dylan. Welcome to the club. It's called being a creative person," she said, looking so proud, it made me feel proud too. "I try to shock the senses, take people out of their comfort zones. For the work. I find that a good dose of terror can make you students let go of the conventional and go toward the truly original in your writing. I thought you most of all would get it. Maybe, in the case that you're imagining things, you should, I don't know, lean in?" she said.

This concept was riveting to me, especially coming from a grownup. Lean into the monsters, the ghosts? I liked it.

"Okay," I said, allowing her to link arms with me and guide me back into the classroom.

Shay shot me a comforting smile as we walked back in.

"Class pet," Cash mouthed, but not with any real threat.

I smiled because the moment seemed to call for it, sat back down, selected the robin's-egg-blue pencil, and started doodling as Ms. Burgess banged her huge tote bag onto the desk in front of her.

Ms. Burgess put the monster mask next to the bag, and proceeded to pull out books, folders, a large sandwich, markers, glitter glue. As she banged her stuff on the table, I took a sort of inventory of her teacherliness: the pencil that held the bird's nest of her bun together, the safety pin that secured her shirt in the back, the not-so-discreet coffee stain on her collar, the pen mark on her forehead. These all struck me as the kinds of quirks you had to have grown up a hot girl to pull off and still look, well, hot.

Then there was her habitual huge cup of coffee, matching the one Shay always had. They must go get mother-daughter coffee together before school. The cup was no doubt cold by now, and Ms. Burgess would at some point spill it all over the desk.

Even in her disarray and recent assault on the class, we could all sense that Ms. Burgess meant well, that she cared, that she was just trying to stun us into accessing something most people never reach for.

"Apologies if I scared anyone. I just wanted to bring a little levity to class, and Dylan's mother Jane just kindly donated this mask to the costume drive for Ms. Pearson's theater class. But I may have gone too far, and I am truly sorry for that." She was looking at me.

My ears perked up. My mother had donated that mask? It looked just like the one the woman in the photo in her closet wore as she stood in front of that burning dollhouse. Why did Mom have that mask? Had she taken the photograph? Who was the woman in the mask? What was her link to Simon? Could he be my dad, or was that just a fantasy of having a famous artist as a father?

Ms. Burgess went to sit down and, right on schedule, spilled her coffee everywhere. As she swore under her breath and grabbed the paper towels she kept in the desk drawer for just this purpose, I couldn't help noticing how still gorgeous she was, how much she looked like her daughter.

She said, "Oh, son of a bitch. Pardon my French. Anyway, sorry, but not sorry for hopefully waking you up to the ingenious book you started for today. Now, keep in mind, this is not merely a monster book. Among other things, it's a book about creativity and loss. It's about an absent father," and I'm pretty sure she shot a glance at both Shay and me when she said that part. "Here's this guy who, in an act of sheer brilliance and creativity, makes a monster and then regrets it, abandons it."

"So," she continued, "Mary Shelley wrote a text on different kinds of creativity: making a text, a baby, a monster. Then Shelley herself was treated like a monster for writing the book in the first place, especially while caring for an infant herself. She even referred to the book itself as her 'hideous progeny,' her own kind of monstrous baby. So when I re-read Frankenstein for today's class, its ties to questions of creativity and parenthood seemed all the more pressing now that I'm a mother myself." Here she shot a look at her daughter, and Shay blushed but blew her a kiss, which Ms. Burgess pretended to catch in a corny way that was also kind of adorable.

Ms. Burgess scrawled, "Art Monster" on the board. Then she turned her eyes to the class, not letting up on the eye contact, asking, "What does this term mean? And, no, I'm not talking about Mr. Ambrogio's photograph," she said, and Hilda lowered her hand.

As she waited on someone to answer now that Hilda was out of the running, she opened the drawer of her desk and pulled out a trash bag. She reached inside and started walking from desk to desk, depositing plastic Halloween Frankenstein masks that resembled the one she'd worn earlier. We all took them dubiously, most of us shoving them into our backpacks, not wanting another monster visitation that day.

"Here you are. Wear them often, maybe even as you're writing, to really unlock your inner art monster. But, again, what does that term

82

mean?" she asked.

Shay raised her hand. "Well, I sort of cheated on this quiz since you never stop talking about this stuff at home, but maybe an art monster is someone who gets to be really into their art," she said.

"Right," said Ms. Burgess, scribbling more stuff on the board, looking like she might start levitating she was so excited. "And this person is usually assumed to be a man. But what happens when the art monster is a woman?"

There was silence. But I got what Ms. Burgess was saying. I wanted my own art to be monstrous, always. I wanted to put the different pieces of me behind glass, let you feel what I feel. Let you look, say, "Here lies the artist's spleen," maybe even make a hole in the glass where you could hold it. For a single shattering moment we'd be one throbbing body before I cracked the glass and ran away from any sort of enclosure.

I hoped some part of my paternal conundrum could be understood by what Ms. Burgess was saying. I was taking notes so fast my finger was getting a weird callous. And I could see from Shay's epic notetaking laced with Frankenstein doodles that she was really feeling it, too.

Ms. Burgess was saying, "In the case of Mary Shelley, the monster is a character in the story, but it also represents the writing process and the way that writing will be treated by society, especially when that writer is a woman, and especially when she's treading on the supposedly masculine territory of genius and monsters. The public acted almost as if to write about monsters is to become one. Let's not forget the same actor portrayed both Shelley and the lady monster in the movie *Bride of Frankenstein*." Shay looked spellbound.

Ms. Burgess then got that crinkle in her forehead that signaled she was about to change direction. "I think I'm getting too theoretical here. You guys look lost. Let's change gears and do some group work. I think we need to make something concrete, but in the spirit of the book—let's create some Frankensteinian art objects. And don't forget to think of a framing question your object answers. Who's with me?"

The class looked buoyant. It was always fun when Ms. B. whipped out her wacky craft stuff and let us play with it.

"I am," said Cash, winking. He was the kind of confident where he would hit on the lady teachers. Maybe it came from being the son of an artist famous for making paintings by dipping his butt in paint and then sitting all over the canvas. I'm serious. Perhaps this was at the root of why Cash had turned out to be such an *asshole* in particular—albeit a talented asshole. Although he hadn't, to the best of my knowledge, utilized his posterior in his art making yet.

Thankfully freeing me from thoughts of Cash's ass, Ms. Burgess gave her directions. "Okay, let's start by pairing off and asking each other a question to get the old creative juices flowing. You can ask your partner or the class in general. Whatever works."

I automatically turned to surly Saint Bernard Jeffrey who was sitting to my right. Since we were both socially awkward and didn't talk much in class, Jeffrey and I perennially got stuck working together. We were always the ones left unclaimed at the end of these little pairing-off sessions, so at some point it got easier to just pretend he was my first choice. Teachers never realized how not-fun group work was for shy or unpopular kids.

There were always a few open seats, and today I noted there was one to my left. Shay was sitting next to it, and then Greta was sitting on the other side of Shay. Greta was hard to miss because she wore a lot of purple. Today she had added a purple headband, which sat on her fiery red hair like an eggplant crown, and her cat-eye glasses rested on her cute little beak-like nose. I wondered if this was what Mom had looked like in high school.

I could see Cash was making a move to get up and sit in the empty seat next to Shay, the wolf about to bust into the chicken coop. I panicked and tried to think how I could put a stop to this. He'd made one gay joke too many and now this was war.

Having come up with nothing better, I shoved my notebook onto the floor in front of Shay, who got up to get it. This gave Greta time to turn to Cash, who was sitting next to her, and say, "Want to partner up?"

He looked disappointed and hesitated. The whole room was

looking back and forth between Greta and Cash.

As Shay was handing me back my notebook, she said, "Are you kidding me, Cash? Just how rude are you?" Cash looked cowed, and therefore agreed to work with Greta. I had to resist a smirk, lest I turn into a movie villain.

Then Shay turned, found the empty seat beside her, and slid into it, so that she was sitting next to me. "Great," she said. "Let's get started. Okay, framing question. Let's see. Quick, what's the most beautiful thing you've ever seen?"

It took the entirety of my self-control not to answer, "You."

My head spun. Sitting so close to Shay and being asked a direct question made me so nervous I found myself reciting the Lord's Prayer in my mind, or what I believed to be the Lord's Prayer, even though I'd never set foot in a church in my sinner's life. *Our Father in heaven, hallowed be your name.* I was speechless. *Your kingdom come, your will be done, on earth as it is in heaven.*

Now the rest of the room was listening for my answer about the most beautiful thing, which made it harder, running the risk that someone else might snatch up the precious question Shay had meant for me.

Sure enough, Cash was first to respond, with the very thing I'd wanted to say but stopped myself: "Ms. Burgess, may I respond?" asked Cash, in a rare show of respect.

Ms. Burgess nodded, "Yes, as you know, students are always free to respond to any question posed in this class. Democracy, folks," she said.

Cash turned to Shay and said, "Your face."

Shay shot him this look that shut him down, and I felt a fleeting victory before remembering that I still hadn't spoken.

"So not gonna happen. She's still not into males," said Malcolm.

Jeffery surprised us all by answering: "The most beautiful thing I've ever seen would have to be this dying bird I saw in Prospect Park recently," and everyone but Shay and I looked repelled. But I got him, and Shay was nodding in a way that told me she did, too. If Shay's photos of dead animals were any kind of evidence, we had both seen beauty in that kind of wreckage.

"I guess the city where I was born, Paris," said Hilda. Of course she was born in Paris.

Give us this day our daily bread and forgive us our debts as we also have forgiven our debtors.

Since I was still floundering, Shay, empath that she was, offered, "I'm obsessed with taking pictures of the Wonder Wheel. What about you, Dylan?"

I was searching for an escape hatch when the answer came to me. Suddenly it was obvious. "I—I think I would have to say that place in Brooklyn Bridge Park where you can see both bridges at the same time," I said. Right where I'd seen her standing, months ago when I first became obsessed with the spot.

Shay looked thunderstruck. "That's—that's my place. It's … just mystical. I've definitely seen you there."

"It really is. Yeah, I'm always there," I said, wondering if she thought I was a stalker. I mean, I was, but I didn't want her to know that.

Even Malcolm and Cash had to nod.

"Nothing like those bridges," said Cash, shooting a look to see if he'd gotten Shay's attention. And it looked, unfortunately, like he had. She gave him a surprised, approving little glance like she hadn't expected him to care about bridges. To be fair, he probably didn't.

"Excellent. Anyone else?" Ms. Burgess asked. Total quiet.

"Okay, I'll go," Ms. Burgess said after a full minute of awkward silence. "My most beautiful thing was a man with a rare condition called epidermodysplasia verruciformis in Bangladesh, which caused him to have what looked like trees growing from his wrists. He didn't understand his condition wasn't considered beautiful. To him, and to me, it was the most beautiful thing. He told me he alone was a forest and I couldn't disagree. I've never been the same since. Okay, great, so not everyone has to share, but let's use these images in our work now, and feel free to share any other questions that come up."

She handed out her usual assortment of oddities—glue sticks, googly eyes, broken mirrors, old dolls, and so forth. I could guess where Shay got some of her hospice art material donations from. We always passed Ms. B's items around trying not to laugh but also thrilled, our sense of childish play awakened.

At the end of class, I gathered up my stuff quickly, so I wouldn't have to deal with the awkwardness of socializing.

As I was hurrying out, Shay stood in the door to intercept me.

"What's the rush? You got a date or something?" she asked.

"No rush. No date," I said, laughing too loudly, shaking.

"Want to go see the bridges together?" she asked.

Cash came up behind her. "I'm in," he said.

My heart sank.

"Another time. We have something we need to talk about," Shay said.

"Next time," Cash said, looking vanquished.

I felt victorious again and, finally, part of a world outside myself, my many dads, and Mom.

Chapter Ten

"What did you want to talk about?" I finally asked Shay as we walked down Front Street. I still couldn't believe she'd invited me on a walk.

"Oh, that's just something I said to get rid of Cash."

"Ah," I said, the wind going out of me. Well, at least she wanted to hang out with me and not Cash?

"How are you doing since, well, the stuff with your dad?" she asked.

"Okay." I wanted to tell her about everything that had happened lately. But the only word that made it out of my mouth was *okay*.

"So you don't talk much, huh?" she asked.

"I just have to get comfortable first. Then I'm quite chatty," I said as we hit the waterfront.

"So, I make you uncomfortable? But I'm so warm and fuzzy." As she walked, she touched the railing that separated us from the river, her fingertips gliding over the stainless steel.

"No, it just always takes me some time." I stopped for a moment and rested my elbows on the rail, gazing out at the water.

"I'm on it. I love projects," she said, resting her elbows beside mine for a minute before we walked on.

"Ha, okay," I said, feeling a sliver of hope that she could one day love me back.

"Has anyone ever told you that you look kind of like Winona Ryder in that old movie *Beetlejuice?* I love that freaking movie. Mom had me watch it and I was like, 'Doesn't that look exactly like Dylan?' and Mom totally agreed," she said.

I managed to make eye contact for a second, feeling fizzy inside. Shay had thought about me. She'd thought about how I looked, enough to have opinions on it. "Wow," I said, "no, I've never heard that, but that's definitely hands down the best celebrity comparison I've ever gotten."

I could feel the Brooklyn Bridge coming closer with each step. It always felt like going home.

"Lydia Deetz—you know, Winona's character—is super Goth. I feel like she would have appreciated reading *Frankenstein.* She would've liked the whole monster thing Mom was talking about in class today, don't you think?" she asked.

"Totally. It's like my favorite book ever," I said.

"Mine, too."

Emboldened, I replied, "Really? I made a little Bride of Frankenstein doll for myself as a child. It was hideous. I think it scared my mother." Only half my brain was saying the words; the other half was trying to ignore the sight of Shay's collar bones above her T-shirt and how much I wanted to trace them.

"Yeah, scaring my mom is like my favorite hobby. That Bride is awesome, and Frankenstein just destroys her. Not cool. But you know what else I get?" she asked.

"What?" I asked.

"Why Dr. Frankenstein made his monsters. How he just had to sew all that shit together. How it felt so right. Made him feel better, you know?"

I was silent because I suddenly felt so seen. She seemed to take my silence badly, though.

"I shouldn't have said all that. Do I sound nuts?" she asked, blushing.

I enjoyed how she was a maverick but also turned red like that. I had to say something. She was waiting. I watched her take out a spliff and I became mesmerized by the sight of flame so near Shay's lips. My breathing became labored until I finally blurted it out. "You have no fucking idea how much I get you," I said. Something I'd been wanting to tell her since freshman year.

She looked relieved, touched even, took my hand and squeezed three times. I was stunned, and not only because Shay Burgess was holding my hand, touching me. It was somehow my father's special hand squeeze. Like a sign from him that Shay was the one.

I felt the need to fill the silence, so I said, "I'm still not sure about Winona but has anyone ever told you that you look like Jane Morris?"

"Like Jane who? I didn't know there was any actress I hadn't heard of."

"No, no. Jane Morris, William Morris' wife, who was the model for the Rossetti painting of Proserpine."

"Oh, so you're an art nerd?"

"Definitely."

"Me, too. Oh yeah. What we learned about her in Mr. Pheder's art class last year was—what's her name again—?"

"Proserpine."

"Right. The one where the god of hell kidnaps her. Mr. Pheder said she looked like she felt bad about eating the pomegranate, but he's an idiot. That Proserpine was a fighter. She showed no remorse. She wanted that fruit all to herself, even if it was her downfall, and maybe because of it. She was like Eve, or maybe Lilith. She, like, ate of the tree of the knowledge of good and evil. She was super wise if you ask me. It's like with the Bride in *Frankenstin*. What happens to the woman monster in the book. But, see, if I'd written the story, she'd have been the star and she wouldn't have been punished for it."

"A hundred percent."

"I knew we had something in common. Anyway, I think that *Proserpine* is a sad painting. She looks trapped to me."

Shay got a weird look in her eyes, lit up a joint, took a long hit, passed it to me, and said, "Maybe that's you."

"Maybe," I said, surprising myself with my own honesty.

She looked thoughtful. "But what about this," she said, "what if Proserpine didn't actually want to go back to earth? What if she fucking loved the underworld and its dark knowledge. We also just read *The Odyssey* obviously, and there's a reason that Odysseus guy purposefully goes down there to hell. That witch—"

"Circe?"

"Yeah, that one who told him to go there was a genius. The villain women always get the good roles. Anyway, she's like, 'go down there and feed those motherfuckers blood and they'll give you wisdom,' and that's exactly what he does. Do you get what I'm saying?"

"I really do. I also really get Telemachus."

She looked surprised at this. "Like you know the guy personally?"

"Hilarious. No, I just mean I get that search for your father that could just, like, take you to the ends of the earth."

"Me, too. You want to shotgun?"

I felt alarmed. "What?"

"Here, make your hands like this," she said, joining our hands to create a shelter against the wind, and then blowing her smoke right into my mouth. She smelled like jasmine and liquor. Had she been day drinking? She left her eyes open while she did it, and so did I.

Momentarily, I felt I was receiving something from her eyes through the smoke. As if enlightened with dark knowledge, suddenly wise as Frankenstein's monster, who was a big reader, though nobody remembers that. Or maybe it was just Shay's good weed. Whatever it was, it was sublime, like Shay, like those bridges in the distance.

"Okay, you ready for this one?" she asked, placing an earbud in my ear. Sex Pistols. We walked along to "Anarchy in the UK." I looked out over downtown Manhattan, *I wanna be Anarchy in the city / How many ways to get what you want* roaring in my head. She had pumped up the volume as high as it would go. Although it hurt my ears and I worried about my future hearing, I didn't ask her to turn it down.

As we walked on, we kept smoking and listening to music. I felt like maybe we were walking in a parallel Brooklyn I'd never seen. I decided I'd tell everyone all about it as soon as I got the chance.

Needless to say, the revelation didn't hold up when the spliff ran out and my high started to fade, surreal edges sanding off the world and leaving just familiar, slightly garbage-smelling Dumbo. But Shay was still holding my hand, and I could feel our pulses careening together where the skin touched, knocking at the walls of their fleshy confines.

After neither of us had spoken for a while, Shay pulled out our earbuds and said, "What I didn't say before was I had a thing for her."

"For who?" I asked.

"For Winona in *Beetlejuice*," she said, giving me a naughty sideways glance.

The notion that Shay could have a thing for anyone who even possibly resembled me was mind-blowing.

"Thank you," I said formally, turning toward the bridges.

As I looked out at the Brooklyn Bridge and the East River, I made the wish I always made lately. We'd read Hart Crane's *The Bridge* last semester with Mr. Boswell and I heard those lines whenever I looked at it: *O Sleepless as the river under thee, / Vaulting the sea, the prairies' dreaming sod, / Unto us lowliest sometime sweep, descend / And of the curveship lend a myth to God.* We also learned that Crane had committed suicide by throwing himself into just such a body of water. It wasn't the East River but the Gulf of Mexico. I wished for my father to come back to life. I wished to make a great work of art one day. I wished to marry Shay. And I wished to fix my mother, to rebuild whatever had broken in her, through losing my father, and who knows what other heartbreaks she had suffered that caused her face to fall the way it did sometimes when she thought nobody was looking. Why did life break so many of us? What was the point of all of it?

As I stood by the water, some mixture of wind and waves caused it to splash up in my face a little, like it had heard my wish. My face was coated in dead fish scent, and I felt located by some primeval force.

When I looked back at her, Shay's face was entirely transformed. An illumination. When she saw my hair was wet in the front she smiled, looking overjoyed in a way you only get to look in childhood, before the world steals it from you.

"I think the river likes you," she said, coming up and hugging me from behind as the water continued to slosh around beneath me.

She ran her fingers through my wet hair. I took an uncharacteristic risk and, in one surreal instant, put my arms over hers, right where they wrapped around and met in the front, and we both got a little damp.

Our entwined arms grew borderless.

"You gonna apply for the Clay?" she asked.

"I don't know," I said, without even thinking about it. Yeah, I had filled out the paperwork. But no, I didn't seem capable of making the art object right now. Plus I wasn't going to get the scholarship anyway. What was the point of inviting failure?

Her arms stiffened around me. "What? Your stuff is so good. Why the hell not?"

"I think I'm going to have to go in a different direction with my life," I said, hoping that sounded appropriately vague and glamorous.

She spun me around so hard it hurt.

"No, don't do that. I saw those weird structures of yours Mr. Edison exhibited in the student-work museum. Stopped my heart. When a person has talent like yours, they owe it to the world to use it," she said.

This made me glow inside. "What about you? I heard you weren't applying either. And weren't you some kind of prodigy? Don't you owe it to the world too or whatever?" I asked.

"Yeah, but the difference is I'm not applying, but not in a defeatist way like you. I know I'm talented but I'm going to be an outsider artist, do it my own way," she said.

I nodded. You had to respect confidence like that. I envied her ability to need nothing but her own powers of invention, to pander to no one.

"Can I ask you something and you'll be honest?" she asked.

"Sure," I said, my heart beating faster.

"Did you draw that portrait of me I found in my locker?"

I wanted to lie, but ... "I did," I said.

"I fucking loved it. Dylan, why did you do that?"

"Because I fucking love you. You must know that," I said, feeling almost angry at being forced into saying it.

"I know," she said, putting her hand on the side of my face. "Your eyes are almost golden," she said.

I felt like I might collapse.

"You working on anything right now?" she asked.

I had to look away from her, out onto the water, where some kind of yacht was passing by full of drunk, waving tourists. "Since Dad died I've actually been blocked," I admitted.

"Oh God, Dylan. I've been meaning to check up on you more since then. That was such a moment to share with someone. But I get it. I do. I went through it. You're broken. You're furious. You feel abandoned and then guilty for feeling abandoned. But don't take it out on your talent. Life is short. You know what can help with being blocked? A good shock, a wake-up call. For the sake of your art. My mom's all about those kinds of shocks, as you know. I guess even that dick Mr. Ambrogio is going for shock value, which is why I still respect his work even though he's so disrespectful. Have you ever seen *The Godfather?* This is me sending you a message, a bloody horse head in your bed that says, 'evolve.'" As she said this, her eyes grew wild.

I was shocked. Was she some sort of thug? Actually threatening me? Was I unsafe? But did I even care? Did I like it? A little? Maybe even a lot?

"I'm not sure where you're going with the whole horse-head thing. That's a little over-the-top, but I will say I'd do anything to make my own *Frankenstein*-level masterwork."

"Anything?" she asked, still looking somehow spooked.

"Anything," I said.

"And what about for me? Would you do anything for me?" she asked, running her finger over my lips.

"I would," I said, looking directly into her eyes, no more sidestepping around the matter, kissing her finger lightly in response.

"I know you would," she said. She quickly squeezed my hand three times again, this time much harder, and then released it.

I felt elated. But then suddenly she was climbing up onto the guardrail.

I felt my legs get shaky as I watched her, and then was overcome by a terrible helplessness. For one godforsaken moment she was teetering on the edge of the rail.

I felt more scared but also more alive than I ever had, that I would now be able to divide my life into before and after this moment, that it would change me from a wimp into hero who takes action.

I made a slow move toward her, but she had already thrown herself into the still somewhat shallow, quite pungent part of the river in front of where I stood.

I hadn't believed she'd do it. Or maybe some place in me knew she would. Maybe I knew from the horse-head comment, or maybe even from that first moment I saw her, saw that mermaid on her back eating that ship, and knew she was trouble, knew she would someday go off the rails and take me with her. Today was that day.

Seeing her body sink reminded me of the moment my father died. The pain of it paralyzed me as she floated there, face-down in the river. If the water hadn't been there, she would have looked like she was levitating.

I had to snap myself out of it and realize that, yes, she had really done this and, no, she was not coming back.

I'd felt like I should have been able to save my father. And I still felt guilty for not being a hero in his time of need. But I would save Shay.

So I scrambled up over the rail, splashed in, and felt the shock of the river against my skin. My body went cold, then hard, then most disturbingly soft. I thought of the mermaids Shay's mother had told us about who saved drowning sailors in myths, but also of the sirens who drowned them. Some said the sirens were avenging women, taking out only the bad men like bounty hunters. I needed to save the mermaid on Shay's back so she could eat still more ships with shitheads on them.

Then I thought of Jonah inside the whale and longed to be consumed, to wake up inside a body and call it home. What would that feel like? Like being inside my mother? I tried to remember it. I wanted to live inside Shay. But first I'd have to save her.

Then I felt I might just sink to the bottom. Shay and I could both live down there together, surviving on a diet of only ships. I almost gave into that image, but the tender face of my father suddenly overtook me, buoying me up. I had to survive. I swam toward Shay who was now face-down and floating away from me.

I felt like my heart would stop, and maybe it did—the old one, at any rate. But what might replace it? Something mightier than a heart, that bloody muscle we'd all projected so much meaning upon. It was not that I wanted to die, but that I so badly wanted to be reborn—as someone not in mourning, brave enough to save this girl, talented enough to make a work of art that could change the world in some small way.

And where better to be reborn than in the whale belly of the filthy East River? I let myself relax a moment, then allowed my body to drift toward the great mother, go home again. I was startled by the sound of a church bell. It felt like an eternity, but it took only a couple seconds before I recalled that I was there to save Shay.

I grabbed her from behind, terrified as to what I might find—a carcass, eyes blackened in eternal rest, arms crossed over the chest? But I felt prepared to swim us both to safety. I couldn't have another dead body on my conscience.

Then as I touched her back, she flipped over with an elfish laugh and blew out a spritz from her mouth, like the whale I had just hallucinated. Right there, treading water in what was basically diluted sewage, she threw her arms around my neck, said, "My hero," and placed a long, cold kiss on my lips.

I longed to climb inside her belly and let her rebirth me, but I was now too pissed. I shoved her away, screamed, "Are you fucking kidding me?" and swam furiously for the shore.

Behind me, she was splashing her way back. Some tourists spotted us and ran away as though we were city swamp things, but not before snapping pictures of just how screwed-up New Yorkers really were.

As we climbed over the rail, another tourist couple took pity, draped us in beach towels, and provided huge neon sweatsuits from their suitcases for us to climb into after we'd dried off. If I'd been a deity, I would have blessed these two homely, fanny-packed tourists and smote the ones who'd run away.

After we thanked them, they looked like they were waiting for something, and I wondered if we were supposed to tip them in exchange for the horrible outfits we were now wearing. The woman looked sheepish as she asked, "Would it be possible for photo?" And it dawned on me that all they wanted in return was for us to take a picture of them in front of the Brooklyn Bridge.

What was it about photographs? These deathless artifacts. It always weirded me out to think the person in the picture could be dead, but the picture lived on. Last year my mother had taken me to an exhibit of nineteenth-century spirit photography, and I found nothing creepier than ghost hunters with photo documentation. We take these photographs obsessively, endlessly, in order to prove that we are still alive, that we have been here at all, that it has all been worth something, that we will leave something behind, that we can control how we are received while we are here.

I still had a picture of Dad from a night not long before he died. He'd looked powerful, even though his body was on its way out. That was the closest I ever got to spirit photography. But now he was gone. Because I had failed to save him.

Shay grabbed the tourists' camera and thanked them by providing a professional photoshoot. They were thrilled. She posed them, taking rounds of pictures, and giving them ornate direction, saying things like, "Yes, dahling."

She even produced a soggy lip gloss out of one pocket that she applied to the woman's thin lips, then took out a small compact from the other pocket to show her the results.

Who knows if the woman even wanted this? But Shay had a way of seeming undeniable. It was vaudeville and over the top, but the tourists seemed to love it, perhaps because it was the Broadway play for which they hadn't shelled out the money, enacted in their own lives, with themselves as stars—the modern American dream of transformation into commodity spectacle, celebrity, even if only for a few minutes. I stood back, shivering a little in my damp sweatsuit, watching the extravaganza, glad Shay had thanked them properly. But I was still furious at her for jumping into the effing river.

When the tourists left, she asked, "So aren't you going to thank me for our little adventure?" She looked like the cat who swallowed the canary. She had the sorry, not sorry expression of people who get away with anything because they're show-stopping lovely, but I wasn't about to let her get away with it. She seemed to be taking a jokey tone to test me, and I wasn't going to sugarcoat it.

"Are you fucking kidding me? How could you scare me like that?"

"Oh, lighten up. It'll be great for your art. Unblock you for sure," she said.

"That's it. I've had it. I'm done," I said, turning to go, not expecting what came next.

Shay was pulling me back to face her, saying, "Please don't walk out on me." She looked terrified that I might leave.

"I'm not walking out on you. I just can't handle this right now. You jumped into the fucking river. You scared me to death. I smell like garbage. How did you think that was at all an okay thing to do to me?"

She switched tacks yet again. "Grow up. It's not so crazy. People swim in the East River every year. It's called the Brooklyn Bridge Swim. Mom and I do it and it's awesome. I just thought you needed a wake-up call. Haven't you seen *Vertigo?* Who would Scottie be if Madeleine hadn't jumped in the water? Ever thought of that? The man was too scared to stand on a chair and suddenly here comes Madeleine, and, boom, he's a detective again, rescuing her from San Francisco Bay. But you're right. I took it too far, and I'm seriously sorry. Let's just chill about all this, okay?" But her face didn't match her nonchalance. She was clenching her jaw so hard I could see the muscles at work in her face.

But I didn't want to hear her apology or chat about *Vertigo.* I'd had it with Shay and her mysteries. I was not Scottie, and I wasn't in search of a femme fatale. Hitchcock was a misogynist who abused his leading ladies so why aspire to recreate any scene from his movies? I just wanted to go home, put on my sweatpants, and never take a chance on socializing ever again. Maybe I'd stop attending Brooklyn Arts altogether, make my mom homeschool me, become a nun or something.

"Are you crazy or just mean? I can't even figure you out. You belong in a mental institution. You're just—you're dangerous," I said. I was about to turn to leave again.

She appeared to be struggling with some topsy-turvy feelings she didn't know what to do with. And then she shoved me.

Or at least, it seemed like she attempted to shove me. She was not a coordinated fighter, aimed too high and ended up hitting me in the mouth.

A profound sting spread through my lips. I touched them and was shocked when I drew my hand away to find blood. She looked surprised herself, gazing in astonishment at me and then at her hand, then at her hand and at me again.

But she'd chosen the wrong person to shove. I'd grown up play-boxing with Dad. Mr. Ambrogio had just trained me further; he'd had us all donning gloves and sparring in the chalked ring for the last couple of classes. The metallic tinge of blood on my teeth was my place of residence. It activated me.

I shoved her back. But then she pushed me again.

A small crowd started gathering to watch us, and Shay roared at them, "Fuck off. This isn't a porno." They looked frightened and dispersed.

We both had an instinctual knowledge of how to hurt each other, but also how to defend ourselves. She was a fellow survivor. I could see that now.

This had been part of what had drawn me to her, not that I'd known it until that moment. I was about to retaliate when I caught a glimpse of her face. This was something else that linked us: a wound underneath our wildness. She looked like a sad little girl, and I lost my nerve. I raised my arms and she cowered, but I was just trying to hug her.

I wasn't expecting this show of vulnerability from her so soon after our fierce exchange. What was it that had wounded her so completely? It was a mystery I felt compelled to explore, but right now I just needed to comfort her.

We collapsed in a heap together on one of the benches overlooking the water, intertwined in an awkward post-battle embrace. I collected her in my arms gently, stroking her hair. When she pulled her head back to look at my face, I contorted my lips into a clownish grin, not sure what else to do. She surprised me by smiling back. A real smile, huge and warm and wide.

I imagined we were both astonished by the ease of our recent viciousness, how it had flowed out of us so effortlessly, more natural than those things supposedly native to women, the monthly blood now, the milk for babies later.

I'd sat through class after class on creative violence as written, as painted by men. But those guys didn't know from violence—guys like Hemingway who said there was nothing to writing but sitting at a typewriter to bleed, guys who wrote about the creative act as necessitating violence against women, like William S. Burroughs who said, *Shoot the bitch and write a book,* guys like Mr. Ambrogio with his whole boxing-as-creative-exercise schtick, claiming that it would especially empower the girls in the class, and then patronizing us about how society had done us wrong. None of these supposedly genius men had any knowledge of what it was to be a girl in this world. Of what it was to live in a body that could be violently entered at any time, a body that must be shrunken and torn apart to become supposedly beautiful. A body that bled regularly. Women were constantly told to take up less space. Literally. Figuratively. We had to fight tooth-and-nail to be ferocious. To become artists. To take up space at all. To do anything other than joyfully conform. Men had their own struggles, sure, but they knew nothing of that.

Jumping in the river had been freaking nuts, but I realized I did finally feel unblocked, like the whole goddam East River might come flowing out of me any minute now. Jumping in had made me even less willing to contort to please everyone but myself anymore. Shay had showed me another path, a way of off-roading it as far as "womanhood" was concerned, and I was ready to follow.

Shay moved so her head was in my lap, and she was looking up at me with these enormous, innocent, baby-cow eyes. She looked like a whole different person. I realized I was seeing something very true about her, the other self we all have inside. She had forgotten to put on her persona, and beneath it she was much softer, more nuanced.

She gazed at me with sheer tenderness. It broke my fucking heart.

So I lowered my head and kissed her. I thought if I did it swiftly enough, maybe even at warp speed, she wouldn't be able to process it, and it would stay my little secret.

But she did notice of course. And then, reader, she kissed me back. Maybe "kiss" wasn't the word for it. More like she ate me alive.

There was some powerful tongue action.

She twined that tongue of hers around mine, creating a suction effect. It was octopus-like, yet unutterably sexy and moving. This was no half-assed caress right here. I was curious to find out what the full-body version of this sensation could be, like without clothes on, how her tentacles might entwine me, and how I would be okay with it, how we might both transform.

I wasn't sure if this was the way normal people did kissing since, full disclosure, I'd never kissed anyone. I suspected, though, that Shay was technically a bad kisser. Not that I didn't enjoy it. It was like beauty: one magazine article I'd read said the most hauntingly beautiful faces weren't the perfectly symmetrical ones, but the ones with a maddening flaw that affected the viewer profoundly. This was what turned a pretty face into a gorgeous, unforgettable one. Not the perfection. The flaw. Not the whole. The broken parts used to build it, to make it haunting.

Some perfect, silver-screen goddess with boring, proper snogging technique could have been anyone, but there was no mistaking Shay's kiss for anyone else's. Like the rest of her, it was entirely and emphatically her own. It scared me. It reminded me of her art. And I fucking loved it, and I fucking loved her. So, I did it her way, sucking back hard on her tongue, out for blood again, but this time in a spicy way.

She surprised me by jerking her head back abruptly and asking, "Am I a good kisser, Dylan?"

I wasn't an idiot, so I said, "Yeah," and some of the tension eased out of her face. Who even knew she cared what anyone thought?

She then sat up and took out a little one-hitter and smoked thoughtfully. Apparently, the kissing part of the proceedings was done now. That was okay, I thought. I probably needed a minute to put my insides back into their proper places.

As our eyes met, we finally took in the whole harebrained scene—our wet hair, her smeared lip gloss, my fat lip I could feel with my tongue, the redness on her neck—and we cackled; there was no other word for it.

"What the actual fuck?" she said, through hysterical gasps.

"I'm sorry," I said, using my neon sweatsuit to mop a little trickle of blood from my nose, and when that was done, I just kept stroking and stroking her hair.

"Sorry? That was awesome. Coolest thing I've done in a while. Now, if you'd hurt me bad, we'd be having a different conversation. I started it anyway. I should be the one saying sorry." But I noticed that she didn't.

"And yet—" I prompted.

"I am sorry. I'd never want to actually hurt you. I've never seen that side of you before, though. Pretty cool. In class you're so—passive."

"I know. It sucks. I hate it," I said.

"It doesn't suck. It's mysterious. I'll never be mysterious because I let it all hang out too much. But if you hate it, change it."

"How?"

"I don't know. Take action. Like this? Just haul out and fight people sometimes. You're a freaking badass. Who knew?"

"Not me," I said.

"This is some feminist fight club shit. Sun Tzu says war's enlightening. Do you feel enlightened?"

"Sun Tzu? Where'd you pull that one from?" I paused. "And you know, I sort of do feel enlightened. Maybe that's fucked up."

"You know, this is how guys work stuff out," she said. "They don't carry it around while smiling and planning each other's baby showers and shit. They just duke it out and move on."

"Are we taking guys' advice on anything these days?"

"How about just on this one thing? Don't tell the members of the Genders and Sexualities Alliance I said that, though, or I'll be ousted as leader, ha-ha. Why don't you ever come to meetings, anyway? You are queer, right? Or, how do you identify?"

I bit my lip. "I don't know. I'm still figuring that one out, but I think so."

"You *think* so? It's as simple as who turns you on. How can you not know about a thing like that? Maybe that's why you're blocked, like with your art. But didn't you just declare your love for me back there? And didn't we just, well? Doesn't that make you at least a little bit queer? It sure felt like it to me," she said, with a teasing smile

"Well, I, yes, but I thought you of all people would understand how these things are, er, fluid. Like just because I like a girl, must I then officially categorize myself as a lesbian? Why do we need labels, anyway?"

"Dylan, nobody says lesbian anymore. And I hear you, but that just sounds like good old-fashioned shame to me. Plus, like, we haven't come far enough with this stuff where we can afford to be hazy about it, you know? People are still getting killed for being queer, so it becomes, I don't know, personally but also politically important," she said.

"Now you're dragging out that dusty, old-school feminist motto like we're living in a textbook. How progressive is that?" I asked.

"It's not dusty; it's classic. And we need it now more than ever."

"I guess. But accusing me of shame? Really? At our school? In our city? Being queer or whatever would probably just make me cooler, or just the tiniest bit cool for the first time ever. No, it's just that I feel confused. You're the first girl I've had these, um, feelings for, or that I'm aware of. And also, how can I explain it? I just don't want to use any word other people use when I describe the way I feel about—you. I want to invent a new word just for you. And nobody else is allowed to say it." I reddened, but I was proud I'd gotten it out. If I'd had feelings for other girls, those feelings didn't strike me as being the same species as those I had for Shay.

Here, she gave me a look I'll remember for the rest of my life. She looked touched and turned on at the same time, and I thought she was going to kiss me again. Instead, she angled herself to brush her eyelashes against my cheeks as she said, "Now, that's a butterfly kiss for you."

It seemed like the perfect word for it, and it made me love butterflies, kisses, and language just a little bit more. It thrilled me to the point where I got uncomfortable and blurted out a stupid question; "How about you? Are you—queer?"

"Me? Is that a joke? I literally have *DYKE* tattooed on my knuckles, Dylan," she said. A tattoo I'd always admired for its certitude. I wished I could steal the way she announced herself to the world like she knew what that announcement meant, and the effect it would have.

"Duh, I know that. I just mean, did you always like girls?"

"Since the day I was born. I probably made a pass at the nurse."

"Ah. And yet you still assumed the nurse was a lady."

"Touché," she said, taking one of my fingers into her mouth. I let myself enjoy the squirmy sensation of it for a second, but then a straight couple passed by and I had to pull away, feeling their eyes on us.

"There it is," she said, "the shame. See, what I would worry about with you is that you're just a tourist, taking me for a joyride but bound to marry some stockbroker and have all his puppies in the end."

"Look, all I can say is that I'm full-on Shay-sexual. If I could choose a more pictorial term, I'd choose something like *heterochromatic*—possessing multiple colors. Or something like that …" I trailed off, feeling silly. But she rewarded me with a little peck on the cheek.

Again, we realized what we looked like, eyeing each other: ugly tourist suits with a few stray blood droplets, drowned rat hairdos, faces so recently screwed up in fury, hands minutes before curled into fists.

"Whatever. I need to shower and sleep," I said, not wanting to talk about how I wasn't queer enough anymore.

"Want to come over? You could shower at my place."

Was Shay Burgess asking me to shower with her? All the fantasies I'd ever had about her vied for prominence until I felt dizzy. So many times I'd watched this creature of lust unwind herself from a post-shower towel like a rare delicacy, and here she was seemingly offering me a taste. I almost burst out of my skin right there, rushing toward her, a miracle of blood and muscle.

"Uh, sure. Let me just call my mom. She'll be worried," I said, impersonating a normal human.

We limped back to Shay's apartment, and I wondered if Mom would be watching us from across the courtyard.

"I'll have to buzz. I lost my keys when I went for my little swim," Shay said.

I still didn't enjoy her making light of it. Too soon.

Chapter Eleven

Shay pushed the buzzer. We waited, and then an older woman with short gray hair, who I'd always assumed was Ms. Burgess's mom when I saw her from across the way, opened the door. She wore a powder-blue track suit and bunny slippers, and immediately threw her arms around Shay.

"Shay-Shay! We were so worried. Oh my goodness. What happened to you and your friend? Have you been attacked? I'll call the police," she said.

"Nana, I'm fine, just wearing lipstick. Did it smudge or something?" Shay said. She looked at me as she said this.

"I'm calling 911 right now, peanut," said the woman.

"Nana, no, we—we did it to each other, like all in good fun. Just playing around," she said.

Her grandmother peered at her critically for another second, but then apparently accepted the idea that Shay and I had had a fun little makeup-smearing party. She seemed very used to Shay's antics.

"Well, well, look at this little spark plug," she said then, eyeballing me.

"This is my grandma, Thelma," Shay said.

Thelma had white hair, but was still a knockout for the geriatric set, with those same unforgettable emerald eyes that both Shay and her mother had. The few non-white hairs that remained revealed she'd once had that same blackout hair as her daughter and granddaughter, and she retained the same beautiful, though now wrinkled, features. She was also, I could already tell, feisty. I wanted to thank her for passing on her genetic material.

Instead, I said, awkwardly, "Nice to meet you, ma'am."

Thelma gave us a sassy look that said she wasn't going to ask about the makeup-smearing or any other hanky-panky.

"This is Dylan," Shay said. "From school."

"Oh, welcome. Are you hungry, honey? I make a mean chili, and no animals are harmed in the process. Here, sit down. Oh, and this over here is Darrell."

An old man with thin white hair and a shy smile emerged from another room.

"Evening," he said, a man of few words. He was bald, with just a few wisps of hair crisscrossing the shiny orb of his head, and milky blue eyes that appeared wise. His belly hung over his faded pajama pants.

Maybe someday I could become the Darrell to Shay's Thelma, the paunchy bald person in faded pajamas who gets to escort the bombshell around. I was okay with that, if she would insert her teeth-grinding night guard and sleep next to me every single night for the rest of her life.

"Pop-pop," said Shay, and flew into his arms.

"My little peanut," said Darrell. He was old but, paunch aside, might have been wiry and athletic back in the day.

As grandfather and granddaughter embraced, I took a moment to look around. Although I'd stared through their windows like a creep, I'd never actually been in Shay's apartment. I wanted to memorize every detail. Their apartment was decorated in a very Ms. Burgess manner: a hodgepodge.

I could see at least three eye-catchingly red things from where I was standing—the toaster, the carpet, and a painting of a naked woman touching her own breasts that made my face feel hot. But the other colors clashed with the red, like Ms. Burgess had just bought things she liked without thinking about how the whole room would look together. In the corner stood a strange cabinet of curiosities with what looked like travel relics. The room also boasted a random furry rug, a huge stuffed Paddington Bear, and a dreamcatcher. I respected Ms. Burgess greatly, but I would never let her decorate my apartment. Or the one I imagined living in with Shay in the future.

Shay and Darrell finally broke apart just as Ms. Burgess came out from the kitchen to call us to dinner. It was the first time I'd seen her not wearing a brightly colored scarf. She always wore them—heavier ones in cold weather and lighter in warm, but always a scarf. It was strange to see her bare neck. Mind you, I caught glimpses of her all the time from afar, in nightgowns and pajamas even. But seeing her scarfless, standing close enough where I could see her breathe, was an odd reminder that my teacher existed outside class, and was a real person all her own.

She did a little doubletake when she spotted Shay and me, damp and filthy in ugly leisurewear streaked with blood and lipstick. "Oh, Shay, what happened? Are you girls okay? Let me get the first-aid kit," Ms. Burgess said.

"Not necessary. We just got in a little tussle," Shay said, biting her lip innocently.

Ms. Burgess raised an eyebrow, saying, "Hello, Dylan. So glad to have you over."

"Hi, Ms. Burgess. Thank you for having me," I said.

"Dylan, you're in my home, having done whatever it was with my daughter that's left you looking … like that. I think at this point you can just call me Darby," she said, grinning. Like her mother, she was clearly accustomed to Shay's outlandish behavior. But she did head over to the bathroom and return with that first-aid kit. I tried to conceive of a world in which the mythological Ms. Burgess who taught us about art monsters became merely *Darby*. I mouthed the word to prepare for the next time I addressed her, but it still felt odd on my tongue.

From the back, I recognized her red cat pajamas as a pair I'd seen a few times before. They were adorable and I felt a little weird about having spied on her often enough to have opinions about her pajamas.

Darby herded me over to the kitchen sink and cleaned up my lip with soap and water, absentmindedly tousling my hair.

"Sorry, Dylan," she said, belatedly pulling her hands away from my face. "I should have asked first. Once you're someone's mother, it's just second nature. It's hard to explain it. I have to resist wiping my students' noses. I hope that was okay."

"No, no, thank you. I really appreciate it," I said. And then she hugged me, something she'd never done. Her pajamas smelled like mothballs, and I suddenly started enjoying the smell of mothballs.

Darby and Mom reminded me of each other in many ways, but there was a warmth to Darby that wasn't there in Mom. Mom wasn't exactly warm and fuzzy. I had a fantasy of never going back across the courtyard, just living here with Darby as my new mother. Except that would make Shay my sister, which would make the things I wanted to do to her illegal, so maybe scratch that.

Darby and Mom were friendly as far as coworkers go, but they'd never become the kind of friends who spent time together outside Brooklyn Arts. I suspected Mom was jealous of Darby. Judging by Darby's youth, she'd also had a baby young, but even with the maybe-unplanned pregnancy, she had still graduated from Yale. She taught high school English instead of being a *New York Times* bestselling novelist or whatever, but she'd also published a critically acclaimed experimental novel with a well-respected independent press—a weird book called *Vagina Dentata*. I'd tracked down a copy in the school library and tried to read it, but the prose was too dense, too heavy with references I didn't understand. It felt like the book needed me to be older to understand it. My favorite part, though, had been the illustrations: stunning black and white photos of Shay that Darby had taken over the years. The poses varied: Shay shaving her legs, Shay mixing paint, Shay looking off into the distance, and Shay looking right back at the camera with those rebel eyes of hers, challenging its very right to exist. It had taken some willpower not to tear those pages out and tape them to my bedroom walls.

"Mom, start feeding the girls. I'm just going to grab some drinks," Darby said. She squeezed my shoulder and Shay's. At home Shay looked so young, a little girl again with her Mama, Nana, and Pop-pop.

We sat down together at the dining table, Shay sitting next to me, close enough that our thighs brushed together. Thelma and Darrell had put out place settings and everything, knife and spoon on one side, fork on the other, napkins folded in laps. It felt way more formal than recent dinnertimes at my apartment, with just Mom and me. I was dazed at the sight of my femme fatale inhabiting this cozy domestic sphere. Even though I had seen it all from afar, some part of me had pictured Shay living in an abandoned tattoo parlor with the Hell's Angels or something.

Darby returned and said, "I got some wine instead of soda. You girls can have just a little, almost adults that you are. But don't tell Ms. Cyllene. Wink-wink."

Shay grabbed the bottle and took a sip right from it, her lips coming out red.

"Hey, hey, behave or I'll take it back," said Darby, giving her a little nudge.

"Okayyy," said Shay, again seeming so adolescent suddenly.

"I'll take some," I said, and poured myself half a glass to drink with my chili. I wasn't a big drinker, choosing weed every time as my ticket to oblivion. I just didn't love the taste. Wine, especially, left my tongue unpleasantly numb.

The chili itself was like tasting a page from a downhome cookbook, and I fell into the polite near-silence of sharing a dinner with someone else's family. I photographed everything with my eyes just in case I was never invited back: Shay shoveling cornbread into her mouth with astounding pleasure; Darby surreptitiously removing cornbread crumbs from her daughter's hair as she shoveled; Darrell silently spooning chili into his mouth; Thelma clearly enjoying the wine.

When the initial burst of eating slowed down, Darby and Thelma were so talkative they didn't notice Shay had gotten a third bottle of wine, and that we were all starting to get drunk.

After I-don't-know-how-many glasses of merlot, and in the middle of Thelma telling a totally unrelated anecdote, I blurted out, "My father died too, and he wasn't even my real father."

The table went still.

"Maybe the wine was a bad idea," said Darby, with that wrinkle she got in her forehead whenever Cash pulled one of his asshole moves.

111

"Let's just eat, honey. I've never met a problem my vegetarian chili couldn't fix," Thelma said, smoothing things over, patting my arm affectionately.

I felt supremely grateful for her existence and did an awkward prayer-hands-bowing thing in her direction that I instantly regretted. Luckily, she had plenty to say for a while. I was pretty sure, though, that her vegetarian chili couldn't fix the problem of my father's death.

"Now, as I was saying," Thelma said, "there's no love like a mother's. I must have bought Darby a bookstore's worth of books as a child, and now look at her. She could teach English to the Queen of England." Thelma let the compliment hang there for a second, beaming at Darby.

The next time there was a pause in conversation, Darrell surprised me by saying, "Here's a good icebreaker. If you had to pick, which front would you've wanted to be on in World War II?"

"Ah, why must we talk about World War II at every meal like heathens?" Thelma asked.

"The Western front for sure," said Shay without hesitation. It was clear she was a pro at discussing war with Darrell. She shot him the look of a co-conspirator as Thelma was looking beseechingly at the ceiling.

Darby really seemed to consider the question, sitting back with a thoughtful expression. Then she said, "I'd want to be wherever Shay was."

Shay reached over and touched her mom's face. The ease between them baffled me. There was so much softness to it, no turmoil. At the same time, it weirdly made me miss my mom's spiny embrace.

I considered Darrell's question for myself, but it didn't strike me as a very interesting one. "I wouldn't want to be at war to begin with," I concluded.

"Don't lie," said Shay, thrilling me by putting her hand on my knee under the table. It rested there for a bare second before Darby raised an eyebrow at us both like, *who do you think you're kidding?* and Shay pulled her hand away. I was surprised that my little anarchist listened to her mama.

"Sometimes we can't choose when we are going to go to war and on what side we will be fighting, though. That's the point," said Darrell.

"I'd want to be on whichever side the women were. That's the winning side in any battle," said Shay.

"The women?" Darby scoffed. "They were too busy being used as forced sexual 'comfort' for the men. You have a lot to learn about the way the world really works, missy. World War II wasn't a high-school movie with a dance battle." That raised eyebrow again.

"Oh, please, Mom. You weren't alive then either," said Shay. "Nana, you're the one who knows how it was for women in those times. Tell us."

"During the war, I for one," said Thelma, as though she hadn't really understood Shay's question, "would have gone wherever I could to get some delicious chili. There was that one time in Abilene. You see, in Abilene they eat lots of chili and have this wonderful relaxed, spiritual way—"

At that point I experienced another merlot-induced bout of word vomit: "What I want to know is, how do you live in a relaxed, spiritual way when it's a total shit show, basically World War II every single day? When dads get cancer and moms lie, and the world's a complete violent mess, and I just don't even know anymore?" I put my hand over my mouth, blubbering a little, wishing I could sink into the floorboards.

Darby pulled her chair over beside me, putting her arm around my shoulder, taking me seriously. "I hear you. Life *can* be a shit show. But sometimes when it feels like we're heading into war—I know that's how I felt when Marco died—it's like that moment in the movies when the star has to defuse the bomb. She needs to take an extra second to clear her mind and be calm, or else she'll just blow the whole place up, you know?"

I loved that, saw in it all shades of wisdom. I'd never heard her mention her dead husband before. Shay's dead dad.

"Thank you," was all I said.

As the family cleaned up after dinner, refusing to let me help, I stumbled around the apartment. I worried that they would kick me out for snooping, but I couldn't resist the opportunity to open cabinets, look behind doors, see all the little crevices that were hidden from my usual vantage point across the courtyard. The door to Shay's room was open. My heart palpitated as I walked in.

I'd stared at it endlessly but had never been inside. Up close it had contrasts I'd never noticed: a play between Shay's two sides—dark and sweet, deadly mature and very little-girlish.

She appeared to favor red, just like her mom. She'd swapped out her lamp lightbulbs for red ones that gave the room a burlesque touch. She had a red record player with a bootleg old Sex Pistols album, Spunk, all set to play, and a knife collection prominently on display.

But at the same time her bed was covered, every inch of it, in ragged stuffed animals she'd clearly hugged until their fur wore off. Then, framed on her bedside table was the pencil drawing she'd done of her mother holding her when she was little.

All the black-and-white photographs she'd ever taken adorned every non-chalkboard inch of wall, and even the ceiling. These, too, I'd glimpsed from afar, but I'd certainly never been close enough to make out the details. I leaned in to admire a striking image of a pigeon sitting on a nest on the subway tracks, and then … near the corner, I spotted an unexpectedly familiar face.

The photograph was of me in my room, across the way, gazing at Shay. Had I been so high I hadn't noticed Shay pointing her camera in my direction? I was flabbergasted. Shay must have known all along that I watched her. Did this mean she liked it? That she was an exhibitionist? Or just flattered by the affections of a loser?

I turned to find Shay standing behind me.

"Oh, hi, sorry to be snooping," I said, moving in front of the photo of me, as if that could make it, and the questions it raised, go away.

"I totally get it," she said. "Looking at someone else's room, their art, is so intimate, isn't it? Like reaching out and petting their mind. Better than sex," she said.

I nodded slowly. Then, deciding to just ask outright: "Um, why do you have this photo of me?" as I gestured toward the upsetting image.

When she realized the one I was talking about, she reddened. "I guess I was just curious about your curiosity about me."

"Okay," I said, feeling like a freak.

"But I do—" she said.

"What?" I interrupted, too eager.

"Like you back, in case you're wondering," she said.

She'd kissed me today. It shouldn't be a surprise. And yet I lit up to hear the words spoken aloud. Shay liked me. Shay *liked* me. *Shay* liked *me*. "Are you asking me to go steady?" I asked, covering up my internal meltdown by attempting to be funny and flirty.

For a second, she looked offended, like she thought I was mocking her. But then she picked up the vibe and started laughing. I laughed too, more a release of tension than any actual humor. "Pretty much, I have a corsage here in my bag," she said.

"Perfect," I said.

She ran her hand over my hips, and it felt like my whole body was breathing.

"Is that an X-Acto knife in your pocket or are you just happy to see me?" she asked, one hand lingering at the right-hand pocket of my jeans.

It was, of course, an X-Acto knife. I'd stuck it in there after attempting a cardboard project that morning and never taken it out. I'd jumped into the river with it still there. I couldn't even bring myself to be embarrassed; surely Shay could relate to carrying around random craft supplies that could serve as weapons.

"Want to be blood sisters?" she asked, and my brain short-circuited as she wormed her fingers into my pocket to pull out the knife.

"What?"

"Like I cut my hand a little and you cut yours a little and we rub them together? I did it with my little-boy-best-friend when we were little."

"Am I your little best friend now?" I asked, joking, testing out how she'd be pushed to define us, thrilled by the prospect of being linked to her by blood. Also wondering if you could still make out with your "blood sister."

"Yup. You good with that?" she asked, grabbing my hand, flipping it palm-side-up.

I nodded. She made a small slit in my skin, and I winced at the tiny bloom of pain, droplets of bright blood welling up. She did the same to her own hand, then rubbed the two cuts together with a look of supreme concentration. I hadn't been sure if she'd go through with it, but there it was, our mutual wound—the loss of our fathers, everything that had ever hurt us made literal right there on our hands.

She put down the knife and ran a gentle finger along the edges of the cut. It hurt, but in the best way. "Your hands are so soft," she whispered.

"That's what they all say," I said, trying to keep the tone light even though I didn't feel that way at all, seeing as we'd just engaged in a magical ceremony that joined us bodily. It felt better than I imagined even sex to be—almost.

"So, this happens to you a lot?" she asked, laughing and poking me in the ribs. But then her voice got throatier, and she whispered close to my ear, "People touch you like this a lot?" She playfully lifted me under the arms and threw me onto the bed, ending up on top of me.

I poked her back and shook my head, most of my brainpower occupied with Shay's body heat radiating through my hip, my breast, my armpit, all the places where we touched. "No, silly. They just say that in the movies. That's what they all say.'"

"But we're not in the movies. People's fathers don't kill themselves in the movies, or if they do, they're just actors pretending. They pick themselves up out of the water, laugh, crack open a beer, hit on the hot production assistant," she said.

I turned toward her so our faces were almost touching. I could feel her shallow breaths. She leaned closer and I felt her eyelashes opening and closing again, as I had by the river. Then my brain caught up with her words. "Wait, what?" I said, pulling back. "That's not how my father died, and you know that. You were there," I said.

Shay pulled my face back close to hers, eyelashes moving against my face, too quickly. I drew my face back again so hers became something more than a much-loved blur, and the way she was looking down and not making eye contact seemed off.

"Oh, Shay. Were you—were you talking about your father, honey?"

I could see a single tear pooling in her eye, suspending, and then falling down her cheek.

I leaned in to lick the tear off her skin, tasting the tang of salt and Shay on my tongue. I pulled back a second later, a little worried she'd be grossed out, but then she pulled me in and kissed me so mightily that it reopened the cut on my lip.

"Oh shit, sorry," she said. She got a tissue from beside her bed and dabbed at my lip, leaving a tiny white tissue mustache. She peered at my face and giggled. "You have to look in the mirror, Dylan. It's comic gold."

I stood up to peer at myself in the full-length mirror over Shay's door, and sure enough, I resembled a fascist Father Christmas. I turned away from the mirror, thinking I'd find Shay still laughing about my Kleenex mustachio, but she looked gloomy. "Oh," I said dumbly, and hurried back over to put an arm around her shoulders.

I held her tighter and tighter, like I was trying to keep her from flying apart, returning to some other form I could no longer grasp. After a few minutes I worried I was hurting her, so I eased up, but she pulled me back to her, saying, "No, squeeze me again," so I did.

"Squeeze me like you're angry, so it hurts," she said.

"Absolutely not," I said, and she looked disappointed. I hurried to explain. "Sometimes I think girls say shit like that but they're really just saying, 'I'm sad the world abuses me so keep abusing me.' It should be the opposite: the world abuses us but the cycle stops here."

"I really don't need you to culturally critique what turns me on right now, Cyllene," she said, looking pissed.

"Sorry, I was just trying to help," I said, feeling pushed away.

"Truce. How about a big sloppy hug with some liberal squeezing thrown in? Deal?" That, I was happy to provide.

"Deal," I said.

Before today, her skin had never been on mine before like this. A heat that felt close to pain ran over me. It was all so much I felt like I might throw up

Then she said, "He—"

"You don't have to talk about it," I said, my lips moving against her cheek.

"No, I want to, I need to. He jumped—he jumped. From the bridge."

"The Brooklyn Bridge?" I asked, slowly letting it sink in. Shay might love to swim in the East River or whatever, but nobody just pretends to drown themselves and then tries to shove you without some backstory there.

She seemed to be waiting for me to react somehow, but I didn't know how. There was no right thing to say. I guess she read that in my face, because after a second she just burrowed into my shoulder, muffling wounded noises against my skin. I petted her as she howled.

"I'm just saying," she said, the next time she came up for air, "it's hard to know how I feel about anything right now, including you, because I'm still so fucked up about losing him, by what he did, that he chose to leave me like that," she said.

"I get it," I said. "I'm fucked up by losing my dad, too, and he didn't, well … But when people do stuff like that, I don't think it's really a choice. Who would ever choose to leave you, angel?" I said, touching her face.

"Lots of people. You said I belong in a mental institution," she said.

"I didn't mean that. I was just pissed," I said.

"No, but you're right. There is something wrong with me. I'm sorry as hell for jumping into the river and scaring you like that. Sometimes I don't even know why I do the things I do. To live life with a capital L? To feel something? To not feel anything? And I have been in a mental hospital, by the way, or at least rehab with shrinks asking how I was feeling every fucking five seconds. It was in the summer, after my father—" she broke off.

"Oh, Shay. I'm so sorry."

She got that wild look in her eyes again. "I still see him, though, you know," she said.

"Who?" I asked.

"My father," she said.

This floored me. "You're fucking with me, right?" I asked.

"Nope. Should I not have told you that? You must really think I belong in a mental institution now. You're not going to, like, have me committed, are you?" She was joking but also not.

"What? No. Of course not. Me, too. I mean, I see him too. Not your father, I mean, mine. But it's not like I think it's an actual ghost," I said.

"No, totally." She was excited now, a little spit flew off her lips as she spoke, the words coming out almost faster than she could organize them. "It's just, this really concentrated form of wishful thinking, mostly when you're fucked up."

"Something like that," I said, thinking, *exactly like that.*

Shay grabbed a red pen from the bedside table, uncapped it with her teeth, and drew a little cartoonish ghost on my hand. She took a second to examine her masterpiece and then blew on it lightly, saying, "All dry." Then she added, "I wish I could see him."

"You wish you could see your dad right now? Yeah, I wish I could see mine too, but I can't really control it yet. It's kind of like a dream," I said.

"No, I mean I wish I could see your dad. Your ghost. Picture him right now, like really powerfully, and let's see if it works," she said.

"Seriously?"

"Seriously."

So I did it. I closed my eyes and invoked Dad. The few other times I'd seen him, he'd just come upon me. This was the first time I was asking to be haunted. I was sure it wouldn't work. It felt like trying to jerk off in front of someone else, not that I'd ever been asked to do that either. But I kept my eyes screwed closed, and finally just spoke to him directly: "Dad? Hi, it's Dylan."

Shay and I both giggled nervously.

"Wait, wait. Let me light some candles," she said. She ran around gathering little half-burnt candle toadstools and placed them strategically around me. The flickering light and Shay's frenetic movement felt like a distraction when I was just trying to hold onto a mental picture of Dad's face, but I smiled because she seemed to be waiting for it.

"Please come," I said. "Shay's here too. She finally gave me the time of day."

Shay elbowed me at the mention of her name.

"Anyway, as I was saying before I was rudely interrupted," I gave her a mock-serious look. "Shay's here and we'd really like to see you. I need you. Please come back. Why'd you just leave like that? To be honest, I'm kind of pissed at you about that. I feel awful, but that's the truth. Come back?" And then I screamed it: "Come back!"

And he did. I hadn't expected it to work, but there he was, right in front of Shay's bed, his feet hovering just above the floorboards.

He looked as he had on his last day of life. He had the scraggly facial hair that sprouted after he'd stopped letting them shave him. He was wearing that same blue hospital gown with the abstract pattern that was definitely not art. His normally curly hair was flattened by lying on a pillow. He had tubes hanging off him like Jacob Marley's cash registers in *A Christmas Carol*.

I reached up, threw my arms around the air where I imagined he was, and thought I could feel him hugging me back. I caught a whiff of my dad's skin, and just a hint of sea salt.

"Daddy," I breathed. The word hurt my mouth. The violence of saying something you no longer have, then holding it beneath your tongue like a knife.

"Bear," he said, "I've missed you. I'd do anything to get back to you. I hope you know that." His voice was like it had always been but different now, richer, something warm that covered me, seeping into my ears.

"Is he here?" Shay asked, her face wreathed in awe.

"He is," I said quietly, afraid to scare my memory of him away.

"Where is he?" she asked.

"He's right here," I said, gesturing to the space where I could still see him, wavering in and out.

Shay gazed at the space I'd indicated with reverence, her hand on her heart.

I stretched out my arms to embrace him again. He pulled me in tightly, his face illuminated with feeling. The sensation of his holding me was eerie in its very lack of sensation, a painful reminder he wasn't really there.

Then Shay surprised me by wrapping her arms around the space where I'd pointed. Actually, she was a little off by my admittedly fantastical calculations. She looked absurd forming a circle with her arms around nothingness while I probably looked the same to her, but at least the whole thing made me feel closer to both Dad and Shay.

And there we were, two grown ass people each embracing someone, something we knew very well wasn't present. We both held onto our respective patches of empty air until I finally said, "He's gone now," because I could no longer even imagine I saw him there.

As I opened my eyes and focused back on that room in the real world, I saw a light go on across the courtyard, and there was my mom, looking at us like we had lost our goddamn minds.

Shay turned to follow my horrified gaze. Mom raised a hand with a confused little wave. Quickly, Shay turned off the lights and we jumped under her covers, like this was a reasonable adult response to the situation. Shay's face was pressed into my neck, and the heat of her breath was exhilarating.

We had entered yet another alternate universe. The space under her covers was semi-dark and smelled like shampoo. It was filled with all the stuffed animals she, like me, was too old to have. I never wanted to leave. My voice somewhat muffled, I said, "Well, thanks for going to crazy town with me."

"Always. I live there too. I'm like the mayor," she said.

"You really are," I said.

She lightly punched me in the arm. "Hey."

"But, seriously," I said, "I do feel a little better after that … whatever it was. But let's never breathe a word about it to anyone."

"Yeah, losing your dad sucks, but even fake ghosts do seem to help."

"They really do. And, you know what else? The whole thing is even more confusing now that I apparently have this other father. My mom said at first that he was dead. What if he really is dead? I'm not sure I can handle two ghost dads," I said.

Her eyes were huge now, or what I could see of them. She whipped her head out from underneath the covers, leaving me alone in our dark, musty under-covers world, until I poked my head out to join her.

"Yeah, you mentioned at dinner, not so gracefully. But, you know what, excuse me if I don't feel bad for you that you might have a living father. Do you know what I'd give for one of those?"

"Oh, I'm so sorry, Shay. I never thought of it that way."

"Clearly." Then, softening, "How did you even find out about that, anyway?"

"My dad told me not long before he died. And then I overheard my bitch of an aunt talking to my mom about my 'real father.'"

"I've always wanted to be a detective. We have to get to the bottom of this," she said.

"Agreed. I've done some Internet searches and something else, but I probably shouldn't tell you," I said.

"I don't really see how you could be ashamed to tell me anything after tonight. Am I right?" she said, and I cracked a smile. "Anyway, you should do whatever it takes," she said.

"Well, I thought this family friend of ours might be my father, so I broke into his apartment, or used the key under the mat really, haha," I said.

"Well, what did you discover?"

"Not much. He actually caught me and assured me he wasn't my father. But then I found this picture of my mom in his bathroom, and it made me wonder," I said.

"So you think the family friend is your father?"

"I'm just not sure what I think anymore. And it's probably going to be pretty weird between the family friend and me now that I broke into his house and accused him of being my secret sperm donor. But also … there's more."

"Do tell," she said, leaning forward, alert now.

"Well, it's a long story, but I also found out that my father had been one of Mom's teachers, or taught her a lot about art or whatever, and then Google told me that someone we both know taught at her art school right around the time she was there."

"Jesus, stop stringing me along. Who is it?" She was engrossed in the caper.

"Simon Ambrogio," I said.

"Don't fuck with me. You're kidding, right?" she asked, her mouth hanging open.

"I'm serious."

"Oh, man. It sounds like you've been a little, well, passive about this. We have got to investigate," she said.

"I think so too. But what do you have in mind?"

"You've already broken into one potential dad's apartment, why not another?"

"Wait, are you saying…?"

"Yeah, clearly we can't ask these adults anything pointblank because they're all liars. So, what I'm saying is we need to hit up Simon's place and look for some clues to see if you're right about this. Because if you are … it will be huge," she said.

"I agree. I'll scope out where he lives. Deal?" I asked, kissing her cheek.

"Deal," she said.

Chapter Twelve

When I got home, Mom was doing dishes. She gave me a *what on earth?* look as I came in but said nothing. I lingered at the threshold of the kitchen, watching her. I wanted her to ask about what she'd seen. To care. I wanted to tell her about Shay, because I wanted to tell someone, and Dad was gone, and it wasn't like I had any other friends. But I also wanted to share this with her in particular. But the elephant in the room, the secret of my origin, always hovered between us now.

So I didn't say anything either. I came up behind her, grabbed the other sponge and reached over her to get the dish soap. Our hands met in the suds as we fought a particularly caked pot together.

"Okay," Mom burst out, "I can't hold it in anymore. What were you doing over there? I mean, I'm glad to see it's finally happening between the two of you. I know how long you've been waiting for that, but what on earth were you doing?"

I was glad she had asked. Really. I wanted to talk about it. But I didn't know how. So I just said, "Nothing, Mom."

We'd left the water running and the sink started to overflow, sudsy water sloshing over the countertop and hitting the floor.

Mom jumped back, turning off the faucet. I turned away to grab a towel to mop up the mess. "But really," she said. "You both just had your arms up like you were receiving rapture from on high. Is this some new artistic exercise I don't know about?"

"If you want me to answer questions about Shay, you have to answer one of mine," I tried.

"Okay, any question but *that* one," she said.

Of course, *that* was the only one I really cared about. But instead of getting pissed at her, I pivoted because I remembered something else I'd meant to ask about. "Why were you screaming at Mr. Ambrogio, on his first day of class? It was so bizarre," I said.

"Oh, I used to know him back in the day, and he's simply not a nice person," she said.

"Care to elaborate? Not nice like he cut you in line or like he's a deranged puppy-murderer?" I asked.

"Ha, Dylan, you're too much. Neither. And, no, I don't care to elaborate," she said.

"Of course not," I said. "But you know what, it doesn't matter. I'll find out on my own."

She looked concerned but then pivoted herself, "Are you still going to answer my question?" while playfully putting a soap bubble on my nose. I smiled in spite of myself.

"Okay, me and Shay were hugging Dad's ghost," I said, unable to look at her as I said it.

"Is that supposed to be funny?" she asked, sounding stern now. "Are you making a joke about your father's death?"

"No, Mom. It's just something we share. A sense that we can still see them. Our fathers."

She looked stunned and said nothing.

I jerked my hands out of the water. "You see? This is why I didn't want to talk about this with you. Like whenever I would set a fire, you'd always act like I was crazy. Did you ever think to talk about it with me? Find out what it meant to me? Did it ever occur to you I might need *your* attention?"

She pulled her hands out of the water and ran a wet hand over my hair. "Oh, Bear. I never thought of it that way. I just always got spooked because when you set fires you reminded me of someone," she said.

"Of who? I'm so sick of hearing that. It's high time you talk to me about that and all the other stuff. How do you expect us to be close if you won't let me talk to you about either of my dads? Anyway, I don't need your input, I think I know who my father is," I said.

This seemed to get her attention.

"Oh yeah, who?" she asked.

"It's Wally, right?"

She actually laughed. "You know full well that Wally and Dad used to joke around about how they both 'shot blanks,'" she said. As she said it, I did remember those jokes. I'd been young enough at the time not to know the saying. Back then, I probably thought they were talking about guns. But now it all came together. Okay, so not Wally.

"It's Mr. Ambrogio, then," I stated.

I tried to read her face. She started laughing in a forced way.

"Simon Ambrogio? How absurd," she said, as she walked away.

A second later I heard the door to her bedroom shut. I was left standing in the empty kitchen with a sink still half-full of dirty dishes, and no clear answers. I turned the water back on and finished up alone, pouring all my frustration into scrubbing each plate like it had personally wronged me. But in the few minutes it took to get everything clean, guilt started to set in. Sighing, I dried my hands and went to stand outside Mom's closed door. "Mom?" I called. "I'm sorry I upset you, but we do have to talk about this."

For the second time in one night, I felt Dad's ghost appear behind me. "How can you talk to your mother like that?" he asked.

I wasn't in the mood for an apparition anymore, and I definitely wasn't in the mood to be chided by a second parent that night, ghost or no. "Fuck off," I said.

He looked hurt.

"You were in on this too, you know. You could have told me all those years that you weren't my real father. You lied to me. If I had that information—"

"What? What would you have done with it? You were my daughter, in every way that mattered. What more did you need?"

"I would have had the truth," I said.

"The truth. What a quaint human idea. Do you really think things are so easy to categorize?" he asked.

"I think whether you donated the sperm to make me is a pretty clear question," I said.

"Don't be crude," he said.

"You're so much less fun as a ghost. You would have laughed at that when you were alive," I said.

"Why are you so angry?"

"Because you left me. And because I know you're not really there now. In theory, this is rich creative territory, but in reality I just want you back. I'm angry at you for leaving even if it wasn't your fault, and I'm mad at you and Mom for lying to me. Just tell me, who is my father?" He looked hurt. "Okay, my biological father?"

"I can't answer that," he said.

"Ugh, why won't you and Mom tell me anything?"

"For one very simple reason, kiddo," he said.

"And what is that?"

"Well, as a product of your imagination, I can't know anything that you don't know," he said.

It was one thing for me to know Dad wasn't really there, but it was another for him—or my imagining of him—to say it outright. It felt like the end of our time together, which had mercifully been extended by my visions.

I reached out to touch him and, poof, he was gone.

Mom's door stayed closed. If she'd heard me out here talking to some figment of my imagination, she wasn't going to say anything about it.

Maybe it was the disappointing interactions with Mom and Dad, but I felt driven to investigate this other possible parent more. I Googled "'Simon Ambrogio' address," and in thirty seconds had located it. An article came up that was all about the cool darkroom and studio he'd made out of an old shack in back of his Brooklyn apartment. It was settled. I would tell Shay and we would break in and discover the truth like two modern-day Nancy Drews.

Perhaps it was feeling like I was on the path to cracking my father mystery, but I suddenly felt a burning need to make something. I was searching around for inspiration, for a catalyst, when I remembered how Darby had bought us all Frankenstein masks like hers.

I reached into my backpack and placed the Frankenstein mask over my face. As the band snapped behind my head and I looked in the mirror, I felt the first stirrings of an intoxicating power. Unlike all other Halloween masks, it hugged my face bones perfectly like it had been made for me.

My eyes burned out of the mask's holes, looking totally natural. I took off my clothes so that I was standing naked except for the mask. It sent a shiver through me to see myself standing there in the full-length mirror in my room.

The rubber felt cool against my skin and had that smell I can describe only as childhood antics. I then thought I caught a hint of someone else's pepperminty breath and some sharp jasmine scent that had recently been inside this mask and wondered if it was Darby's smell since she'd given us the masks. Or Shay's.

There's a moment in every book or movie with a female character where she studies herself in the mirror intently. Even Mrs. Dalloway does it, though in that case, it was Empire she was really considering. Women are taught to study one subject more intently than any other— how we're seen.

All people are self-focused, sure, but with girls there's this added level where we've been taught to surveil ourselves, and everyone else is also surveilling us at the same time. It's difficult to explain to guys.

So, instead of learning to see and survey the world from the inside-out—what do I see and how do I feel about it—I'd learned to see from the outside-in—what do they see when they look at me and what do they feel about it? Is it what they should see? What they want? And, if not, how can I transform? If I'm not what they want, do I even exist?

What do well-behaved, beautiful, good girls get to create? Only and always themselves, their perfect girlhood. I wanted to build something bigger. My mirror scene felt different than all those women in all those stories. But it wasn't.

I rolled a joint and inhaled deeply through the hole in my monster mask.

As I leaned out the window to exhale, I saw my father levitating above me, and I quickly pulled my bed covers over me to hide my nakedness. He might not be real, but I still wasn't about to have this spirit see me naked.

"You came back," I said.

He floated down to perch as much as a ghost can on the side of my bed.

"You looked sad about how we left things," he said.

"I think I need to stop seeing you, um, imagining you," I said.

"Oh no, don't do that, Bear," he said. He looked sad and it felt like I was hurting my actual dad.

"Because you don't exist and I don't want to end up in a loony bin," I said.

"Oh, come on. They don't do that anymore. They don't have the funds. You know they dumped a lot of those people on the side of the road and gave them a bus ticket and that was it?"

"You know what I mean," I said.

"But aren't I exactly what you should be doing with your mind? You're inventing, no? Playing fast and loose with the old imagination, using a way broader color palette than the rest of those pretentious Instagram-friendly artists. You'll outdo them all one day, my girl, but you must stop worrying how other people are going to judge you. If you really want to make great art, you must be an art monster yourself. Now, I'm not saying that means being a bad person. You could never be that. But you need to put aside the whole complex root system of thoughts and messaging designed to stop you from bleeding onto the canvas and creating that rip-roaring work of art that has been trying to come out of you since you glued Elmo's head onto Big Bird. You loved monsters for a reason, kiddo. They're hybrid and that's the greatest kind of creativity. Do you know what innovation is? Making unexpected connections. That's all it is. In any industry. So go glue Elmo to Big Bird, or whatever the older form of that is. But just do it already. Stop using me as an excuse for procrastinating. You got this," he said, throwing a huge and now weightless arm around me.

"But these aren't your thoughts, though. They're mine. Aren't they?" I felt a chill run through me, confusion about where I ended and everything else began. Was that feeling art?

"Yeah, but they're pretty good ones, eh? Maybe you can see that now that you think they're someone else's?"

He had a point; or, I had a point. I rested on his invisible shoulder, and it almost felt like old times. The whole story of us was there in the precise tilt of my head required to rest on my father's shoulders. Except he wasn't there. When I caught sight of myself in the mirror, I was horrified to see only me, but with my head cocked. I shut my eyes against the sight of it.

When I cracked my eyes open, I couldn't see him anymore, but I could still hear his advice in my head. I would do it. I would be the motherfucking art monster.

I thought back on Shay's little pep talk about my talent by the river before she started acting like a maniac. Maybe tonight I could channel my restless creative energy into the final step that would allow me to finish the full application for the Clay scholarship. First: create a genius assemblage. Second: photograph said act of genius. Third: print photographs. Fourth: attach to application paperwork. Fifth: send in mail. Easy.

I rummaged around downstairs and found a certain important document, a lighter, a bottle of water, some stuff people had thrown in the trashcan by the pier at Coney Island, my charcoal, and the paintball gun Dad had given me for my last birthday.

They were doing construction on the apartment complex next to ours, and they had scaffolding up and plywood. I threw on some clothes and went outside with my sack of supplies. Once out there, I pulled out my charcoal and quickly scrawled across the plywood, making ghostly images of my family members: Mom, Dad, me, and a faceless other father who hovered like he meant us harm. The coal dust smearing my hands, I purposefully stretched their proportions until they were misshapen. As I worked, everything around me became a blur, the one vivid thing my plywood creation. There could have been a hurricane and I wouldn't have known, so deep was I in what some annoying people call a state of *flow*.

Next, I grabbed out of my sack the junk I'd gathered from Coney Island—three green mermaid can cozies—and arranged them in a circle to form a makeshift altar for my not-shrine. Then I pulled out a lighter and the piece of paper, my birth certificate, and placed it at the center of the mermaid-cozy-Stonehenge.

Then, in slow motion, to feel the full rush, I flicked my Bic lighter, using my thumb to spin the metal spark wheel down toward the ignition button to release gas. I felt a throb between my legs, watching the tiny blue flame pressing against its plastic prison. I touched it to my birth certificate, and that document full of lies went up in flames. Just what I needed.

When the certificate was ash, and when the mermaids were a touch singed but right before they were eaten up by the flames, I poured the bottle of water over the whole thing, putting out the fire, making a moat for my mermaids, letting the certificate ash dissolve into black rivulets for my sirens to swim in. It was gorgeous, folks.

Then I went across the street and shot up the whole thing with paint bullets, including the plywood wall behind it where I'd drawn the fucked-up charcoal family. If the paintball method was good enough for artist Niki de Saint Phalle, it was good enough for me. I felt a thousand feet tall as I shot the shit out of that ugly wall and its cast of malformed beings.

Then I heard my name being shouted and found Mom standing at the door of our apartment, looking like she might explode.

"That's it," she said. "I don't know what to do with you anymore. That's someone else's property. Just how selfish can you be? Some underpaid person has to clean all that up," she said.

I hadn't thought of that part, which actually did make me feel really bad. Even worse, when I looked at it now, I saw that my glorious masterpiece was just a mess of burnt wood and junk. I'd brought my camera out in the sack too, in the hopes that I might be able to photograph this work for the Clay submission. I'd pictured sending the committee a photo of a piece that spoke of fucked up family and marred birthright, a study in what fire can do. But it just looked like teenage vandalism. Not a masterpiece at all.

"But it's art," I said weakly.

"Only to you," she said. "Come on, it's time for bed." Then she stopped. "Baby, listen. Everything I do is for you. I want the best for you, want to defend you from this cruel world, keep you safe from anyone who would ever hurt you, even if it's you. Do you get that?"

I nodded. She could be so compelling when she wanted to be, face upturned like a painting of an old-time saint. That "mug was irresistible," as Dad used to say. I hugged her, even though I still felt angry. I shoved it down.

I said I forgave her, but I still slept in my own bed that night. I was relieved to finally be alone. There are those who can assimilate into any crowd, but that's not me. I force myself to smile and laugh at the correct times, to ask about people's parents and dead pets. But all the while I'm just waiting to slink back to my room where nobody can see me. My whole day is spent waiting for the exact minute when I can stop impersonating a human, put on my comfy pants, and stare at the wall until my vision goes blurry, and I start to see flashing what I can only imagine to be my own inner stars.

Chapter Thirteen

The next day at school, I ran into Shay by our lockers. I went for a kiss on the lips, but she kissed me on the cheek. The whole interaction was so uncomfortable as we both tried to readjust our heads to accommodate the other's intentions that I had no idea if Shay just wanted to be friends or what. Were we two people who had just engaged in a near-drowning, meeting-the-parents, and séance who would now never hang out again?

As she pulled back from the tragically awkward kiss hello, I saw that Cash was watching us. He looked both jealous and aroused. I wasn't sure which disturbed me more.

I was still focused on my plan to snoop around Simon's place, so I slipped in to see Ms. Sloane in Mom's office before first period.

"Morning, Ms. S. I have class with Mr. Ambrogio later. I wanted to see if you knew his schedule so I could see what the best day for a private tutorial might be?"

Ms. Sloane gave me a look like she knew I was lying. I was in her office all the time since, as the other school secretary, she shared it with Mom. She knew me well enough to joke around with me but not well enough to know that I liked girls now. "Does someone have a crush on Mr. Ambrogio?" she asked.

"Ew, Ms. Sloane, he's old enough to be—"

"Your father?" she finished.

"Um, yes. Anyway, about his schedule?" I didn't tell her I needed his schedule to find out if he actually was my father.

She rifled through her desk and then pushed a paper toward me conspiratorially.

I saw that on Friday, two days from now, he had classes all day and then was giving a talk to donors at night, so his house would be magnificently empty. That would be my moment. I still couldn't wrap my head around how I was planning my second potential-father-related break-and-enter job in a week, especially after the first one had gone awry—but as Shay had said, if I wanted to bypass all these lying adults then it was time to get serious.

I got to Mr. Ambrogio's class just as he was herding us into our seats. While I was plotting my ambush of his studio, Darby surprised me by slipping in through the half-open door, wearing the Frankenstein mask. She'd been wearing it around the school a lot, ever since that first class. We'd grown accustomed to it. Like anything you're exposed to long enough, it had lost its shock value.

"Mind if I audit?" she asked. Then she removed the mask, streams of her black hair pouring out.

Mr. Ambrogio stared at her a little too long and then made a grand gesture that seemed to indicate his classroom was hers. "Is the mask a nod to my *Art Monster* work? I'm touched," he said, baiting her.

"Not everything's about you," said Darby, as she sat down between Shay and me.

"Glad to have you sitting in," said Mr. Ambrogio. "Perhaps you'll pick up a thing or two."

Darby gave him a death stare. It was not uncommon to have observers; Mr. Edison often sat in to make his teaching reports. But it was unusual to have another teacher sitting in. I figured Darby wanted to check out Shay's art idol.

Today's lesson was on photography. Mr. Ambrogio asked, "Does anyone know what depth of field is?"

I raised my hand, and then immediately regretted it. I didn't normally volunteer in class; I was more the *wait till the teacher demands participation* type. My heart was pounding, my face hot. I started to lower my hand, but it was too late. Mr. Ambrogio had already spotted it.

There he was, moving in on me. "Yes, Dylan?" he asked.

I fumbled. "It's, well, it's basically how much of the photograph remains in focus."

Darby and Shay shot me reassuring looks. The others were less helpful: Hilda twirling her hair and Cash mouthing "class pet" yet again.

Then Mr. Ambrogio delivered to me my exact fear: the confirmation that I was a worthless idiot. "Nope. Depth of field? Anyone else?"

Even Cash saw the injustice. "Er, but what Dylan said *is* the definition of depth of field, though, *right?*" he asked. Darby and Shay nodded their heads vigorously.

"That's the textbook definition, sure, but this isn't Photography 101. What's the context? What are the deeper implications? What's the history here? We don't live in a vacuum. Do your homework, Ms. Cyllene," he said.

"That's bullshit and you know it," Shay said.

"It's not bullshit at all. Mr. Edison didn't bring me here to say, 'Oh, you all have nothing to learn because you're absolutely perfect just as you are.' He brought me here to shake things up and extract your brilliance like crude oil. Do you know how one of my favorite writers describes brilliance? He compares it to diamonds being incinerated. You don't get incinerated diamonds by playing it safe with textbook definitions of art," said Mr. Ambrogio.

"But you can teach me to go deeper without shutting me down," I forced myself to say.

The whole room, including Shay, looked stunned that I had spoken back to him.

"I'm not shutting you down, I'm just trying to teach here, and have a little fun while we're at it."

I had accepted belittlement by boys and men too many times, and this time I just couldn't do it. I'd saved Shay from a river, or from her pain, whichever. I was feeling my oats. "A little fun? That's what guys always call it when they're putting down girls, but it's not fun for the girls."

I practically cowered, waiting to be sent to Mr. Edison's office. Cash sniggered. Darby and Shay looked proud. Hilda actually shot me a look of solidarity, which I greatly appreciated. Malcolm was sleeping.

But Mr. Ambrogio shocked me by pounding his fist down on the desk and snarling, with spittle shooting out of his mouth: "I don't care what's fun for you girls. I'm here to teach and if you don't want to learn, then get out."

"Then I'll leave," I said, grabbing my bag.

He closed his eyes, took a deep breath, and seemed to be collecting himself. "Wait, Dylan. Don't go. Let's continue the lesson. I'm sorry I snapped at you," he said.

I sank down low in my chair, wondering if I even wanted Mr. Ambrogio to turn out to be my father anymore. I wasn't so sure, but I had to know the truth.

On Friday, at her locker between classes, Shay was breathless.

"I can't wait for Mr. Ambrogio's class. I know he was a dick last class, but I heard we're throwing axes today," she said, yanking her locker open.

"Throwing axes?" This sounded terrifying. I loved the idea of throwing axes in theory, but I was afraid that in practice I would suck at it. But Shay was already running into the classroom. I followed behind.

I was not so jazzed up for Mr. Ambrogio's class since I'd tangled with him in the last one. I was also still puzzling over how Mom had said she knew him, that he wasn't a nice person, and how they'd screamed at each other in the hallway like—like what? Like old lovers. How she had a secret photo of his. I had all these scraps of meaning and I wasn't sure whether I wanted them to come together to make a whole. Maybe there was some other explanation for all this that didn't involve my having the same DNA as Mr. Ambrogio who *didn't care about what was fun for us girls.*

I was also not looking forward to the axe-throwing aspect. I was just about the least athletic person and had terrible aim. As I followed Shay in, class was just getting started.

Mr. Ambrogio had somehow managed to turn our classroom into

an axe-throwing range. He'd pushed all the chairs aside and erected a target at the front of the room, over the chalkboard. There were little mini axes on everyone's tables, and he'd set up protective barriers between the tables.

"Thank you for joining us, Ms. Cyllene," Mr. Ambrogio doing a slow clap. "Okay, let's get started. This is an excellent art exercise for both body and mind. To successfully throw an axe, you must put the right level of force behind it so that it flips over once in the air and then lands head-first in the target. Throw too hard or too soft, and it'll hit handle-first and bounce off the wood. Aim is important too, but it's not the whole thing. It's not a linear progression, and that's what makes it intriguing, to me at least. This is an art of patience, of commitment, of learning about yourself," he said.

Cash attempted to throw first, as hard as he could but the axe went nowhere near the target and just jangled to the floor. Clearly he hadn't gotten the message that some things weren't just about brute strength. He cursed softly under his breath and looked around to see who had seen him fail.

My first attempts failed to fly, but eventually I started breathing into it, entering a state like how I felt when I made art. I was starting to think Simon was onto something with this stupid exercise. Or maybe he'd had no idea about this state of flow that might ensue, and I'd just lucked out, learning something profound he hadn't even intended about how to work with an object instead of against it, whether in axe throwing, love, or art. Finally, I got one somewhat close and looked around proudly.

"Ah, Cyllene, always a little off the mark, eh?" Mr. Ambrogio said.

I felt a sinking sensation. But it could've been worse—nobody seemed like they had heard him or cared.

Except Shay, who looked irate. "Why do you keep picking on her? What's your problem? Honestly, it's pathetic," she said.

Then she grabbed up my axe from the floor, and I saw her arm moving furiously through the air. The axe whizzed inches from Mr. Ambrogio's face, and did not land anywhere near the bullseye, but it impressed me deeply nonetheless because she'd stood up for me.

Mr. Ambrogio was speechless. I wondered if it was the first time he'd ever stepped out of the bounds of theory and into practice. He had talked on and on in class about the violence in any good artwork, but I'll bet he'd never so much as thrown a real punch in his life.

Shay sauntered out, but not before picking up her mini axe and handing it to me, saying. "A gal should always be armed."

I was carrying my new weapon as we walked out.

I followed Shay in a daze, out the door and down the hall, leaving Mr. Ambrogio and his casual bullying behind. "Shouldn't I put this in my locker or something?" I asked as I trailed behind her, "Couldn't I be thrown out of school for walking around like an axe murderer?"

Shay responded, "As long as it's in the name of art, I feel like Mr. Edison would be okay with axe murder. And he's the one who brought in this nutcase who has us throwing around axes in the first place. It's an insurance nightmare. But yeah, let's leave it, that thing's heavy."

We swerved down the hall toward my locker, but after I entered my code, I had second thoughts. I turned and gave Shay an imploring look.

"You want to bring it home, don't you?" she asked.

"I really do," I said.

"I guess we're lucky it's a mini-axe. Does it fit in your backpack?" she asked.

I tried. "It does."

"Then we're good to go I guess," she said.

It was only second period, but after nearly chopping off a teacher's head, I doubted anyone would expect us to go back to class today.

"So I really need to talk to you about something," I said as I steered us out the big wooden doors of Brooklyn Arts.

"Shoot. I'm guessing it has something to do with the axe?" she asked.

"Actually, no, but thanks for that. This is something a little bit different," I said.

"Uh-huh?"

"Well, there's something I haven't told you yet. You know Mr. Ambrogio's photo *Art Monster*?"

"Yeah, of course. It's his most famous one."

"My mom has a similar photo that she keeps in her closet."

Shay cocked her head. "Like, she has one of his prints? So what? Like I said, it's super famous."

I shook my head. "I don't think so. I can't find evidence that this photo has ever been publicized."

"I'm intrigued." She tensed as she said this, tightening the shared loop of our interlinked arms.

"So am I, but also a little spooked. So, you know how you wanted to break into his place?"

She nodded. "I like where you're going with this," she said.

"Today's the day."

I'd expected Shay to be immediately on board with anything resembling real detective work, but she looked skeptical. "How would we find his studio?"

"I found an article about it online. It's a building this other famous artist lived in years ago, so I looked it up, and it's on Willow Street."

"Oh my goodness, Dylan Cyllene, are you asking me to break and enter with you?"

"Well, that's not exactly how I would—"

"Hey, I'd love to. Sometimes I wish I'd been born a private eye in postwar America."

"Okay, cool."

Shay reached into her bag. "Here, take Mom's scarf. She shoves extras into my bookbag every morning in case I get cold. It's cute but also annoying. I'll take one, too—our disguise."

I put on a red one, throwing the ends over my shoulders and then another around Shay's head. We looked ridiculous and not at all in disguise. "Okay, good to go," I said, trying not to laugh.

We didn't speak until we reached Remsen Street, perhaps because we were too deep in private eye mode.

When we hit Willow, a middle-aged man walking an enormous Marmaduke dog yanked his beast to a halt and said, "You tell that douchebag he has some nerve letting his garden grow like a jungle and not tearing down that atrocity out back when he moved in."

Because the man was middle-aged, and I always pictured my

biological dad as having a big dog, I automatically wondered if this jerk were him, like I'd been wondering about pretty much every adult male for days now.

"Let's go in," Shay said. Then, turning to me, "Mr. Ambrogio is kind of a douchebag, but is it wrong that I still want to see where he makes his brilliant work?"

"Nope. I get it."

"Thank you," she said. Her face was close to mine, the sun turning her eyes into a hall of mirrors.

As we approached Mr. Ambrogio's studio, it dawned on us two unseasoned detectives that we couldn't get to the backyard without walking through the apartment, and we had no key. Besides the cute red scarves, we hadn't thought this thing through at all in the way we needed to.

"Guess we can't do this after all?" I said, casting an unenthusiastic glance back at the safety of the street. I didn't want to just turn around and go home now that we were so close.

"No, come on," said Shay, "we just have to hop over the fence." She indicated a picket fence guarding the narrow gap between the side of Mr. Ambrogio's house and the neighbor's trees.

I was still just warming up to contemplate it when Shay got a firm toehold and propelled herself over in a single maneuver. "Right," I muttered under my breath, grateful she at least wouldn't be able to see how ridiculous I looked trying to follow her. It took me four tries and, after I finally got that same toehold, I ended up almost somersaulting over.

Chapter Fourteen

As I dusted myself off, I shot a quick glance at Shay to see if she found me ridiculous, but she was too busy looking around in amazement. And the cranky neighbor was right. The garden was eccentric. But also amazing. It just might have been Narnia. Vines snaked around the back of the apartment and the garden was exploding with flowers of all colors. It had archaic statues of angels and fairies, and a fountain with a lion dribbling water from its mouth.

It didn't feel like we were in New York City anymore. The trees were unbelievably green, the bird songs deafening, and the smell of pine so pungent it felt erotic. I touched Darby's red scarf around my neck and felt the hot pulse of being alive. Shay was circling the confines of the garden. Her state of wonder was so charming I imagined the shack was our new home, and I longed to whisk her off her feet, carry her over the threshold.

Instead, I walked up behind her, tapping her on the shoulder. She turned, her hair fanning my face. She looked worried, asking, "Did he come home?"

I touched her cheek gently and kissed her. She quickly pulled away. This was the second time she'd avoided kissing me since the first day we'd made out, and I was worried that she regretted what happened.

"Dylan, we came to do this, let's do this," she said, pulling her long hair back into a ponytail like she meant business.

143

It was then that I fully took in the shack. There it stood, covered in ivy, misshapen with time and maybe with all the art made in there, but to me it was perfect.

I grabbed Shay's hand, got up my nerve, and marched us both toward the shack.

Somehow, I knew a guy like Mr. Ambrogio wouldn't lock it. He struck me more as a *let's bust this door down* type than a *world, keep out* kind of guy—and I was correct.

The doorknob turned. I had a moment of worrying there was some sort of latch, but it turned out to be just a catch in the rusty old door. So I pushed it right in, by which I mean Shay did it.

Entering, I was overwhelmed by a smell I recognized from photography class: the aroma of developing chemicals. Sure enough, I parted black curtains to find an area cordoned off as a darkroom. The Intro to Photography terms circled my head—*dodging, burning, exposing*—as I took in their sharp aromas. Shay looked mesmerized to see all the photo paraphernalia.

It wasn't just photography stuff, though. There was a little area with a desk and a single bald lightbulb hanging from the ceiling above it. It looked like where the cops interrogate the perp in movies, and I gave that area a wide berth as I wandered around.

The huge room was covered, as in every surface, with art materials of one kind or another. I knew Mr. Ambrogio was a mixed media artist but this took the cake: he had all the conventional things you'd expect in an art studio, paintbrushes and paint and so forth, but also pairs of boxing gloves; old typewriters; Holly Golightly-style cigarette holders; ads torn from vintage magazines; illustrations from rare books; clown heads; derby hats; painted animal skulls; exotic instruments; and even what looked to be a pig fetus in a bottle, like Mr. Ambrogio was some mad scientist from a bygone era.

This was Dr. Frankenstein's lab, his "workshop of filthy creation" dragged into the real world. I felt at home here.

When I pictured my inner studio, it looked just like this. It, too, had images developing, and pigs that would never be.

Shay, who had been pacing the place, rifling through Mr. Ambrogio's drawers, snapped me out of my trance by screaming, "Oh my god, Dylan, get over here now."

There are some moments in life that feel unreal. Times when the curtains of reality part to reveal everything to be vastly different than you'd ever supposed. My father passing had been one. And this was another.

I ran over to where Shay was standing: in front of a framed photograph of the same model wearing the Frankenstein mask in front of the burning dollhouse. Except this time, the woman wasn't wearing the mask but rather holding it. She was standing further back from the camera, face streaked with tears. I knew it was the same model because the body was exactly the same as the one I'd first seen in Mom's closet. I'd felt then that this physique was strangely familiar. And now I saw the reason for that.

There, with strawberry hair and delicate features, standing naked and unmasked was, without a doubt, my own mother.

It was shocking to find an image of Mom in this place, and seeing her naked made me feel shame for both Mom and myself simultaneously. I just wanted to get out of there, wash my eyeballs, and forget I'd ever seen it. But I knew I wouldn't forget, not for a second. What did it all mean?

Shay came to touch my shoulder, but I jerked away.

"Sorry," I said after a second, because I didn't want to discourage Shay from touching me. "I'm just trying to process what this even is."

"Yeah, it's bizarre all right," she said.

"Why would Mr. Ambrogio have this? Does this mean they were like a thing?" I asked.

"Isn't that what you've suspected?"

"I guess, but it still feels bizarre to say it out loud." I needed to take this picture and leave. Tucking it into the waistband of my jeans, I made a beeline for the fence where we'd come in. It took me three supremely ungraceful tries, but I did finally propel myself over the fence between Mr. Ambrogio's weird and wondrous studio and the rest of the world.

On the way down I twisted my ankle a little, and then headed for the F train, limping.

Shay caught up with me easily, saying, "Dylan, wait."

"Shay, I don't mean to be rude, but I need to be alone right now," I said.

"Are you fucking kidding me? This has been our thing together. Our plan to uncover the mystery of your birth father. I dropped everything today to go and jump some fence and break into this random dude's shack, and now you're just dropping me like this?"

"You've been blowing me off all day, and I just saw some disturbing photo of my own mother naked and crying. Can you not understand that I need to get home? Ask her about it? I'm digesting how this random dude, as you say, was probably Mom's teacher, and close enough to her to photograph her naked and crying, so this random dude very well may be—my father. And she's been lying to me about it. As usual. I just really need to get home and talk to my mom. Do you seriously not get that?"

"Whatever," Shay said, stalking away from me down Willow Street.

I normally would have run after her, but I was still in a haze and determined to confront Mom once and for all.

When I got home, Mom was in her room watching TV. The lights were off, and I could see she was half-asleep. I was about to barge in when I freaked out. Did I really want to know the story that had caused my mother to appear in that disturbing photograph? I felt at once curious and utterly repelled by the prospect of discussing Mom's nakedness and whatever else was going on there.

But in the end, I had to know. I was working up the courage to confront her when I felt a compulsion to wear the Frankenstein mask Darby had given us, in the hopes that it might give me some much-needed courage for my confrontation.

When I went to get the mask out of my backpack, I also found the little axe and placed it in my underwear drawer. It seemed a good place to hide a weapon. I tried to visualize chopping off one breast with it, becoming an Amazon warrior, Wonder Woman herself even, charging around on a steed, maybe merging with the horse completely so I became a new kind of creature.

The rubber of the mask settled over my face like an old friend, and I did feel better. Bold. I opened the door to Mom's room, wearing the same Frankenstein mask she'd worn in the infamous photographs.

She jumped up from her bed in terror as I appeared to her.

Once I realized, I ripped it off, and her body relaxed a bit.

"Dyl," she said, one hand pressed against her chest like a heroine overcome by the vapors, "why do you have that awful thing? You gave me such a fright."

"I saw something today." I felt mad with grief, with confusion, with the need for truth.

"Oh, honey," she said, "we've talked about this. I've had a tough couple of weeks and I'm not sure how much ghost talk I can handle tonight."

I could see a black-and-white war movie flickering on her TV, and I flashed to a parallel inner TV show, where I would douse this whole godforsaken apartment in lighter fluid, toss a match, and Mom and me and everything around us would incinerate instantly.

"I saw the photos," I said, feeling the rage rising in me, the vision of our apartment as inferno playing on the screen of my mind. I let it play while I spoke to her so that her face fused with the flames in a way that would have made a striking film shot.

"What photos?" But it looked to me like she might have some idea. Her face was growing pale.

"Goddammit, Mom. You know which photos I mean. I went to Mr. Ambrogio's studio."

"You went there?" Her face grew dark. "Listen to me, he's dangerous. You stay away from him, you hear me? He will never put you first."

"He's a visiting art teacher. Why the hell would he ever put me first? The question is, why you haven't been putting me first? The way you talk about him makes it sound like—why were you in that photo?"

She stared at me, jaw clenched, and I was sure she was about to stonewall me again. I was ready to scream, to throw things. But maybe she finally saw how desperate I was because her shoulders sank in surrender. "Oh dear," she said, "let's sit down. I'll make some tea and we can talk."

The last time she'd needed tea to talk, she'd told me Grandma had died. As I placed the kettle on the stove, my muscles were tight. I needed to hear what she had to say and didn't want to waste time making tea. But I saw she needed the ritual.

I put a mint teabag in my I Heart Art cup and one for her in the Best Secretary Ever mug, which Mr. Edison had given her, with great fanfare and no bonus, last Christmas. Mom lowered herself into a chair at our dining room table, where we never sat unless we were eating. Or unless she was telling me Dad was dying.

I brought the tea over and sat facing her. She had an odd look on her face. Was it fear?

I held her hand. "Mom," I said, "please. What is it? You're scaring me."

"I—I don't know how to."

"Please try."

"Well, you see, Ray will always be your father, but—"

"Mom, I know he's not my fucking biological father. I'm asking you for the last time to just tell me already. *Who is my father?*"

"I mean, Ray's the one who did all the fatherly things. Nothing can ever take that away."

"Mom!"

"But, biologically speaking, he is not. You are correct."

"The photograph—did Mr. Ambrogio take it?" I asked.

"What?" she asked, playing dumb again.

"Is he my—" I couldn't bring myself to say it.

I could see she was starting to sweat, and I felt sorry for her, but also so fed up with everyone jerking me around. I wanted to comfort her and to hit her in her delicately pretty face at the same time. But I did neither.

"Yes. Yes, he is. Simon, Mr. Ambrogio, is—your biological father, I mean," she said, biting her nail so hard I could see it was bleeding.

It was at this point that I lapsed into blankness. I had always thought in images more than words, and now my whole inner landscape was just a white expanse.

"If you say you won't tell me the story one more time, I swear to

God I'll just run away," I said, in a haze, getting up so quickly I knocked over the chair.

"Okay, let me explain," she said.

I sat back down. This I had to hear.

"I don't even know where to begin, Dyl. I was in art school and Simon was the hot new teacher. He took an interest in me. I liked it. I thought it was about my talent, which I have to say, even though ladies aren't supposed to, was substantial. I didn't recognize that his interest was anything more because I was with your dad.

"Simon kissed me one day while we were working. I should have stopped it. I know. But one thing led to another. I don't know if it was the proximity to his talent and success or what. And I also felt afraid to stop it. Like it might end all of what was happening artistically for me, that he might take it away. Now, I don't mean to say that he forced himself on me or anything. Not at all. But it only happened once, and I always regretted it.

"When we found out I was pregnant it grew more painful. Your father was furious, and he left me. He didn't come back until you were six months old. But he'd had an accident as a kid and couldn't have children, so you see you were our only chance, and it's a long story, and how much do you really want to know about our lives before you came and what it took to make you?

"I obviously kept the pregnancy. To do otherwise was simply out of the question in my family. I know I brought you up without religion, but you also know I come from religious people. When your father came back, I forgave him as much as I could, he forgave me as much as he could. But Simon went abroad, and I didn't ever see him again—until now."

I'd been waiting to hear this story for so long and here it was. "So he just abandoned me?" I asked. "Of course he did. He's such an asshole. I could kill him," I said, feeling panicky, trying to reconfigure my life story as she spoke.

"Well, not exactly. You see, he claimed he wanted to be there to help bring you up, but I didn't trust him as far as I could throw him, so I told him to get lost."

"You—you told him to leave me?" I asked, stunned. That my mother had driven my father away, no matter what kind of a man he might be, was too much for me to bear. I scrunched up my hands so hard my nails dug into the skin. "How could you do that?" I said, not even sure how loud my voice was anymore. "You've ruined everything."

"Let me explain," she said.

"Oh, I think you've explained enough," I said, grabbing up my backpack, throwing random stuff in it, including my monster mask and my little axe, and running for the door, not knowing where I was going or how life would ever be the same.

"Oh, Dylan, where are you going?"

"To see my father—the living one," I said.

She blocked the door. "Don't you leave me. Don't go to him. He'll only hurt you."

I surprised myself by pushing her out of the way and stumbling out the door. I turned around to see her one more time before I left.

Her wounded look sparked a looped memory of the day I learned to ride a bike. Mom ran behind pushing me for hours, kissing booboos, assuring me I could do it. And then she had given me that one final push and I had glided away from her.

I'd felt elated, but then a sinking feeling overtook me. I became convinced I'd never see her again. I pictured the jagged pain, in horrific, high-definition detail, of the day of her death—an image so searing it shot me out of my delirium, where I was about to crash into a tree.

I quickly rode back to her, and she was waiting with open arms. She'd been standing like that the whole time.

But now, tonight, I just left her standing in the apartment, and didn't come back. I wondered if her arms were still open now, but it hurt too much to picture it.

So there I was on the F train, and then at Willow Street, pushing the buzzer for number 112 until someone answered. Mr. Ambrogio was wearing only boxers and clearly had been awakened by my long ring. He looked bewildered.

"Dylan?" Then, slowly waking up, he stared at my face for a long time like he was trying to remember what a person was.

I looked back, trying to memorize his face. I was reminded of that children's book where the little bird asks all the animals who aren't birds if they're his mother. Was this my father?

I surveyed his square jaw, dark hair with a hint of a sleep-induced cowlick, day-old stubble, full lips, deep brown eyes, slight wrinkle on the forehead. Was this how I looked? How I one day would look?

"You talked to your mother," he said. It was not a question.

I nodded.

"Come in," he said.

Chapter Fifteen

I had broken into his shack but never seen his apartment. I was so distraught, I started obsessively taking in its details to calm myself, the way I used to count when I was nervous.

His was like other Brooklyn brownstones I'd been in, but what was different was the decor. Every inch of wall was covered in paintings and photographs. Everywhere sculptures, probably famous ones if I knew any better. One was of a father holding a little son in his arms, and as I stared at it, I started to weep.

"Now, now, don't do that. Here, take a seat. Can I get you some tea?" he said, putting his arm around my shoulder stiffly.

Well, that was one thing my mother and Mr. Ambrogio had in common at least—the way they broke bad news, with tea.

"I'm good on the tea," I said.

He gestured toward a very bachelor-pad black leather sofa, where I sat down while he sat on a chair halfway across the room. Then he must have sensed the distance because he dragged the chair closer, probably too close now.

"Listen, I can answer any questions you may have," he said.

Faced with this huge expanse, my mind could produce not a single inquiry. But then I forced myself to come up with: "Why were you fighting with Mom at school?"

"We used to know each other and she's not too fond of me," he said.

"Used to know each other? Like biblically? You were one of her teachers, she said?"

"Yes," he said.

"And you are my, uh, my–"

"Your father? Well—um, yes, technically," he said.

"Technically?" I asked. How in the hell could he use a word like technically to describe the way he and I were quilted together by chromosomes?

"I mean, yes, physically," he said.

Physically? "What?" I asked.

"Yes, I am your father," he said.

Star Wars, I thought.

"I get how Darth Vader all this must sound. But your mom and I had, well, a love affair. And then we all decided that it was best to proceed as though nothing had happened."

I cringed. "*Nothing had happened?*" I snapped. "Didn't you have any, er, feelings about having a kid?" I asked.

"Of course, but I wanted to be free for travel and such," he said.

"Travel and such?" It sounded too selfish for words.

"Okay, I'll be honest. I was in love with your mom, and I was hoping she'd leave him and want to bring up the baby—uh, you—with me. But she didn't. And afterward, Jane didn't ever make it seem like I was very, how shall I say, welcome in your lives. She thinks I'm bad news. What do you think?"

"I don't know you. I go back and forth," I said, being honest.

"Would you like to get to know me? I would love that. It's why I came to Brooklyn Arts, you know," he said.

"I guess I would. I mean, I'm dying to, but why were you so mean to me in class?" I asked, now feeling numb.

"Mean? I was just holding you to a higher standard, since you are clearly a way more talented artist than those other teenage wastelands. Mr. Edison, who's in on our little secret by the way, showed me some of your work. It's scary stuff, powerful stuff, especially for a teenager. I'd love to understand what's going on in that head of yours. And I guess I was also holding you to a higher standard because you're my—

daughter. Oh, that's strange to say aloud. Is it okay if I call you that?"

"That is what I am," I said.

"And I was also trying not to play favorites," he said.

"Well, mission definitely accomplished," I said.

"I'm sorry about that, Dylan. I'm not great with people, but I'd like to become better with you. Why don't you start coming by in the afternoons to help me out in my studio, or just hang out? We can get to know each other. You can sleep on the couch tonight if you'd like and then come by after school on Monday. I'll set up a place for you to work," he said.

"Cool. But can I crash here for a little bit, like more than a night? I'm kind of on the outs with Mom about all this," I admitted.

"Sure, but you should work it out with her. Bad blood does nobody any good," he said.

How could he talk about not creating bad blood? Wasn't abandoning your daughter a surefire way to *create bad blood?*

"But what about you two? And me? Didn't you ever wonder about me? Have any interest in getting to know me for the past eighteen years?" It dawned on me then that his lack of curiosity was heartbreaking.

"Of course I did, kid, but your mom barred me."

And this made me even more furious at her. "I'm never going home," I said.

"No, no, of course you are, but you're welcome here as long as you like, until you guys work things out, which you should, which you will." he said.

"Can I ask you something?"

"Sure," he said.

"How does it feel to be a famous artist?" But that was too direct. I felt silly. I had meant to come at it slantwise but then just said it straight out.

"Well, uh, a little empty I suppose. Like you thought the fame would fill you up, and you seek more and more, but the hole just keeps getting bigger. Some call it the god-shaped hole."

"So I guess you could say I have a father-shaped hole," I said, and then immediately regretted it.

"Yeah, I'm sorry about that, kid. You've had a rough time." He actually did sound sorry as he said it.

After an uncomfortable silence, he asked, "And how does it feel to be a girl? Er, a woman?" It was his turn to look embarrassed.

"Honestly, I'm not really sure I know."

"But you must have some idea."

"Squishy and passionate and powerless," I said.

He cracked a smile, seeming impressed. "That sounds about right."

"Can I ask you something else?" I asked.

"Yup," he said.

"What do you do when you're blocked? Creatively, I mean."

"You're blocked, huh?"

"Yup," I said. "What do you recommend?" I asked.

"Well, it's like with everything else, *carpe diem*. Seize the moment," he said.

"But what if I get paralyzed like always?" I asked, holding my breath.

"Just pinch yourself and move forward. You see this rubber band I wear around my wrist? I snap it whenever I get stuck. Can't make art today cause I'm feeling blocked? *Snap*. Need to stay up all night to finish the artwork but I'm tired? *Snap. Snap.* Here. Take it," he said, getting up and snapping the rubber band onto my wrist.

"Wow, thanks," I said, giving it a little pull. *Snap.*

"And by the way, it's fine with me," he said.

I froze up. "What's fine?"

"You know, that you're a lesbian," he said.

"Oh, wow. Okay. We're done with this conversation," I said.

But now that I had shut down the dialogue, I had no idea what to do. I sat across from the man who had emitted the seed of me, and we had nothing to talk about.

Luckily, he filled the silence. "I got you covered. Come with me. I had an eccentric teacher in art school who used to do these exercises with me. They're a little wacky but they do the trick every time. I—I used to do them with your mother," he said.

"It's pretty late," I said, looking at my watch.

"Art is like method acting. If you don't start to believe you live in this world you're building, it won't sing. Do you want to be a famous artist or not?" he asked, a sharpness coming into his voice.

He was looking at me so intently it was uncomfortable.

"Yes, I do," I said. "More than anything. But you know that already, don't you?"

I followed him to the shack. As we entered, I could see he was approaching the place I'd seen when I broke in, which had given me the heebie-jeebies: the desk with a single bald lightbulb hanging over it that had struck me as a space of interrogation.

He pulled a partially broken chair up to it and said, "Have a seat, sport. This is where I interrogate you," like he could read my mind. He was laughing like we were in on a joke together, but were we?

He was so hard to read. It kept seeming like he was messing with me, but there was also a bashful sweetness about him at times. I guess it didn't matter what I thought about him as a person. We both knew I'd follow him to the ends of the earth because he held the keys to the art kingdom.

Still, something was too unsettling about the whole situation. I had a flutter in my chest like he might not let me out of that shack. How could a person simultaneously be so charismatic and so repellant? Then again, they say the most luminous angel of all was Lucifer before he fell.

"You know how I'm obsessed with the detective genre?" he asked. How would I know that?

"Oh?" I said, now trying to plot my escape, wondering if he was going to murder me.

"Are you a true crime fan, Dylan? Of course you are. Look at the mysteries in your life." He paused, maybe noticing the incredulous look on my face. "Wow, sorry, that was rude of me," he said. "I'm not actually going to interrogate you, of course. But I do need to ask you something a bit—delicate."

"Okay," I said, eyeing the exits.

"Promise you won't be offended?" he asked.

"No," I said.

"You strike me as a very repressed person."

157

"Okay, now I'm offended. I might be repressed, but you have no filter. You could afford to be a little more repressed," I said.

"No, no, what I mean is, you have great talent but you're holding it in. It's like a shit you need to take but you keep on clenching. Get my drift? I don't know how else to put it. You do it in your life, too. I've seen you in class. I see that you have this big force in you, but you go around like a frightened mouse, like, *is it okay for me to exist?* I'd like to help you let that lion out of the cage," he said.

I hated how he put it. Didn't like his crassness, his sloppy mixed metaphors, or his male savior aspirations, but I knew exactly what he meant. And I did want to be let out of my cage. Wasn't that what drew me to Shay? That she'd jumped in a freaking river on our first date? That she seemed to live in some wide-open expanse while I stalked the limits of my own enclosure?

So I hesitated, and he seemed to see it as an opening.

"I knew it. Okay, I have some exercises guaranteed to help. Follow me."

And now I couldn't resist. I wondered if he could make me over in his image as an artist, inject me with his genius, our newly realized genetic code.

Thus began Simon's art exercises. It was after two in the morning at this point, and the adrenaline of my fight with Mom was slowly seeping out, leaving me drained and limp. Not the best time to unlock my creativity. But I didn't say anything when he started manically gathering oddities.

"Follow me," he said, and I obediently followed.

He led me out to that extraordinary garden. There were blocks stacked in front of the glorious lion fountain.

"Here, help me lay these pavers in a circle," he said, grabbing up a heap of cement blocks.

"Wait, so basically your special lesson to unblock my creativity is to have me do hard labor at 2 in the morning," I asked.

"Young lady, what you're doing is constructing a fire pit, where I'll burn the artworks I photograph to make my world-famous pieces. Is that something you'd be interested in?"

I shrugged. I was exhausted. "I guess so," I said, not sure where all this was leading.

We worked for a good half hour, sweat drenching my shirt.

"I mean, I get burning art. I burn my own all the time. But I'm not sure about burning other people's art, you know, morally speaking," I said, as we swept sand over the pavers at the bottom of the pit.

"Oh no, don't worry, kid, the artists are extremely flattered to be featured in my photographs. It gets them way more attention than they would ever get on their own. Pass me that masonry chisel," he said, pointing to a tool I'd never seen before, as he pared down some of the pavers with a hammer to perfect the circle.

"But you're still destroying their art," I said.

"Hey, what can I say? Sometimes you have to break some eggs to make an omelet or whatever," he said.

"Um, didn't Stalin say that?" I said, side-eyeing him.

"That's erroneous. It was his crony Kaganovitch who said it," Simon said, caressing the chisel.

"Same difference," I said, plopping down on the grass to survey what we'd made.

"It's not, actually," he said, his eyes blazing. I feared for a moment that he'd chuck his chisel at me, but then he just threw it down into the grass.

"I didn't mean to offend you," I said.

"You didn't," he said coolly.

I took in what we'd constructed with, admittedly, a good deal of pride. I was still trying to make amends. I said, "Ah, I think I see what you were going for with that whole exercise now. It was grass but now it's this space where art can happen."

"Precisely," he said, placated, starting to get excited again. I was learning how to manage him, but should I have to?

"Sometimes, the best thing to do for your imagination," he continued, "is, counterintuitively, something very concrete, something homely, humble, that takes a little elbow grease, to get the more numinous stuff flowing." He swabbed his face with a filthy-looking kerchief, then offered it to me. I declined.

"Still not sold, eh? You need the fancy-pants brand of art exercises. Well, have no fear, Dylan, I have those too. Let's head back to the shack," he said, leading the way yet again, as I followed.

Once inside, he rummaged in the storage closet and came out, saying, "Here, hold this," as he plunked a small statue of Walt Whitman wearing a Santa hat into my arms. I laughed but he looked totally serious.

"Okay, now hold it out in front of you, like so," he said, grabbing the statue back from me, cradling it in his hands like a mother holding her pregnant belly and then flopping it out to the side. I laughed but he gave me a look that said the quest for greatness wasn't a laughing matter.

As he handled this strange baby, I said, "I'm not seeing what this has to do with my sculptures."

"All in good time, young Dylan. So, what I need you to do is simply describe what's happening. Don't judge anything, just chronicle what you see, feel, taste, and touch."

God, if he wanted to enrich me, I wished he'd just take me to a museum or get me a library card or something.

For the next hour, he coaxed me into describing any number of bizarre tableaux that he enacted, involving everything from a collection of clocks with famous royal families on their faces to shirts he'd cut holes in so his "business could breathe."

As we approached hour two, I said, "I see bird eggs?" as Simon noisily assembled more marvels.

I stifled a yawn as he said, "Push yourself, Dylan. Train your eyes. They're trainable, you know. Genius is made, not born. You must be dedicated."

I was getting fed up. "I am dedicated, but I'm exhausted. Give me a break already."

"But I can't. Art is a holy thing. It's like praying to someone out there with your paintbrush. I want you to feel good about yourself, I do, but no Diane Arbus was ever created with the everything-you-do-is-super brand of parenting that's in vogue right now. I mean, religious acolytes flagellate themselves. And I'd absolutely whip myself if I thought it would get me to the next creative level," he said.

"I bet you would, and that's what freaks me out," I said.

"You know what, never mind. I was trying to help but just forget it," he said.

He had a gift for withdrawing at the perfect time to ensure you'd fight to hold on. And now he looked vaguely wounded on top of everything. I saw myself getting ready to care-take, to mind his feelings and leave my own to the side.

"No, no, wait. Thank you for all your efforts. That diorama is very Joseph Cornell," I tried. Bingo.

He looked delighted. "Do you really think so?" He was suddenly a schoolboy seeking my approval, and I loved that. "I'm so glad to hear it. That was exactly what I was going for. Great, now take a seat at that desk and sketch this. Look, I'm certainly not saying you should whip yourself. That would be too easy, ha-ha. I'm getting at something mystical here. You know that moment when you accidentally see something beyond where the seeing's supposed to end? That's what you're going for, you know?" he asked.

The thing is, I knew exactly the space he was describing. I'd lived there my whole life. It was my only real place of residence. "Listen, Simon," I said—finally calling him by his first name, but not ready to call him Dad—"I've never had a mentor, and I appreciate all this, but I really do need to get to bed."

He now looked jovial suddenly, maybe because I'd compared his work to Joseph Cornell's. All egos need stroking. "Of course you do. Let's get you some sleep. Yeah?" he said.

"Yeah," I said.

He made up the sofa in the shack for me. When I went to bed for the short period I had before my alarm went off, the covers smelled like turpentine, but I nonetheless cuddled up to them, in love with the idea of this new fancy artist father I had always fantasized for myself.

My eyes fell shut, and then snapped open again when I felt Dad's ghost enter the room. This time he was not happy with me, more like a typical ghost: scary, vengeful. He shook his ethereal fist at me and floated close so I could really take in his architecture. His face was stitched together from disparate parts: Dad had become the Frankenstein creation he, Mom, and I had been building in the basement before he died. But from the part of the book where he's been rejected by his maker and by the humans he meets and thus becomes murderous.

"So you think you can replace me?" he demanded.

"Dad, it's not like that," I said, cowering.

He saw that I was afraid and softened. "Kiddo, I'm sorry, but I'm just hurt. Don't you love me anymore? Simon is such a pretentious fuck. How can you fall for it? Have you forgotten our car-part miracles? How can you undo me like this?" And he started undoing the stitches of his face, so he began to come apart. Pieces of his mosaic face fell, making a sickening thud as they hit the floorboards. I reached out to gather the pieces of him, trying to put him back together, saying, "Papa, I'm so sorry" over and over. But he was gone.

I slept fitfully. Come morning I felt just as lost as I had before, and a great deal more confused. The night before I had spoken to two lost fathers.

As an artist Simon was what I'd hoped my father would be like, but not as a man. I had always prized kindness over talent, or at least found talent meaningless in the unkind. I had believed wholeheartedly in the superiority of my father's brand of making—outsider, self-taught, unpretentious art, and now Simon's ostentatious art school demeanor was turning my head in ways that made me feel like a traitor.

Maybe Simon was one of those guys with a secret kinder side, and I was happy to be tutored by someone with his gifts. But by trying to be close to Simon, I feared I was betraying both my mother and the man I would always consider to be my father.

I got up before Simon did. When I peeked into his room, he was passed out on his bed facedown, snoring loudly. I snooped around his kitchen to see what he had breakfast-wise, found nothing but vodka in his freezer and leftover eggrolls in the fridge, and decided to buy an egg and cheese sandwich from the deli on the way to school.

Chapter Sixteen

When I got to Brooklyn Arts, Shay was waiting by my locker. She was wearing her usual black, and a technicolor daydream danced behind my eyes. I imagined I was touching her face, she was standing on a beach in a black wedding dress, smoking a huge jay, holding the little axe she'd given me, waves crashing wildly behind her, that glint in her eyes, as we got married. *I do*, she said, *I do*.

But, really, she was standing by my locker, saying, "What's going on? You seem weird. What happened after you ditched me yesterday?"

"I'm sorry I ran off. I was just so overwhelmed. I have a bad tendency to shut off when I feel like that, but I'm working on it," I said.

I snapped Simon's rubber band against the sensitive skin on the inside of my wrist. The burst of pain made me feel braver, more centered in my body.

"Look, I really am sorry for ditching you. I would never actually want to be without you," I said, pulling her into me.

She quickly drew back, and something inside of me shriveled.

"Are you just not into me anymore?" I demanded. "Do you regret what we, um, did together? You keep pulling away when I try to, er, be with you."

"Me? I'm pulling away? I helped you with some important detective shit and you just left me high and dry. How do I know you're not just going to run off again?"

163

"Let me draw you something. I'm not as good with words anyway," I said. I leaned my sketchbook against my locker and sketched a quick black wedding dress and handed it to her, hoping it would say what I could not.

Shay took a quick look at the sketch, crumpled it up and threw it on the floor. "What is this? A funeral dress? Really sensitive, Dylan."

"Uh no, it wasn't a funeral dress. It was—a wedding dress. I just couldn't picture you in a white one." I looked down as I said it. If I didn't make eye contact, it didn't happen.

There was a long silence. When I did finally get up the nerve to look at her, she was staring at me with a tiny smile. She bent and picked up the drawing, uncrumpled it, took out some tape, and put it up in her locker. "I love this dress," she said. "Thank you." She leaned in and pressed a quick, warm kiss to the corner of my mouth. "Okay but update me here. What's going on with the photo stuff?" she asked.

"Well, I don't know how to say this, but Simon is—my father—for sure now and I'm kind of crashing on his couch for a while," I said.

I had never seen Shay struck silent before. Finally, she said, "I can't even process that. I mean, we suspected it, but I never really thought it would turn out to be true. Details, please. What did your mom say?" she asked.

"Ugh, let's not talk about her. I can't trust anything she says anyway. I'm looking outside of her to fill in the blanks in this story from here on out," I said.

"Let's cut our next class and go to Ms. Fuller to get the full story. She knows all," she suggested. I was so used to relying on screens that I hadn't even thought of asking our school librarian, who was practically a professional detective herself. She'd helped me track down a paper for one research project that the Internet claimed didn't exist anymore. Nor had I thought of cutting class, so I was hoping to get this little excursion done quickly. Ever the good girl. We had a few minutes still before first period, so we rushed over to the library together.

The moment Ms. Fuller saw me, she shot out of her chair. "You need me to get you some contraband intel?" she asked, and I loved her for it.

She was wearing her white hair in a tight bun, but pieces had wormed out on the side. She was rocking Reeboks with black stockings and a dress. She reminded me of that Mrs. Piggle-Wiggle who cures all the neighborhood kids with potions, except Mrs. Fuller's magic elixir was her knowledge of the archive.

With her help, we scrolled through tons of old articles until finally we found it—one about Simon and the student he was collaborating with at New York Institute of the Arts nineteen years ago: Jane Rainey. Shay sat next to me, and I could smell her shampoo. I wanted to shrink down and travel through her hair for all eternity. What would I find in that lush hair land? More Shays? But I tried to concentrate on our research.

I put my hand on her knee, but she pushed it off, suddenly strangely prim. "Not right now, Dylan, we're researching," she said. Ms. Fuller gave us a look like, no judgment. But why did Shay seem to be avoiding my touch?

The article's author, Sylvia Platworth, went on about how Rainey considered her professor to be "an absolute genius." Then Platworth spoke of something I'd never heard about or even imagined: Rainey's own "brilliant" project she was working on, which she described as a "haunting piece, a dollhouse in which she'd carefully, lovingly carved the details of Charles Manson's murder of Sharon Tate, down to the last bloodied noose."

"Whoa, Dylan, your mom's a badass, and more than a little disturbing, actually. Who knew?" Shay said.

"Not me."

"So that was *her* dollhouse piece in Simon's *Art Monster* photo?" Shay asked.

It boggled the mind. I nodded, dumbfounded. I almost felt more astounded by this revelation than that of Simon's paternity. It was shocking enough that Mom had been the naked woman in the Frankenstein mask, but that the burning dollhouse had been hers scrambled my circuits. First, it was just the most incredible structure ever. That she'd had that kind of capability and walked away from it was just about the saddest thing. Second, I'd often been drawn to make dollhouses myself without knowing there was a family history there. Third, who had set that thing on fire? Simon was known for burning other artists' work, yes, but why would Mom have agreed to it? Fourth, my mother had been an artist in that photo and not merely a muse or patsy.

Platworth wrote that, "Rainey hopes for her work to be 'an astounding feat of world-building, a visionary commentary on creation and destruction, violence and the art that could grow out of trauma. When asked for comment, Rainey said only that she fears it to be 'an unsightly craft project.' But her professors don't share her doubts, describing her work as even more skillful than her teacher's, Mr. Simon Ambrogio."

So dollhouses and self-doubt ran in the family, at least among the women. I was flabbergasted to discover that my mother had been an artist once considered more brilliant even than Simon, when most of her art these days consisted of sewing my Halloween costumes. *Why had she stopped?* Pregnancy didn't seem like a compelling enough reason to give up on the sort of talent of which most artists can only dream.

I spent the next few days crashing on Simon's couch, staying up into the wee hours every night running through his seemingly endless collection of "Art Boot Camp" exercises. I was still feeling blocked, but on only a few hours' sleep every night, I was starting to be too exhausted to care. Maybe that was the point.

Friday afternoon, I got out of Physics to find Mom waiting outside the classroom door, right by my locker. She looked sad. "I understand you're angry at me," she said, "but you have to trust me that it's complicated. I'm glad you told me where you were going, and I get that you want to get to know him—he's your father, who can blame you?— but I don't want to see you get hurt, honey. And I miss you terribly. I can't eat all that spaghetti alone," she said, really trying, and I saw it, but I was still pissed.

"Then maybe you shouldn't have lied to me for years," I said, slamming my locker closed, aware that I was acting like the typical teenager she'd never had. "You never talked about your art. Never even told me about your dollhouse. We could have bonded over art more, you know? It was usually Dad encouraging me and teaching me. Why was that? When you were secretly Louise Bourgeois or whatever the whole time. It's like I don't even know you, like you're leading a double life."

"Maybe all women do," she said.

"Oh, don't you dare try to theorize right now. Stick to the subject, Mom. Is this not important to you?"

"How do you know about the dollhouse?" She paused, but I just stared back at her. "You know what, never mind. I don't want to argue, Dylan. Let's just go home and figure out where we stand now. We don't have to rehash everything."

"You're trying to make up and get me to come home but you *still* don't want to 'rehash' all this? Of course you don't want to talk about the past. That's what caused this whole mess in the first place." And then, for the second time in my life, I walked away from my mother.

I was brooding in the shack on my couch-turned-bed when Simon poked his head in after school, saying, "Come on, I want to take you somewhere."

"I have homework," I said. I didn't like having my normal after-school snack and homework routine interrupted, even though I knew it was what I needed if I was going to make anything of note. I pictured telling reporters how it all began, in a shack in Brooklyn, with two lost fathers, but one found.

"Kid, this *is* your homework. Your whole class will be there. Let's hit the road," he said.

"Oh, okay. Let me change," I said.

"You're good. Let's go."

I didn't like how he could be so controlling, but I followed behind, feeling younger than I had in a long time.

As we walked, he said, "I think this will help with your whole blockage scenario."

"Cool," I said. "But can we not have everything be about how I'm falling short somehow?" I asked.

"It's not falling short. Is that how you take it? You're as brilliant as your mother, and I want to make sure you never back away from it as she did. So, to that end, let me dig deep here. I'll tell you a little fable I share with my female students—the ones I teach to box," he said.

Oh no. I was getting sick of the special lessons about "having balls" he felt the need to give his female students … and his daughter.

"In Kafka's 'Before the Law,' which appears in *The Trial*—" he said.

"Please don't 'teach' me something right now. I'm not in the mood. Can't we just hang out as, you know, father and daughter?"

But it was like he hadn't even heard me. He just droned on: "— this guy wants to gain entry to 'the law,' as in go through a gate that's a kind of metaphor. So what is essentially a bouncer tells him he can't come through right now. The guy asks if he'll be able to enter in the future and the bouncer's like, *maybe one day, but not today.* Then this poor guy waits by the door for his whole life, this symbol of 'the law,' still trying to get in. He even bribes the guard, who takes it only to make this pitiful guy feel like he has some agency. Then as this man is about to die, he finally asks the guard where everybody else is since they all want 'the law,' too, but he's been here alone the whole time, trying to acquire this coveted thing, its very thingness, you get me?" he asked.

"Uh-huh. Yeah, I've had English class before," I said.

"So the guard says, basically, this door is for you and you alone. And now I will close it."

"Um … okay, not sure what to do with that," I said.

"You can lead a horse to water …" he said.

"What? Just spit it out. What are you trying to say?" I demanded.

"Fine. What I tell women is this: First, if you want freedom, power, creativity, stop bitching about it and take it. Nobody's going to hand it to you on a platter and nobody can keep you from it but yourself. So how are you going to find your own power and space? And if you want that scholarship you keep whining about, go get it. If you want to make great art, there's only one way: just do it. That is, if you still want all of this. I'd find a way to keep making art with both arms chopped off." Well, that was quite the image.

"Still want it? It's *all* I want—to be creatively validated," I said, annoyed.

"Fine, kid, but you need to think about trying to validate yourself. When you leave that choice in other people's hands, they can feel it, and that's why they'll never validate you. You're giving them too much power and keeping too little for yourself," he said.

"Spoken like a famous white man," I said.

"What?"

"Of course you think all I have to do is just *lean in*, just 'go out and get it,' but it's not so simple for the rest of us."

"Okay, I can see you're not getting it, but we can work on that in the ring today," he said.

"No, I get it alright. Wait, what? The ring?" Oh boy.

"Seriously, this is important. Why do you think the guy never stormed the door?" he asked me as we turned the corner at Borough Hall.

"Because the bouncer might have beat the crap out of him?"

"But isn't that better than waiting passively, if all you want in life is to go through that door?"

"Yeah, maybe you have a point there. But just on that particular thing."

"Ugh, you're so stubborn."

"I'm not a horse you're breaking. I'm your daughter. Why don't you act like it?"

"It's time to stop being such a pussy, Dylan."

I grimaced. "I *hate* that word."

"Oh, aren't you the sensitive one?"

"Look, when was the last time you heard a man who respected women use that word? It's especially bad when it's used the way you did. Like, why equate weakness with women's reproductive organs? It's also offensive to cats." I added the last part to soften things because he looked grim. Then I wondered why I felt the need to soften anything for someone who'd just told me not to be a pussy.

"Duly noted. Now, let's hurry up. They're all waiting for us."

As I trotted behind him, I considered his parable. It was disturbing but there was something there. Why, in any given situation, did I cast myself as inferior? And how could I stop? Stop feeling the need to soften things for people who were insulting me? Become the kind of person others softened things for? I'd heard about women doing superhero power poses before giving big presentations—the positioning of the body creating the geometry of self-assurance. But what was my power pose?

"So, seriously, where are we going?" I asked, trying to distract myself.

"To the boxing gym," he said.

"The boxing gym?" This had gotten too ridiculous even for me.

"I'm requiring that all my students do a session there. I'm no boxing expert myself, mind you. I do it for the art. Every woman should learn to defend herself but also how to go on the offensive. Not to mention what it does for the work. Guaranteed to unblock you and help you storm the door of *the law*, so to speak."

I regretted having told him I was blocked. Now I had to hear about it every waking minute.

A couple days ago, while I was still reeling with the revelation that Simon was my father, I took a pilgrimage to see his most famous boxing painting, *Ultraviolence* at MOMA. In general, I found his work to be, superb yes, but also macho and overblown. I'd seen *Ultraviolence* online, but I wanted to be close enough to touch it.

I'm not going to lie; I was riveted. I sat on a little bench in front of Simon's work, giving it my full attention, relinquishing my prime viewing space to nobody.

Simon had taken vintage pin-ups of women in sexy poses, pasted them to a canvas and punched them with gloves dipped in different colors of paint. The result was disturbing but also electric. Slivers of these women's faces and bodies peered out of thick punches of paint, proudly, like they had survived Simon's chaotic process, or like they were the real artists. I couldn't decide whether to be enraged or not. Was this work feminist? Misogynist? Both? Maybe all those words were woefully outdated, or at least sadly limited when it came to encapsulating the mysterious things that any work of art could do. Was it even right to apply words to art?

But there was no doubt that I felt uneasy sitting there, looking at it. I imagined, in far too graphic detail, how Simon's hands had flown against those women's faces. How those same hands had grazed the depths of my mother's sweating body. I had to be careful I didn't become like Judy in the movie *Vertigo*, pretending to be Madeleine at the Legion of Honor museum, obsessively contemplating the portrait of her great grandmother because she was supposedly possessed.

In my favorite Googled articles, Simon talked about how *Ultraviolence* looked like a random act but was, in fact, the most painstaking creative meditation. He went into detail in both the *New Yorker* and the *New York Times* about how many canvases he'd tried before he'd gotten it just right. The tender way he'd had to wield his gloves to achieve the perfectly brutal effect of his final piece. And, let me tell you, it had worked. It was layered, a piece of storytelling.

But it disturbed me how he claimed the work protested the way men treated women. How do you protest violence with a portrait of violence? The way he treated me made me wonder. The pussy comment made me wonder.

Ms. Fuller had helped me find video footage at the library of multiple artists at work, and there was Simon performing the sequence to make his *Ultraviolence*, which looked more like an ancient dance than prizefighting. It was beautiful and ridiculous, and I'd watched it several times, wanting so badly to perform the sequence myself, to become the kind of artist who could seize the audience's attention like that.

As Simon and I journeyed to the boxing gym, on the R train heading toward Bay Ridge, without any weird artistic exercises or Kafka parables to fall back on, just time to kill, we were quiet for a full ten minutes. Hands gripping the same subway pole, but studiously not touching, swaying next to each other in total quiet, until discomfort prompted me to ask, "So, how'd you get into boxing?" My voice came out shrill and the question sounded stupid. Common and not worthy of a great artist like ... my father? I was still getting used to that concept.

"It was a photograph that got me into it, actually. I became a convert when I saw how Dick Halstead captured with nothing but his humble camera the moment Muhammad Ali socked Leon Spinks in the face:

the red of the gloves against the red of Spinks' shorts, the victory of Ali's visage played against Spinks' face so contorted it doesn't even look like a face, the motion, the violent transformation, the brutal creativity of it. I wanted a piece of that, so I started going to Gleason's Gym down in Dumbo. The first time I walked in there, I saw that Virgil quote they have up—'Now whoever has courage, and a strong and collected spirit in his breast, let him come forth, lace up his gloves, and put up his hands,' and I knew I'd come to the right place. You ever boxed before my class?"

"A little bit. With my father. Um, I mean, with Dad. I mean. You know what I mean."

"That's right, he played around in the ring a little, didn't he? I was always afraid he'd come after me and kick my ass after what went down between your mother and me."

"Maybe he should have," I said, surprised by my boldness, only half-kidding.

"Easy there, tiger. Save it for the ring," he said, jokingly holding up his dukes, until the subway came to a halt and sent him veering forward. I grabbed his arm to steady him.

"So, you are strong, eh? That will serve you well," he said, as he took my hand like a child to lead me off the train.

"I can steady myself," I said. But I appreciated the gesture for its warmth, for what it meant in terms of his own grappling with the notion of me as his daughter. Since I didn't want to discourage him from that part, I gave him a strong pat on the back as he climbed the subway steps in front of me, which caused him to spin around and give me a questioning look. I made a *keep going* gesture, herding him up the stairs, and hopefully away from the memory of my awkward attempt at daughterly affection.

Chapter Seventeen

Once out of the station, Simon marched along with me following just behind, until he turned into a dirty-looking storefront. Inside were punching bags, a little boxing ring, and the smell of competition.

A few students were already there already, sitting on the benches. They jumped up as Simon came in. Hilda smiled shyly, moving her carpetbag, and gesturing for me to sit between her and Shay. I sank down, grateful for the invitation. Shay winked at me; she was wearing a faded *Rocky* T-shirt, which I found hilarious.

Then Simon got in the ring and started sparring with the guy who owned the gym. Simon seemed to be a pretty good boxer, as far as I could tell.

"Okay, so let's put some of the theory we've been discussing in class into action," he said once he was warmed up, gesturing toward me. I was immobile for a long, humiliating moment. But then I snapped the rubber band he'd given me, and asked myself, "What if I died at the end of the week? Would I wish I'd done this?"

The answer: a resounding yes, so I took a mouthguard, and a huge chug from the water bottle Simon handed me. My throat burned with whiskey where I'd been expecting water, but I managed to choke it down instead of spitting it all over the gym floor.

"Oops, wrong bottle," he said, flinching.

I wondered if it really had been a mistake, or just another ploy to get me to "man up." I stepped into the ring with an unexpected buzz.

Then, as Simon showed me how to hold my hands and throw a punch, I whipped off my sweatshirt, throwing it aside to feel the cool air of the gym against my arms in my tank top. I'd thought I would feel self-conscious up there with everybody watching, but then I looked right at Shay, and I no longer had any desire to be covered.

Simon and I traded easy blows, circling each other. Maybe there was something to this whole "artistic violence" thing after all. I felt generative. At one point I rode the whiskey train and abandoned anything resembling boxing. I let something else take over, Pandora opening her box.

I beat my chest, writhed on the floor, and then became tangled in my own imagined layers, my hair snaking around my head. It might have looked like I was having a fit if my movements hadn't grown so strangely precise.

It all felt so right. I shot a look at Shay, and she was clapping so hard I thought her hands might bleed.

Simon just stepped back and watched me like I was a rabid animal. I didn't care. I was in the throes of something. When I could contain myself no longer, I jumped out of the ring and circled the room, resting my fingertips on the other students' sweaty foreheads as though blessing them.

"Ew, get off," Cash said, rubbing where I had touched him, but without emphasis, like maybe he'd liked it.

The rest were too shocked to even pull away. I wondered if perhaps they couldn't truly touch me, like I was deranged but also possibly a sage walking in their midst.

I was saving Shay for last. I felt her eyes on me as I circled the room, but I knew a forehead touch wouldn't be enough for her. Everything coursing through me, blood and whiskey and holy energy, drew me to Shay, and finally I came to her from behind, throwing my arms around her and pressing us together front-to-back. Simon started moving toward me, saying, "Okay, okay, break it up gals. This is a school function."

Shay gently pulled away, but didn't seem angry, thankfully. She did say quietly, "Please don't use me as a prop in your little awakening scene," but she was laughing.

Afterward, as Simon toweled himself off, and Shay tamed her hair back into a bun, I sobered up a little. "I'm so sorry. Maybe I went a little overboard," I said to her.

"Hey, never apologize for coming into your own. You were great. I couldn't be prouder," Shay said.

"Yeah, you were terrific out there," Simon agreed. I hadn't realized he was close enough to hear, but my stomach jumped to hear my father say something nice about me.

"Really?"

"Really. Go get 'em, tiger. You felt powerful, huh?" Shay asked.

"Something like that."

"You want more, don't you?" Shay said.

"Always," I said.

"Welcome to my world," she said.

Again, I heard those Mary Oliver lines: *Tell me, what is it you plan to do with your one wild and precious life?* Today I'd found my answer in Shay, in Simon, in boxing, in art, in making my mark on the world.

My next thought, a homely little thing, was that my whole biography was a carefully constructed riddle, at whose center my real, more vital, self was hiding. It was time to let her out.

Simon stayed at the gym after dismissing the class. He said he wanted to practice a few things on his own, and it didn't seem to occur to him that I might want us to head home together. After my time in the ring, I took the R train, and walked home from the Court Street station to Simon's with a new sense of fearlessness. Not that bougie Brooklyn Heights posed any real danger, but just in general now on a dark street I no longer felt afraid. Hell, I pitied the fool who tried to jump me. I'd summoned the gorgeous darkness that had always lived inside me.

That night I smoked pot out the shack's window, feeling like an artist in Paris in the 1920s or something. I clomped around the studio in the huge slippers and pajamas Simon had given me, feeling like I was going as him for Halloween, and liking it.

I thought how much easier life would be if I kept impersonating him. Admittedly, I'd gone a little hard on the weed, but at the time this all made perfect sense. I'd stop being an uncertain teenage girl. I'd travel the world as Simon Ambrogio, still wearing these pajamas and slippers.

Or maybe I wasn't trying to be Simon but just finally settling into my own self, into my flesh and blood container with its inevitable limitations. Maybe what was transcendent about the art I would make was its lack of transcendence. Maybe for so long now I hadn't been making art because I'd been too focused on perfection—creating something good enough to get me the Clay and to be a proper memorial for my dead father, instead of art that reflected who I actually was, in all my fallibility, down to the smallest detail. In the spirit of this new idea, I took off the pajamas Simon had given me and made the rounds of the studio in my birthday suit, as just plain old me.

I was about to go to bed when I had a strong impulse that felt illicit and crept to find the plastic bag in my backpack where I kept my monster mask. In the dim light, the mask resembled some nightmare creature, and I felt inspired.

When I came out, naked except for the mask, I ran around touching every item in Simon's eccentric studio, running my hands over canvases and the bizarre objects Simon had collected. I drew paintbrushes over my naked body, even sucked on one of them.

I put paint in a bowl just to feel it squish between my fingers, and I stayed up to see the sunrise. I didn't want to wait anymore for some famous art guy to set up a space for me to work. I cleared a place for myself. Admittedly I was not ginger in doing so. I shoved Simon's eccentric paraphernalia, pushed ashtrays off tables—just letting them crash and shatter—to set down the paintbrushes and paints I straight-up stole from Simon like I was at Pearl Paint.

I moved the sofa over to the other side of the room, not caring that it left drag marks on the beautiful old wood floor. I grabbed up his boxing gloves he'd rigged with sponges and poured paint into a splattered vat.

Then I went over to his record player (of course he had a record player, just like too-cool-for-school Shay), dropped the needle and decided not to look at the record, just let it rip at the highest volume. Whatever played would have a secret message for me.

When its music belted out, it was The Velvet Underground's "Sweet Jane," and I laughed. Mom's name. What a joke. But it made me miss her terribly. I left it on as I donned the boxing gloves. It was an awkward process. Luckily, I was able to hold one glove with the other hand and push it against my chest to do the other.

Then I found a stack of large canvas pieces. I wasn't sure about the professional way to secure one of these to the wall, but I found a hammer and some nails and decided that would do the trick.

Once I'd hammered the canvas to the wall, with the Velvet Underground's "Loaded" blaring, I dunked my sponged mitts in the paint vat and made my first punch against the canvas, still wearing the monster mask and roaring like a beast. It felt phenomenal.

At first, I was sheepish, barely making contact with the canvas, as though I'd been forced to dance with a stranger. But then I felt a buzzing in my head that told me something might be ready to bust out. I thought about recent events: how Dad's eyes used to catch the light right before he threw his head back to laugh; but then how they'd glazed over right before going out completely; how they'd burned red as he'd recently accosted me looking like Frankenstein himself; how I was the last thing he ever saw in the real world, my terrified eyes reflecting his back to him; how I shamefully screamed at him like I was angry, "Don't leave me; how could you?" I punched harder.

I then thought about the delicacy of Shay's collarbones and how I wanted to pour honey on them and then lick it off, but also how I wasn't so sure she actually wanted me to do that anymore, considering she'd been rebuffing my advances since the séance night. And I punched harder.

I thought of how Mom used to give me butterfly kisses when I had a nightmare, the feeling of her eyelashes tickling my cheek, and how she'd do it over and over if I asked her, until no part of me was scared anymore, and of how Shay had done the same, pressing her eyelashes against my skin that first day by the river. But I also thought of how for eighteen years Mom had lied to me, let me call another man *Dad*—

even if that's what he'd always be to me.

And who was this stranger who'd burst onto the scene with this huge Greek tragedy of a revelation? We all know how those tragedies end. I punched still harder.

I thought of how finding Simon felt like a second chance at having a father, which had seemed impossible after Dad died; but also how he'd showed up out of nowhere, picking on me in class like he was testing to see if I was worthy of being his child or just a "pussy," like I was the hero being challenged in all those fables.

I thought of how Simon had never come to look for me until now. How do you just lose something and not go see where it ended up? By this time, I was punching the canvas so hard I was afraid I'd break through the wall. I was almost foaming at the mouth. But when I calmed down and stepped back, I saw that I really had something this time.

My painting gave me the good kind of chills. There were swaths of paint where I'd run my gloves across the canvas and Rorschach-like blots where I'd punched, demanding that the viewer decipher them but then always slipping out of any neat definition, as we all did in real life.

The paint had dripped in places, like the painting was crying. At the center were two punch marks that hadn't been filled in with paint, like eyes that looked back at you. Like you could see the artwork, but it could also see you.

I didn't care if it pissed Simon off. I was for once plenty high on my own achievements, so I wore one of his robes, left my monster mask on, and rushed over to the main house to wake him.

Chapter Eighteen

"Who died?" he asked, rolling over, his hair spiking. Then when he saw my monster mask, he bolted straight up and said, "Why the hell are you wearing that?"

"Oh yeah, this. Darby gave them out in class. Now, get up sleepyhead. You have to see what I made," I said.

"Yeah, yeah, kid, in the morning."

"No, now. You were the one who told me to beat down the door of the law or whatever. Up and at 'em, as you are so fond of saying," I said.

He looked surprised, then smiled. This was the first time I'd ever taken an authoritative tone with him. He obeyed, rolling over, groaning, but getting up.

When we got to the shack and I turned on the light, he seemed to wake right up.

"Wait, what? You made this, Dylan?" he asked.

"What do you think, I got some elves to come put it here as a prank? Yeah, I made it," I said, still talking to him liked we'd switched roles, like I was now the teacher.

"Okay, well, I think we have the work I can photograph for you to send to the Clay," he said.

It was like he'd given me the gold medal. "Really? You really think so?"

In answer, he grabbed up a camera and started snapping shots of my work, from this angle and that one, with me in it and not. Just snapping and snapping. I stood there grinning, the kid who'd won the science fair in front of her baking soda volcano.

"I'll develop these right away so you can send them in the morning. Good?"

"Amazing. I can't thank you enough." I paused. It was like all the air had gone out of the room now that I'd completed my quest to make the Clay entry. "Um, Simon?" I asked.

"Yeah?"

"Why did you come to Brooklyn Arts?"

"To get to know you," he said.

"You said. But why all of a sudden?"

"I don't want to sound insensitive. Your mom and I agreed that my role in your … creation … should be kept quiet because you already had a father, but when your father—" he said.

"Oh, yeah, yeah," I said. It made sense. I didn't know what I'd expected him to say. He'd showed up because he heard I was brilliant and wanted to be my mentor? No. Of course not. He showed up because Dad died, and he heard there was a vacancy for the position of my father. "Well, thanks for the photos," I said.

"You got it."

Simon shuffled off to the darkroom and I saw a faint outline of Dad standing behind him, shaking his head until I rubbed my eyes and collapsed on the sofa to finally sleep.

The next morning, I dropped the photos, along with the rest of my Clay application, in the mailbox, fingers crossed so tightly they hurt.

A few days later, at breakfast, Simon asked if Shay would be willing to help out because he had something he could use our assistance with. I felt worried he'd hit on her and/or offend her, but I said I'd ask. I knew she thought he was a jerk but would also appreciate the chance to study with him.

When I called, she seemed eager, but then she was late, and I wondered if she was even coming. Simon and I still weren't very good at hanging out just the two of us, not unless there was an art project to focus on, so after about an hour I gave up on Shay and retreated.

"I'll be in the shack," I said. When I got there, I felt antsy, so I put on the Frankenstein mask and roared at myself in the mirror to pass the time. I was just about feeling ready to make something when I heard a knock. I opened the door a crack, and there was Shay, wearing a short jean skirt and combat boots like some B-movie femme fatale. She seemed a little tipsy or something.

"I guess you liked your mask," she said, giggling.

"Oh, this. Yeah, I was just messing around," I said, reddening and going to tug it off.

"No, leave it on, and I'll put mine on, too." She pulled an identical mask out of the messenger bag slung around her waist.

"I guess you liked yours, too," I said, trying to sound casual.

"Hey, it was my idea for Mom to buy them for the class," she said.

She put hers on. As we stood there in our masks, I felt that I stood on some precipice. Behind me were dreary days waiting for my life to begin, and in front of me: Shay and Simon.

Shay came in to sit on my unmade bed, legs crossed, and lit a joint, which she smoked through the mouth hole of the mask. She exhaled fingers of smoke, looking like a sultry dragon.

I imagined this mask hole was the origin of all things, from which everything had sprung. "So," she said, "what are we going to make with Simon, do you think?"

I felt an unexpected stab of jealousy. Apparently, Shay was mostly excited to be hanging out with Simon. I alone didn't inspire this sort of exhilaration in her, or her attempts to resemble a postwar starlet. Were those pin curls?

"Not sure. Let me change," I said. I grabbed the first top and jeans I could get my hands on and headed toward the bathroom.

"I caught you wearing a monster mask just now. I stuck my tongue in your mouth. I hugged your dead ghost father. And now you're embarrassed for me to see you in sweatpants?" she called after me.

"You make a good point," I said, letting the shirt and jeans drop to the floor as though I would be nude without them, extending a sort of challenge. I did my best *come hither* pose. She seemed to accept the challenge and came to me.

She gave me this look like, *you won't believe what's coming,* and then tilted her head to the side, took the joint out of her mouth, and proceeded to kiss my monster mouth with hers. We were caught mask to mask, in mid-monstrous kiss when Simon knocked.

He opened the door with a squeak just as we sprang apart. "Oh wow," he said, taking in the scene, "sorry to interrupt, gals. You want me to come back later?"

I nodded, but Shay said, "No, no, we're all ready to work." She sounded a little too eager to get out of my grasp. I wanted to smite Simon.

"Okay, so if you can pull yourselves away from each other—I mean, who could pull themselves away from a spectacle such as Shay, am I right, Dylan?"

"Ew, stop. Get back to the plan," I said, glancing over at Shay, who looked embarrassed.

"Er, anyway," he continued, "what I need you to do is break stuff. Do you think you can do that?" he asked.

Shay looked thrilled. "Of course. What do you need us to break?" she asked, following him out to the garden, which was in full bloom.

"See these?" he asked, pointing to a set of full-length mirrors and rainbow lanterns lying on the grass.

We nodded.

"Well, take these hammers, put on these protective goggles—an artist always needs to protect the old eyes—and break this shit. I'm going to be using it for a project," he said.

Without hesitation, Shay started shattering the mirrors. She looked like the angel of death. Finally, I followed suit, bringing my hammer against the mirrors and lanterns like they had wronged me, feeling the heat of fury overtaking me until finally we had destroyed everything and were looking around for more stuff to break. Simon stepped forward to wrench the hammers from us.

We were covered in sweat, Shay's white tank top revealing a little too much. I found myself stepping in front, so Simon didn't ogle her, but then wondered if I was being either patriarchal/archaic.

"Easy there, cowboy," Simon said as he took the goggles from me. "Thanks for your help, gals. That was … thorough. I think that's all I need from you for right now, though. Feel free to stick around if you want, Shay, but I'm going to go grab a shower."

Shay and I were alone again, and I felt fluttery.

She went back into the shack, flopped down on the couch where I slept and then pulled me down on top of her, saying, "Have I told you yet today how much I like you?"

Every inch of me tingled. "So you do? Sometimes I worry," I said.

"No, I do. But there is something I need to tell you," she said.

"What?" I asked, touching her face.

"It's just that, well, I've never been with anyone before. I know people make other assumptions but they're wrong. I just don't know how to do … anything," she said.

"What? You've never been with anybody? What about your dyke tattoo? Is that just propaganda or what?" I asked, stunned. I regretted joking about it when her face fell. Who was I to mock Shay in the not-having-gotten-laid-yet department, anyway?

"No, no. Unlike you, I know exactly what I want—lots of pussy. Well, no. Just yours, actually. But let's just say I haven't explored that whole territory to the extent I would like," she said.

"Ugh, I hate that word. Why is everyone saying it this week?" Although it did have quite a different valence coming out of Shay's mouth.

"Sorry, so do I. I was just trying to be salty. To be honest, I feel kind of lame about the whole lack of experience issue," she said, fiddling with her skirt hem.

I must admit I was surprised. "And I don't? Shay, you were my first anything. And it's not like I've been fighting off the suitors with a baseball bat. Do I seem like anything but a virgin to you? There's no pressure for us to go any further than kissing if you don't want. I respect you. Whatever you're comfortable with," I said.

"You sound like a priest or something. What if I don't want to be respected?"

I laughed nervously. "Well, I can't help you out in that department. I do respect you, and that's that."

"So you've never fantasized about not respecting me?" she asked, touching my hands so softly with her fingers, running them in little circles over mine. She smelled like fireplace. I could tell she also felt my body in the air around her.

Her eyes looked greener in the neon light of the bar sign Simon had hung over the couch, a flying Pegasus.

She reached over, drew a bit of hair out of my eyes and back behind my ear. Her touch carried an extra special degree of grace, like when a pianist barely touches the keys before starting to play.

My body tensed. A whole minute passed probably with her hand frozen in time and space by my head, and words nowhere to be found, and maybe language had stopped, and nobody could tell us because language had stopped. How were we to know? We had lost contact with the outside world.

"Show me your fire," she said softly. "I've been wanting …"

"We shouldn't talk about that," I interrupted, still feeling it was too good to be true.

"To do this," she finished, touching the group of freckles on my arm, tracing its circumference, map making, topography. Then—in a motion I memorialized the minute it happened, safe from the ravages of both time and death—she licked my constellation.

I said, "Topography," and she said, "I'll map you," and, bang, that was it. The limits of control.

Then her face was right there again, her eyes so close I couldn't see them clearly anymore. They had become lands unavailable to sight, like how your home from an airplane looks like strange sets of squares.

She bent to lick my arm again, this time more slowly, holding eye contact the whole time, looking like she might eat me alive. In my mind's eye, I kept catching glimpses of water, as seen from an aircraft. I visualized her as that mermaid eating my ship.

I said, "It's like an airplane," and she said, "shhh."

Then she bit me. Not that hard, but still, I was astonished.

"Oh no. That was weird, right? You didn't like it?" she asked, looking embarrassed.

"No, no. I did. I was just surprised. Do it. Do it again," I said.

And she did. Then she was kissing my face all over while barely making contact. I was reminded of a butterfly, but this time definitely not of my mom.

She moved so she was on top of me. The entirety of her black hair fell over my face, feeling like silk, just like I'd always imagined. I saw it cascading around me as some sort of cocoon and felt the two of us were about to metamorphose.

She kissed my neck and bit me again, harder this time, and for all I'd imagined her looking like a vampire, I hadn't expected this. I liked it, though. It wasn't too hard, and there was a lot of tongue involved the last time she did it.

I wondered if this was what they meant when they sang about *the Monster Mash*. Then I tried to squelch that unsexy thought; I was relieved my inner monologue was silent, and I really wished I could mute the whole thing just for this one historical event, so I could fully commit every detail to memory. If anyone had told me there was any universe in which I got to make out with Shay, in which she would one day pull down my Hogwarts sweatpants, I wouldn't have believed them.

She touched me. A lot. And for someone who didn't know what she was doing, it didn't take her long to figure it out.

Then it was my turn, or at least that's the way I saw it, both from a sense of wanting her body to feel properly cared for, and from an all-encompassing curiosity about her flora and fauna. She still had clothes on, and I needed to rectify that. I'd been largely passive up until now. So I tugged her t-shirt over her head, unbuttoned her jean skirt. And then Shay was naked. It was too much to bear.

What broke my heart were the homely details of her body nobody else would love. I collected them with care: the angry red bumps where she'd shaved her bikini line; the darker wisps of hair above her lip; one breast slightly larger than the other; stretch marks on her thighs; and up close her eyes had a strange shape she told me

185

was sun damage: *pterygiums,* she called them. Have you ever heard a more beautiful word?

There was just so much going on there in her body. From the porn I'd watched during my voyage of trying to figure out if I liked men, the male equivalent was a lot more straightforward, and not in a good way. This was its own ecosphere, and I went voyaging.

Being with Shay reminded me of her breathtaking drawings. Her body came at me slantwise; I wasn't even ready for the things I saw and felt; sex with Shay was a labyrinth. Granted, I had smoked a lot beforehand, but I had this high-definition vision of entering her body. I mean adventuring around in there like it was Atlantis. Like parting the doors of her skin and daring to go inside with my whole body. She was in there and I was in there, and we were making a mural featuring the face of photographer Francesca Woodman. In short, I'd finally gotten laid and gone off the deep end. I was snapped out of it when we heard the creaky shack door, and there stood Simon.

"What the, what's going on here? I, uh, came to check on you guys," he said, actually blushing.

"We're great, Simon," Shay said, not making any move to move from atop me, just staring at him.

I don't know why he looked so shocked when he'd supposedly had such an adventurous sex life, as chronicled in every art blog.

Simon was just standing there staring, dumbfounded, at Shay in particular. I had covered up immediately but not her. He appeared to be enticed but also possibly a little turned to stone, maybe how all men feel when faced with a woman unbound. But I was sick of sheltering men from our horrifying femininity.

I was about to apologize to Simon but then I took a different tack. I gently moved Shay aside, got up off the couch, took a cigarette out of Shay's bag, lit it, inserted it in my mouth and took a long, deep drag. I coughed furiously as I was not a smoker.

Simon looked amused. But then I took another drag, walked over to where Simon was standing by the door, exhaled the smoke right into his face, and said, channeling a femme fatale, "Scram, buster."

When I glanced at Shay, I thought I detected a delicious glow of approval. But then I tried to see anew. Not how I was being seen, but how I was seeing. Not how others were feeling about me but how I was feeling. I was feeling pretty fucking good, that's how. Simon said, "Okay, then, you girls enjoy yourselves," and walked out.

Chapter Nineteen

After that time in the shack, I would call Shay up, with her making fun of me for not texting, and say stupid shit like, "What's that light in the window over there? It is the East, and Juliet is the sun." Miraculously, she still kept sleeping with me afterward.

She taught me how to make my own paint, brought me vibrantly colored stones from the stream in Maine where she went over break, then showed me how to rub them against the cement of the Brooklyn promenade until they turned into a sort of cream, which we would then collect in little bottles. When I got home, I'd put them in front of the windows and the light traveled through them until my heart sputtered.

We spent a lot of time at Muse Café where the barista gave Shay free coffee, sketching across the table from each other. When a good image arrived, I might say something like, "I feel like I'm losing my mind," and she would understand I meant the inspiration that was exploding me. She'd say something like, "Ride it to its endpoint," and keep working on her own stuff. Then in the afternoons, we would go on adventures. To Coney Island with its Wonder Wheel, Cyclone, and haunted houses. To Chinatown, with its secret shrines, perplexing window seafood, and fruits that looked like blowfish, so Shay could get squid ink from a lady at a market to make me drawings and write me love letters.

Darby let me sleep over in her daughter's bed whenever I wanted, which I greatly appreciated. I could never be just conventionally curious about people. I needed to know what they wore to bed, if they were photogenic, what their sex face was, who they were when nobody was looking. I wanted to be able to download their experience, know what it was to wake up in their body, make coffee. Shay was the only person I knew all these things about, and this was tenderness to me.

My personality had never been well-suited to being a "desirable woman," to guys, at least. I was always flowing over the edges of my own structure. But then Shay asked me to be louder, urged me to build myself up rather than attempting the feminine art of disappearing. She even fed me. Whenever I talked about how I felt too large, she would bake me pies or roast me her mom's ingenious vegetarian take on those huge turkey legs so we could pretend we lived in medieval times. I was more than happy to be Shay's wench. When I felt too large on a more metaphorical level, Shay would pump me full of information, causing me to grow still more until I thought I might burst with knowledge. She would buy me Susan Sontag's *On Photography* and Roland Barthes's *Camera Lucida*, after hours at The Strand, and then we'd discuss the books together, arguing, getting fired up, interrupting each other, traveling the history of photography.

I got to know Shay's patterns so well. Her grossness: nose picking, shower avoidance, and a sick enjoyment of leftover takeout food too long in the fridge; the daredevil exhibitionist behavior she performed like clockwork whenever she started to hurt inside; her flurries of art production followed by dry spells that led her to smoke too much pot and watch too much reality television. We shared a bed so often I started to think we absorbed each other's thoughts through the skin. One night Shay had a dream about a black widow spider who was trying to bite her, and it turned out I'd had the same dream. I tried to remember if we'd seen something like this on television that night or what. And by what mechanism had these dreams shuttled back and forth between us? Was there a sort of umbilical cord that developed between people who loved each other as much as Shay and I did?

One night she put her hands on my pudgy tummy and asked, "Do you ever want life to grow there?"

"I think it might already be," I said, taking a shot at my own rotundity. But then, getting serious, I said, "I definitely do, but I want to be a different kind of mother than mine. I want to be the knight's guard for my daughter's weirdness."

"You don't think you'd have a son?" she asked.

"Not possible, no penis is ever growing in here," I said, rubbing my belly.

"Yeah, but would you finally call it a pussy if you had one growing inside you?" she joked.

"In that case, definitely," I said, grabbing her ass.

We laughed but she got serious. "I wish I could plant a baby in you, like with garden seeds. It would be our joint artwork. It would be so beautiful. If I had a kid, I'd never kill myself and abandon it," she said.

I embraced her, saying, "Oh honey, I know you wouldn't. And I'd never get cancer or be a famous artist and abandon it. But you have to chill with the weed, ok?" I pulled her onto my lap and started tickling her to distract her from further thoughts of baby pussy. Or our fathers.

But she still looked thoughtful, and said, "That baby would be our fucking masterpiece."

"Slow down there, crazypants," I said, and kissed her. She tasted, as always, of weed, kombucha (she claimed the alcohol buzz added up if you had like ten), and Skittles.

I thought about Mom all the time while staying at Simon's, even more so after Shay and I joked about motherhood. It was the first time I'd ever been away from Mom. Despite our differences, our constant bickering, we'd always been inseparable, two hens pecking each other into infinity.

I'd been wearing Mom's NYIA sweatshirt the night I'd fled my house, and these days I slept with it wrapped around me, sniffing it as I fell asleep, imagining I could still smell her signature scent: Fracas perfume, Nicorette gum, Nivea cream. Mom never knew, but I started sneaking home for just a few minutes every night, to check our mailbox for an envelope from the Clay scholarship people. But also to spy on her. To smell Mom's burnt cooking fumes. To read her post-it note reminders arranged like an investigator's murder wall. To touch the teabags, she always left on the counter because I couldn't touch her.

I know, I know. When does my spying end? Have I no shame? I haven't. So, I would snap open the mailbox filled with hope, only to slam that empty thing shut. Then I'd peer into the window. If Mom wasn't home, I'd go in; if she was, I'd watch her eating dinner alone or poring over an art book. I willed her to look up, to see me standing there by the window. But she never did. I felt lonelier than ever, a monster without a creator.

Meanwhile Simon seemed to want me thinking about neither Shay nor Mom. Only art. In particular, my relationship with Shay seemed to bother him. He grew even more volatile after walking in on Shay and me, as though he were jealous that my attention was going to anything but art, to anything but him as art sage. He kept making comments about how I had to stay focused on my work, how I shouldn't let any girl turn my head, and did I see him married? No. Because he was a real artist.

About two weeks after Shay and I, uh, consummated our relationship, I'd had it with Simon's comments. One night when he made a big deal about my need to shut people out and stay focused, I finally came back at him with, "So that's how you became famous, huh? Ditched the baby to make the art? Leave the mom artist to take care of the kid and give up her career?"

"Oh God, Dylan. Is that how you see me? I wanted to be there. But your mom was in love with Ray, and she wanted to bring you up with him. Do you have any idea how that broke my heart? I would have given up all the art stuff just to help change your diapers and rock you to sleep," he said, looking genuinely upset. "But it's a valid question, and one I've asked myself every day for the last eighteen years. I'm sorry for all of it. But what's done is done. Dylan, I can't take back the past. All I can do is be here for you now. And I'm here. And I love you in my own cockeyed way, my daughter." He gently cuffed me under the chin.

This was the first time he'd ever said anything like that. Love. What a force. His comment did melt something in me, and I gave him a shy hug.

He surprised me by hugging me back heartily.

"I'm so glad you're sweethearts with Shay now. I know how much that meant to you," he said.

"It doesn't seem like you're glad. Seems to bother you somehow," I said.

"Hell, maybe I'm just envious. In a way the two of you remind me of your mom and me back in the day. She may hate me now for how things went down, but don't let her lie to you. We were madly in love," he said. I hadn't expected that. The thought of Simon and Mom carrying on like Shay and me was hard to stomach, so I didn't try.

"You're right that I'm driving you hard. But, Dylan, that's because you have the kind of talent that doesn't come along often," he said.

It was hard to ignore something so affirming of my work, something I'd been waiting to hear my whole life.

"Now, let's get back to the work, champ," he said, slipping on his second boxing glove and boxing the canvas alongside me. There was a poetry to action painting with your famous artist father, not gonna lie.

"Now hit the canvas like so," he said, walloping it with his glove.

"I'm doing it, just in my own way," I said.

"Did you come here to apprentice yourself to me or to just keep making the same mediocre crap you were before?" He ripped off his glove to grab my arm, a little too hard, as he said it, exhaling liquor vapors. I felt, for the first time, genuinely scared of him. That word, 'mediocre,' made me wilt inside. And right after he'd just talked me up. It was all too confusing. Simon was always careening between moods, leaving me running along behind.

"Let go of me, and don't say that about my work. I hoped to learn something from you, sure, but I'm not your art servant. And I don't feel like learning anything now that you're, like, assaulting me."

"Assaulting you?! Are you fucking kidding me with this #metoo bullshit? That's the problem with you young women artists, you're all a bunch of pussies. You need more trials by fire."

"I told you I hated that word," I said, glaring at him, wishing I were more physically intimidating so he didn't feel like he could just push me around.

"Is there another word for what you are?" he asked.

"Yeah, a fucking artist," I said, whipping off the gloves and throwing them to the ground.

"Fine, fine. I see you're not up to making art today, so I'm out of here. Let me know when you're ready to stop being such a little cunt about everything and get serious about your work," he said, heading for the door of the shack and then back toward the main apartment.

I stood very still, watching him walk away, horrified by this exchange. I felt queasy and contemplated leaving that very minute. But I still had my big boxing painting hanging in pride-of-place on Simon's studio wall. I didn't want to abandon that. It was my baby. I decided that running out in the middle of the night was unnecessary, but I planned to head out the next day with my precious painting. I was done with what he'd called this "apprenticeship" if he was going to be calling me the C word.

But then, about an hour later, as I was wearing my monster mask and painting, he didn't even knock on the shack door as he always did, but just busted in. When he saw me in the mask, he said, "Take that fucking thing off," and pulled it roughly off my head.

He had smelled of it a bit earlier, but now he reeked of booze. He was in a darker mood than I'd ever seen, and there had already been some dark nights.

"There's somewhere I need to take you," he said, as though I should have always known this was coming. I felt partly afraid of him, partly intrigued. I guess I wasn't totally done looking up to him, hoping some of his sparkle would rub off on me.

"Now?"

"Now, Dylan. It's important for your artistic development. None of this is easy. It's not supposed to be. But do you want to look back ten years from now as a housewife and know you could have been more than just okay? You could have been brilliant and you just ... walked away?"

And now he'd dangled before me the one thing that could have gotten me to stick around: the possibility of being a brilliant artist like him one day, my fear of ending up domesticated and disappointed like my mother. And he knew it. He was right about me. I couldn't stand the idea of missing my chance at greatness. Not to mention that he was the only person who really understood the part of me that would have done almost anything for the sake of creativity. There was a preciousness to that understanding. And you know what? He might be right that I was a cunt. But I meant this as a reclamation: I was an art cunt.

As we walked down Montague toward the R train, he had a stony expression and didn't say a word to me—no diatribes on art tonight.

Even on a subway car full of people with bleak expressions, Simon's was the bleakest. He kept taking swigs from a flask. He wouldn't tell me where we were going. But in a way I didn't care.

We got out in some neighborhood in Sunset Park, Simon practically jerking me off the subway car.

I thought of turning back a few times, but I was somewhat entranced, still somewhere the little girl who wanted to please her daddy.

Simon said, "I need to make sure you're cut out to be the great artist you want to be."

"I'm not a great artist already? But you said—"

"Of course, of course," he said, without conviction.

He gripped my hand so hard it hurt, leading me along the empty, shadowed streets. I was too baffled to say anything, so I just kept walking like the undead. But I did pull my hand from his. I could walk on my own.

The place Simon finally stopped looked like a flophouse. Slats covered the windows, and when we entered, an unsettling smell, something I identified after a moment as blood. I recognized it from play-fighting with Dad, and also the nosebleeds I got in cold weather that brought Mom to my room with tissues and hugs.

It took a minute to adjust to the sensory overload and make sense of what was happening. The room was afire with feathers and beaks and blood and men. I couldn't even think of the word for it at the time, but Simon had taken me to a cockfight. The birds were released upon each other and then launched into a frenzy of pecking and scratching. I'd never felt sicker in my life.

"Now," he said, "I know it's awful to look at, but see if you can learn to face life at its most elemental. If you can allow this very upsetting scene to be but an aesthetic experience." He leaned over me and offered up some peanuts from his pocket. I pushed his hand away.

I looked on as these roosters did battle, and soon felt the sting of tears coming on, tasting them in the back of my throat the same way I imagined the salty blood of the sparring chickens would taste. I hated myself for not rushing out to rescue the poor wounded birds. How could I just sit there like that? I was afraid these guys would kick my ass if I interrupted their little entertainment. But how was this entertainment?

What I hated myself for most was the tiny shard of exhilaration running through me as I absorbed the energy in the room. If I took my eyes away from the frenzied birds, an image that was breaking me, I could see the crowd. Total immersion on a grand scale. The audience members' eyes were trained on combat like it was the kind of inventive artwork Simon was inviting me to create, like it gave them that same heart flutter I got when I looked at Louise Bourgeois' Mother sculpture.

These spectators were in awe of something larger than themselves. They were facing the inevitability of death: the roosters', their loved ones', their own. But in this brush with mortality, in these violent emotions, they were locating a kind of fucked-up poetics, a creative euphoria that I recognized all too well. This realization was what put me over the edge; I leaned over and threw up into Simon's lap.

"Shit," he cried, jumping up and trying to brush the mess off himself. Worse still, he was essentially raking it onto the big, tattooed bald guy in front of us.

The guy looked over his shoulder at the vomit on his back, then at Simon like he was the most disgusting person in the world. I'd never seen Simon look so small and scared, and there was something kind of great about it, a majestic and much-needed leveling effect. But then this bro spun around and decked Simon right in the face.

Simon grabbed at his nose, making sure it was still there, blood trickling from it.

"You motherfucker," I screamed. "Don't you ever hit my dad again." The guy froze. Simon froze. I froze.

Dad's ghost froze. Yes, he too had joined the scene, probably summoned by my carnal sin of calling another man the word I'd only ever called him.

"How could you?" demanded his ghost.

"Did you just call me Dad?" Simon asked, blood leaking into his mouth as he spoke.

The bald guy had already lost interest in the whole scene and turned around to watch the fight.

"Dylan?" asked Simon.

"Dylan?" asked Dad's ghost.

"Dylan, eh? Isn't that a dude name?" asked the bald man, turning back for a moment.

"Fuck off," said Simon. And the guy did. He shrugged, brushed his shirt off, took a chug from his beer can, and went back to watching the cocks annihilate each other.

"Did you? Call me Dad?"

"I did," I said, "I didn't mean to. Sorry."

"Sorry? I'm delighted," he said, taking a flask out of his pocket and swigging from it, teetering, clearly really drunk now, blood drops spattering on the flask.

It was all too much. Dad's ghost looked devastated, and I didn't have the energy to deal with either of my fathers, especially after the recent blood bath for both the roosters and Simon.

"I gotta go," I said.

Simon and Dad both reached for me, but I broke free and ran toward a longhaired man who was picking up the bodies of the dead birds and chucking them into a trashcan. He looked up, surprised no doubt to see a furious girl come hurtling toward him with maybe the saddest look he'd ever seen.

"Give that to me; how could you?" I yelled, wiping remnants of my vomit and Simon's blood from my cheek.

The guy looked briefly freaked out but then just went back to his bleak work.

I jumped between him and the body of the next bird he was preparing to throw away, then stopped, uncertain what to do. After a second, I grabbed the dead bird and hugged its bloody, limp body to my chest with an intensity that surprised me, as though I could somehow give it back its shitty, caged life.

Simon finally came over and gently took the body out of my arms.

"Life is tough," he said. "You must make things happen. You must be able to face these things and record them. You must be able to kill with your brush. Hemingway was obsessed with bull fights. This was as close as I could get. Sorry it got so intense. Before we got here it seemed like a good idea."

In that instant I suspected I couldn't move or speak even if I'd wanted to. But I knew too that I must fight, must rise up against Simon who was not, in fact, trying to help me. Who in all the world could possibly be so bad at mentoring?

"I'm truly so sorry. I didn't realize how upset you were getting," he said.

"You never do. I want to go home," I said.

"Of course, let's head home, daughter," he said, putting his arm around me.

"No, I mean to my real home, with Mom, who doesn't take me to fucking cock fights," I said.

"Oh, sure, okay. We can head back and grab your stuff and I'll take you," he said.

"I can go myself, Simon," I said. Calling him Dad had freaked me out and made me feel guilty. My only real Dad was floating around my head, still moping; Simon looked miffed at being called Simon again.

But before I left, I grabbed that poor bird's bloody body from Simon. Though I'm sure it was a health hazard, I put it in my backpack and rode all the way home on the subway with it, reaching into the bag to pet and comfort it periodically, whispering, "We're almost home, baby." I never thought I'd be the craziest-looking person on the subway, but there I was, cooing to the dead animal in my backpack.

When I got back to Simon's place, I took out the bird's body gently. I stroked it, sang it "Twinkle Twinkle Little Star" as Mom had done when I was little. Finally, I kissed it, not sure if that was a good health move, but unable to stop myself. Then I dug a little hole and laid it to rest in Simon's astonishing garden, with the perverse hope that it would one day sprout, make more roosters. I found a little rock and put it where I'd planted the bird, as a gravestone, so I'd always remember.

Dad's ghost looked proud.

Chapter Twenty

I wrenched my canvas off the shack wall. He got back about an hour later, after a trip to the bar from the looks of him. He drunkenly teetered toward me across the garden, but I wasn't about to talk to him right then. I went in and gathered my things from the shack and put them down in the main apartment.

My painting was big enough to be unwieldy, and I was trying to figure out whether I could bring it in a Lyft without angering the driver—debating whether I should say goodbye to Simon or not. I decided it would be a good idea to use the bathroom before I left.

As I was washing my hands, I smelled something burning. As angry as I was, I couldn't let Simon burn to death if there was a fire. I wasn't a murderer.

I ran out to find Simon burning something in the fire pit we'd set up to photograph flaming works of art. He'd only ever burned his own work since I'd lived there, though, so I hadn't seen any ethical issues at the time.

As I grew closer, I saw he was so drunk he was almost falling over as he madly photographed the burning work, pausing only to take more swigs from his flask.

"Isn't it gorgeous? Aren't you flattered? Now you can be involved in great art even if you never get there yourself," he said.

It took me a bit to make sense of what he'd said through the slurred words. Even when I did, I couldn't believe I'd heard him right.

I walked slowly to the fire, knelt closer and saw my painting—the one Simon had said he admired so much—on fire.

"You jealous motherfucker," I screamed. I ran to grab the painting out of the pit with my bare hands, singeing my knuckles in the process, barely noticing, just trying to protect the smoldering canvas. Luckily, I was in time and the painting was only burnt around the edges and a little bit in the middle. I stomped out the flames, laid it carefully down, then lunged at Simon, grabbing away his camera.

"Careful with that," he slurred, "it costs more than you do. I've done this with countless famous artists, and they've all been flattered. I only do it with brilliant works, so you can rest assured that this painting is, in fact, top notch. Let me just clarify about the aesthetics of—"

"Shut up. God. I'm not some other artist. I'm your goddamn daughter. Or at least that's what you tell me, but how can we be related? You're cruel. That's my work. I finally made something I could be proud of and you're burning it?"

"Well, if you see it from another perspective, in the history of art—"

"Oh, just shut the fuck up. Stop lecturing me. You're a tiny, wretched thing, aren't you? The Wizard of Oz with his curtain pulled back is just a sad old man. You will no longer make me feel small. I don't have to be like you to be a great artist. Why on earth did I ever even think that? With zero training my father, my *real* one, was twice the artist you will ever be. And I have that in me, too, somewhere. Plus your work is so woman-hating it makes me want to puke. Who punches naked women and photographs ladies while they're crying?"

I threw his camera in the fire, heaved up my burnt painting in my arms, and stomped away from him. I could hear him screaming and cursing over his camera in the distance. I felt like a winged avenger. Dad's ghost linked arms with me, and we walked away together.

I left my bag of clothes and other stuff, but I carried my painting out over my head, so I had what mattered. It felt so good to leave Simon standing there with his mouth opening and closing like a landlocked fish, holding a melted camera that cost more than me. I found a cab driver willing to let me push my painting into the backseat, with part of it sticking out into the front (bless him) and headed home. I listened to every detail about all five of his kids with reverence. He had helped me save my art, after all and I loved him for it.

The lights were on when I got home. I jangled my keys to give Mom a warning and even knocked on my own door after it opened to give her enough time to gather herself.

Mom was at the kitchen table reading one of my art magazines, the light above her head revealing her gray roots, reminding me of her mortality. When I came in, she ran over to me and practically picked me up off the ground as she embraced me, which, given our relative size, was a herculean feat.

Smelling her neck brought everything about her back to me, making me realize how much I'd missed her.

Even though I'd been sneaking over there regularly, it felt like someone else's home now and I kept looking around to check that everything was the same. Except for the unnecessarily ugly new flowered tablecloth, everything seemed in order. I guess it was just me that had changed.

"My girl! You came back to me. I knew I couldn't force you. You had to come on your own, but it's all been so hard. It was all I could do not to steal you back in the night like a changeling," she said.

"I'm so sorry. And you were so right about Simon, or about parts of him anyway," I said.

Now she looked aghast. "Oh God, what has he done?"

I held up my boxing painting, charred on one side, but luckily saved before being destroyed. And it actually did look better. The swaths of paint where my gloves had hit the canvas were now sooty. The two punch marks at the center were blackened, and the edges of the canvas has become almost lacy in their burnt quality. The painting had become seasoned, a surface that had known trauma and lived to tell about it.

Not that I would ever admit that to Simon. He'd claim it as an aesthetic win, and I could not have that.

"That monster. I'll kill him," she screamed. "I'm going to go destroy his art for once. It's high time he knew what that felt like." She surprised me by actually going over to the coat closet and pulling out a baseball bat nobody had ever used.

"Oh my God, Mom. Please calm down. Put the bat down. This is not the answer," I said, taking the bat from her. She looked like she might protest but then did go sit back down at the kitchen table, breathing heavily.

"Look," I said, "he did teach me things, and in his own sick way I think on occasion he might have meant well. I don't think he's evil, just hopelessly selfish, and I have to say I'm going to be pretty pissed if you still won't tell me what happened, your side of the story, the rest of it, I mean. You chose to have a child with this maniac. Look at this painting. You owe me this," I said.

She cringed. "Don't make excuses for him. But, yes, it's time. I'll get some tea. And that painting is amazing, by the way. It's good you rescued it. You have guts I never had, kiddo," she said.

Tea, tea. All this tea to just get to my familial truth. Though, I was touched by her praise. "Thank you, Mom," I said.

She sat across from me at the dining room table again, holding her tea.

"What happened with the dollhouse?" I asked.

She was silent.

"Mom?" I asked.

Silence.

"Mom?" I repeated.

"Well, basically you already know. Why rehash it?" Her bottom lip trembled, and she bit a nail.

"Mom, this is the big piece of the puzzle, of something about me, that I've been trying to figure out."

"Fine, Dylan," she said. Her voice weary. "I haven't been completely honest," she said.

"Obviously."

"It's not lying. It's just. People, and especially people your age, want a black-and-white story and things just don't happen like that in real life."

"Thanks for the life lesson. I've had enough of those lately," I said.

"Anyway, Simon and I, we were art partners in crime. Well, not literally but you get what I mean. The feelings were complex and ran deep. We admired each other's talent but were also competitive," she said.

"I do get that part," I said, reaching over and squeezing her hand. And I guess for the first time I saw that she'd been chasing the art, just like me, just like Shay. *Art monsters.*

"And Ray was great, but he wasn't *an artist in that same way,*" she said.

I disagreed but this wasn't the point of her story. I could see how at first a rising art star would seem more obviously creative than a down-to-earth mechanic.

She continued. "I was working on, well, you know about it now, my dollhouse. It was going to be in my first show that Simon had organized for me. Simon had been sculpting famous murderers and I'd been creating large-scale dollhouses with realistic down to the very last detail crime scenes. Our work was complementary, that was why it made sense to collaborate. There was this one day when we borrowed a truck from his friend to go through a warehouse in Red Hook for supplies. I went to warehouses all the time, found all sorts of great things, a faded family photograph a child had drawn over with crayon, a broken weathervane. That sort of thing. As I held these, I could already see flashes of their future transformation in the studio. In childhood, while other kids wanted apples, I wanted the cores. Does this make any sense? Do I sound nuts?"

"You've never sounded saner. I totally get it. Keep going."

"Simon and I," she went on, "had been driving around all morning trying to find this place. A guy had called looking to unload what to him was a bunch of junk. This happened often. I needed materials and Simon would come along to photograph. As we walked in, I told myself these discarded objects would sleep in my dorm room that night. And after the rest of the city had gone to sleep, I imagined—it sounds weird, but—speaking to them. Then I found this Frankenstein mask, well, you know it well by now, the one I finally donated to the Brooklyn Arts because I just couldn't have it in my home anymore. Anyway, I found it in that warehouse. I loved it.

"We got back to Simon's—the same apartment where you've been staying. He rented it out when he left, but he's had the same place for decades now. I'd been working on my dollhouse there; it barely occurred to me how intimate it was for me to spend so much time in his home. I thought it would be funny to surprise him by wearing the mask, but when I came over, he took it off, kissed me, and, um, the rest. When it was over, he asked if I would leave Ray to be with him, and I said no.

"He stormed out and I could just feel he was going to destroy something. I put the mask back on before even getting dressed. I realized I'd just ruined my relationship with your dad, so I was pretty upset, and it just felt right at the time. When I realized Simon was taking pictures of my burning dollhouse, I was in such shock I didn't even try to stop him. I just cried, took the mask off, ran away like a coward. And, as you've seen, he photographed that as well.

"There he was photographing my burning art. Not even a hurried shoot, either. He was concentrating so hard, focusing each shot perfectly. And then, almost as soon as you were old enough to work a lighter, you started burning the art you made, and it terrified me. I'm sorry, but it was like seeing a ghost.

"My problem was I had the same will to art as Simon, but I also had human decency, and I felt like it held me back. I think I wanted to be the photographer, the art burner, rather than the photographed, the one whose art got burned. That photograph was the one that would make Simon famous. And I never made another real work of art of my own," she said.

"Oh, Mama," was all I could think to say. Then, "But what you make is still real art, even if you've stopped calling it that. You're not a hundred years old. You have to get back to it. I'll help you," I said.

She just shrugged. I went over to her, stroked her hair, and said what she'd always said to me when times got tough, "It's all going to be okay, baby." I wasn't sure I believed it, but it seemed like the kindest thing.

I went out to check our mailbox for a letter from the Clay people, but nothing. I tried calling Shay, but she wasn't picking up. I texted her:

"SOS. Really need to talk," but she must have already been asleep. Her lights were off.

I felt shaken up after my talk with Mom, and not sure how to feel about all of it. The whole thing put me in a hazy state that only could be broken by the arrival of a certain, very important letter.

The morning after our chat, Mom went out to the market to buy stuff for a special breakfast. I guess she felt guilty for laying all that on me the night before.

When she returned with the groceries, I was already up and about, draped over the kitchen table, doodling. I'd woken up when a call came in from Shay, probably responding to my SOS text from last night, but I hadn't known what to say yet. I figured I would call her back once I got my head together.

Mom looked a bit disappointed that she couldn't bring me breakfast in bed, but then she remembered what was in her hand.

"Dyl, a letter came from NYIA!"

I grabbed it so fast I made her drop the milk, which cascaded over the floor. I prayed it wasn't a sign. I went to grab the mop to clean it up, but she said, "Come on and open it already," and I dropped the mop, grabbed up the envelope again and broke the seal.

It had been weeks now of rushing to the mailbox to find just another one of those brightly colored coupon bundles. I knew the scholarship finalist announcements would go up on the Clay website pretty soon, but the official notification came first by mail, which I liked. It was calming to have something I could touch.

I held the opened letter in my hands but felt too afraid to look.

"You want me to read it to you, Dyl?" Mom asked, reaching for it, but I felt a sudden protectiveness and snatched it away.

She looked surprised, but like she understood.

"I'm sorry. I just don't know how to do this," I said.

"I get it, honey. This is your big moment. Whatever you need," she said.

Finally, I read from it: "Dear Dylan Ann Cyllene, we are delighted to inform you that you have been selected for the interview process for the Marissa M. Clay Scholarship of the New York Institute of the Arts. A representative of NYIA, Dr. Delphine Alderman, will be coming to meet you and the other interviewees at your school at 10 a.m. on March 4. Please meet the representative in the office of Mr. Oscar Edison." I was in shock, like a practical joke had been played on me. This, after all, was the golden ticket.

While Mom was making breakfast, I dialed Shay immediately. She didn't pick up, but instead just texted me back: "Where are you? We're waiting for you."

In all the chaos, not only had I not gotten in touch with Shay yet to tell her all that had gone down last night, but I'd forgotten Shay, Simon, and I were supposed to meet up so Shay could use the darkroom today. I dialed her number again, but still she didn't pick up. I texted: "Don't trust him. Get out of there now." But when I didn't hear back, I decided I had to head over there myself, frenzied, filled with absurd images of Simon setting Shay on fire because I didn't get there on time.

When I got there, Shay and Simon weren't in the main apartment, so I rushed toward the shack, hoping I wouldn't find Shay or her work smoldering. I got there just as Shay was coming out.

But something was wrong. I took in the scene quickly and added up its elements. Shay was heading out of the studio with Simon close behind her. When she saw me, she looked guilty. Her lipstick was smeared like it had been the night of the river and her hair was mussed. Something in me snapped.

"Betrayers," was all I could think to say as I stormed away from them.

She said, "Dylan, wait. Let me explain," running after me.

But I was off. I ran through the main apartment and found myself hyperventilating on Willow Street with no idea where to go or what to do. As I wandered down Willow, my phone beeped repeatedly with Shay's texted protests until I silenced it. But I was still able to see her words lighting up the little phone screen, so I threw the damn thing into a trash can on Middagh Street, not even considering how much babysitting I'd done to afford to buy that darn phone in the first place.

Of course Shay wanted to be with a hot famous grown man artist and not with me, some teen girl doodler who worshiped her so hard I wanted to voyage in her vagina.

Chapter Twenty-One

When I got home, I pushed past Mom's questions about what was wrong, claiming I was fine. Not knowing what else to do, I went down the basement stairs, picked up the Frankenstein shadow box and my lighter, and headed out to the courtyard grill. I placed the box, with its creature and creator and their vividly rendered features, gently on top of the burner and I lit that shit up. In the book, when Dr. Frankenstein encounters the monster he's created, this is the moment of father meeting child symbolically, and I'd had it with all my fathers at this point. I was embracing my orphan status officially, at least in the paternity department.

I was something of an expert pyromaniac by this point. Some stuff goes up so fast you barely have time to enjoy it. But a wooden box? Even with liberal application of lighter fluid, it blazed for a long time, paint blistering and cracking off the figurines inside while I stood and watched. It lasted long enough for euphoria to wear off and regret to creep in.

I felt horrible for burning Dad's final work of art, which he and Mom and I had all done together. I was a horrible art-burner just like my father after all and hated myself for it. But then I thought better of it, and rescued that burning art beast from the flames, knocking it off the grill with a stick, throwing dirt on it until it was merely smoldering, and then entirely without flame. I picked it up, carried it like a hurt animal, and left it on Shay's fire escape. An offering, a warning, a final love letter, a parting gift.

Between fathers lost and found, girlfriends had and lost, and mothers whose art careers I'd ruined, when I woke up for school the next day I was in a mood of, as Shay might have put it, *not giving two fucks.*

I got to school to find that Shay wouldn't so much as look at me. I had figured I'd be the one spurning her, while she groveled for a second chance after breaking my trust. But she looked so angry I started to question my own stance.

I approached Shay by her locker, saying, "Morning, stranger, did you receive my fire escape gift?" She didn't acknowledge me, just walked away without a word.

Darby's lecture in English class about the destruction of Frankenstein's Bride felt a little too close to home after that, considering I'd just left a burnt Frankenstein monster on Shay's fire escape like a cat delivering a dead frog.

Darby was saying, "What happens to the Bride is really a tragedy. Dr. Frankenstein finds the notion of this creature procreating and making monsters so terrible that he rips her to pieces."

Shay was sitting next to me because that was the only option. I tried to catch her eye when she turned toward me while getting something out of her bookbag. She totally iced me out, though, studiously looking through me as though I'd ceased to exist. It made me feel desperate.

I scribbled "speak to me, my love" on a paper and passed it to her under the desk, but she crumpled it up without even a glance. My panic was rising.

Shay was taking notes but also seemed to be creating an ornate labyrinth there along the transcript of what her mother was saying. I thought I could make out an abandoned monster at its core, and I pictured the two of us little fatherless ghouls there at the center of the nightmare land she'd constructed, just the two of us against the world, making a home there, staying forever. On it, she wrote, simply, "Fuck off," and I felt all was lost.

Darby continued, "In the movie *Bride of Frankenstein*, the Bride gets to live only for a short spell, and this time it's the monster himself who destroys her because she doesn't want him." I shot a beseeching look at Shay. She rolled her eyes at me, but at least she hadn't avoided eye contact altogether like earlier.

"Man, that bride is one piece I'd throw out of bed," Cash said.

Cash had made so many stupid, sexist, infantile comments in so many of my classes. Normally they just faded to background noise. But this, today, made my blood boil in a way I found hard to explain. I knew it had something to do with Shay rejecting me, and every offensive thing Cash had ever said to me to date. I tried to calm myself down, reminding myself that Cash and I both came from the same stuff as stardust—a mantra Mom had taught me for when I felt angry at someone. But it didn't help. If we were both made of stardust, then why was he such an entitled fucking asshole?

I didn't know now which part angered me most: Cash being an idiot, dead fathers, lying mothers, cheating girlfriends. Cash was suddenly everything that stood against me in the universe. I snapped.

"Even if you were the last guy on earth, the Bride would never have had sex with you," I said.

He looked stunned, like no girl in his entire, handsome life had ever spoken out against him. He fired back: "You're just bitter because even if you were the last guy on earth, Shay would never sleep with you. Plus, everybody knows I'm going to get the Clay this year."

I wanted to hit him, but I took a deep breath and merely said, "Take that back."

"Whatever," Cash said.

"Fine, whatever," I said, putting the hood of Mom's NYIA sweatshirt up and slouching in my seat, wishing I could disappear completely.

Darby didn't chide us but she did glance back and forth between Cash and me, eyebrow cocked like *are you finished?*, before getting back to the lecture.

English class finished off without further incident, but next I had Special Seminar with Simon. Cash and Shay were also of course in the class. The whole combination seemed inflammatory given the state I was in. Maybe that's specifically why I didn't cut class.

When I walked into Simon's class, he jumped up and came over to my desk. "Kid, I'm so incredibly sorry about everything. I can't even say how sorry. I've made such a mess of things," he said quietly.

"Don't talk to me," I said.

He looked hurt but went obediently back to the front of the room and started lecturing, looking right at me.

"Class," he began, "what is the role of betrayal in art? I ask you this. Can some betrayal be artistically *necessary?*"

I was no longer in the mood for his lectures, especially ones in which he tried to make aesthetic excuses for being a sociopath. I stood up, cutting him off mid-monologue. "I'm done listening to your art advice. Why don't you just admit that you're a fraud who steals other people's work and other people's girlfriends?"

Shay looked surprised. Cash's mouth was hanging open. And now Simon looked furious.

"Well, little lady, you don't have to listen to my advice, but you won't get very far without it," he said.

I saw red. I took the mini-axe from my backpack, and brandished it as I walked up to Simon, well beyond the barrier of politeness, so that I was holding the axe about an inch from his face. "How dare you," I hissed.

"Well, what are you going to do about it?" he asked. It occurred to me that this whole public-fight thing fit into his plan perfectly, forcing me to act, to embrace my inner art monster, and blah blah blah. I didn't care. I moved closer to him, feeling like a feral creature.

I pushed him, gently almost. He pushed me back in what seemed an instinctual way, also tentatively, but I could feel his hands against my ribs. I dropped the little axe, and it hit the floor with a dull *thud* that seemed to echo in the silent classroom. The students were silent. Frozen in place.

I grabbed him by the collar of his expensive shirt and snarled, "You've made a mistake," snapping the rubber band against my wrist, though I didn't really need the extra boost of adrenaline right now.

He looked actually scared, which thrilled me, sent a hot tremor through my body.

I stepped back to get the right distance, wound up, and prepared to bring the full force of my weight, of my disturbing past, of my wretched present, into the swivel that would bring my fist to his face in a swift punch.

And, boy oh boy, was he floored when he saw this. I felt awful, but also something else. Power.

Dad had been an amateur boxer. He went to a gym where he sparred with some friends after he finished up at the auto shop. The first night Mom met Dad, he invited her to come see one of his little matches. She describes the vision of his body in motion as being "revelatory." I had never understood what that meant until I watched my own fist in slow motion floating toward Simon's face. For the first time I understood all that talk of the aesthetic of violence, the power of opposing forces. I didn't want to understand, but I did.

I could hear Cash screaming, "Holy shit, she's gone ape shit. She's going to, like, assault him," in the background. I didn't give two fucks. I understood now that sometimes I didn't have to give, give, give; that I could take. That sometimes it wasn't about being nice. Sometimes to make art, you had to break shit.

Then I felt a coldness run through me, fear that I would end up an asshole like my biological father and not a mensch like my real one. I looked up, instinctively seeking out Shay, my north star even now when I was supposed to be pissed at her. The expression on her face almost floored me. She looked disgusted, like she'd seen inside me and found how ugly and twisted-up and wrong I was in there. Wrenching my gaze away from her, I stopped myself. What was I going to do? Hit Simon? Here in class? In front of everyone? This wasn't the answer. I let my arms fall to my sides.

Simon looked stunned, seeing as he had almost just gotten hit. I watched his mouth opening as if in slow motion. Then the word came out, the one I had somehow expected all along. It was just a matter of when. "Bitch," he said.

We looked at each other. After calling me both a bitch and a cunt, something had broken between us, something that couldn't be fixed.

Shay was the first of my classmates to kick into gear, jumping up to put herself between me and Simon. "Okay, break it up, guys," she said.

Mr. Edison burst in. He was accompanied by Cash, who had apparently run off and summoned him. As always, thank you, Cash.

"Good God," said Mr. Edison, "I can't allow near fist fights here, folks. What were you thinking?" he asked.

When we arrived at his office, Mr. Edison looked back and forth between Simon and me with a more serious look on his face than I had ever seen. In a few seconds, though, his seriousness started to dissolve, and what began as a chortle turned into a full belly laugh, which sounded like a cat choking.

Simon and I looked at each another, willing ourselves not to laugh until there was really no trying anymore, and we were all hysterical.

"A father-daughter skirmish between two brilliant artists at Brooklyn Arts? Yes, I'm in on your little secret, young Dylan. One a darling of the New York art scene and the other destined for it herself, almost coming to fisticuffs during Special Seminar? It's just too marvelous to be believed," said Mr. Edison.

"So, can I go now?" I asked, rising.

"Well now, you may be talented, young Dylan, but you did almost strike a teacher in my school. There will be consequences. Now, let's see. What would be fun?" asked Mr. Edison.

"Fun?" I'd had enough for the day.

"If you two are so intent on a battle, then a battle you shall have," Mr. Edison said.

"Come again?" asked Simon.

"In lieu of doling out what I would say is a very justified punishment, I will use my years as an educator and thus an amateur mediator and analyst—let's not forget that I chair our psychoanalytic workshops—to solve this little problem. So, I think I'd rather have you work out this conflict in an artistic forum. I say we have an art battle. We can stage it when the representative from NYIA comes to interview young Dylan and Cash. Yes, it has come down to just the two of you, as we predicted it would. There needs to be a live art-making activity and I'd say this would do just fine. You and Cash have your own little tensions to work out, and I know Mr. Ambrogio has been schooling you in the dark arts, Dylan. He himself, I'll have you know, was a star of the art battle scene, so I am confident you'll all be well prepared. You, Simon, can be the M.C and you, young Dylan, can battle Cash. I believe that collaborating with each other in this way, in your shared artistic passion, will help you work out whatever is going on between you as father and daughter," said Mr. Edison.

We both looked at him blankly.

"An art battle at a high school, really, Oscar?" Simon said.

"Yes, yes, you know the term battle here is sheerly metaphorical. You'll make some nifty art is all while donning boxing gloves. You know the drill. Now, off with you both. It's time to start preparing for the festivities," Mr. Edison said, and that was the end of the meeting.

As I left Edison's office, Shay was waiting outside.

"Can we talk?" she asked.

After all that had just happened, I wasn't in the mood. "I don't think that's a good idea. But thanks for ignoring me all day," I said, still angry at the world.

Shay sighed. "Do you remember my mom's good advice a few weeks ago at dinner, about defusing the bomb? In that scenario back there, you almost let a bomb blow up the whole school. And in this scenario between the two of us you're doing the same," she said.

"Yes," I said, "I remember her excellent advice about taking a second to clear your mind or whatever, but I wasn't exactly thinking rationally back there in the classroom. I lost it. Hasn't that ever happened to you? And I didn't actually hit him, so maybe your mom's advice sunk in more than you thought."

"Of course it has happened to me, Dylan. You know it has. But almost punching a teacher, your father, in the face? What was that about? That's not you. Me, maybe, but not you. And what ever happened for your love for me? Your trust in me?" she asked.

"What happened to yours?"

When she walked away from me this time, it really did feel like something had exploded.

That night, I climbed up Shay's fire escape and tapped on her window. In the hours since we parted ways at school, I'd had time to think, to calm down. I didn't want to leave things all blown-up. I wanted to fix us. Somehow.

When she cracked the window, looking supremely annoyed, I said, "You're right. We need to talk. I shouldn't have brushed you off today." I thought about apologizing for that, but right now I couldn't make my mouth form the words *I'm sorry*. Shay was the one who should be sorry for canoodling with Simon, and I wanted to hear her say it.

She stared stonily at me, and then closed her shade with an angry *fwump*, leaving me staring at a blocked-off window. She had never done that before; all through my months of peeping-Tom creepiness, the window had stayed uncovered, a beacon. Something was wrong. I kept tapping on the glass until she peeled back the shade a few inches and opened the window even less than last time.

"What the fuck do you want?" she asked.

"We have to talk about what happened with you and *my father*."

"No, we don't," Shay said. But then, after a minute, "Fine, you know what? You're right. We really do. Because you don't seem to get it at all. Come in. Or whatever."

I did. It felt wrong to sit among her special things while I still felt so angry at her. "How could you—with Simon?" I asked.

"How could you think that? I don't even like guys, and you know that. You didn't even give me a chance to explain. You acted like I was some cheap slut. You didn't even check if I was okay or ask what was going on. You were just like some angry, jealous, macho boyfriend," she said.

The words sank in slowly. She didn't sleep with him? She didn't sleep with him. I couldn't convince myself it was true. My mind just kept throwing up images of Shay naked for him like she had been for me, kissing him like she'd kissed me, trading me in for someone more famous, someone with half my genes and a penis.

"I'm sorry," I said, trying out the words. If she was telling the truth, if she hadn't slept with him, then I'd been a huge asshole to her for no reason. "It's been a really hard week for me," I said.

"For you? Do you ever stop thinking about yourself? It's always a hard week for you, Dylan. Always drama. You know what? It was a hard week for me when your father, your fucking biological father, tried to kiss me and I had to run out of there. And then, instead of comforting me, you shunned me. Do you have any idea how that felt? So fuck you. Enjoy hanging out with your ghost dad. You just lost the one living person who ever hung out with you." With that, she slammed her window shut and let the shade fall.

Right before it all closed completely, I tried to say, "I'm so sorry, honey. I'll make it up to you, I swear." I felt bereft, and furious with Simon. I sat on the fire escape grappling with the revised mental image not of Shay cheating on me, but of Simon pushing himself on her. What kind of a "father" does that?

I tried to imagine Dad in that same position, but it was not possible. He wouldn't. He wouldn't have cheated on Mom at all, but he definitely wouldn't have done it with someone half his age, someone his daughter was in love with, someone who didn't even like boys. I stayed out there for a long time, shivering, and finally pulled an emergency blunt out of my pocket to try and get high enough to see Dad. But nothing came. Not even my ghostly father would hang out with me anymore.

No matter how much I smoked, though, I couldn't get away from Shay's point about how selfish, how self-absorbed I'd been. She was right. I'd spent so much time trying to figure out how to come into my own, to stop being uncertain, to blossom artistically, that I'd been a jerk to Shay along the way myself … just like my alive father.

I vowed then and there to make my next artwork a tribute to Shay, a way of properly saying sorry for being an asshole.

I thought back on the conversation we'd had by the bridges about how cool the Bride of Frankenstein was, how she shouldn't have been destroyed, and an idea started to form.

Chapter Twenty-Two

The night before the art battle, Mom came into my room and sat on my bed in that way that told me she had something important to say.

"Bear, I wanted to say …" she swallowed, like the next words were hard. "It's not that I don't want you to pursue your art dreams, to the ends of the earth if that's what you want. It's just that I don't want you to get your heart broken by all of it the way I did."

"But Mom, that's just what you don't get. What would break my heart is not pursuing it to begin with. I'd rather be ripped apart by it, just knowing I tried. And anyway, it's not a decision. It's just the only way for me. Like breathing. Do you see what I'm saying?"

She sighed but then patted my head and said, "I do. And I have something for you."

She walked out of the room for a second and returned holding what I recognized as Dad's boxing gloves. She looked tentative. "I thought we could rig these up with sponges and you could use them for your big day tomorrow?"

I ran over and threw my arms around her, Dad's boxing gloves hanging over my shoulders as we embraced.

"Yes, please," I said.

Amateurs that we were, we got the huge sponges we used for sponge painting when I was little and jimmied them to Dad's gloves with twine, just winding it around until we had the ugliest pair of boxing gloves on the planet. But I adored them.

"Make me proud," Mom said. I felt seen.

On the morning of the battle, I was ready. Mr. Edison had gussied up the gymnasium to resemble a boxing ring meets gallery opening. It was impressive.

Cash wasn't there yet. I tried to picture the ring we had been given as a sacred space, the opening to the temple. I tried to believe we were performing sacred work there.

Mom took out Dad's gloves and helped me lug a vat of paint over to my little area. She gave me a quick hug and then headed over to the bleachers, sitting down in my little cheering section beside Hilda, Darby ... and Shay. Shay didn't so much as look in my direction, but she was wearing my favorite combination—torn fishnets and Doc Martens. How could that not be a message for me, a ray of hope? I made a mental note never to forget this image just in case she never spoke to me again. She moved nimbly up and down the bleachers, saying hi to people before things got started, and then settled back down.

I tried to get through the crowd to say something highly romantic and apologetic, but I got side-checked by Cash, who was blowing Shay kisses as he finally arrived. She rolled her eyes and mimed a yawn.

Cash did a dramatic lap around the room making little air punches, and then shed a robe like he was a prizefighter. The crowd roared, and it was hard to distinguish it from the howl in my head as Simon entered the gym.

Simon was grandstanding too, really feeling his fame. I was only feeling my blood boil. I almost lunged at Simon right then and there. And Simon must have felt it because he jumped back as soon as we locked eyes. I looked over at Shay to calm myself. She was crossing and uncrossing her legs, and I started to wonder if she was doing it on purpose.

For the first time all week she caught my eye, and mouthed to me, "Defuse the bomb." I grinned, feeling something relax in me. *Defuse the bomb.* I could do that. I hoped Shay's advice was proof that she hadn't given up on me entirely, that she still liked me somewhat.

When Simon caught sight of Mom, he did a dramatic bow thing.

She crossed her arms and gave him her siren look—and not like a hot lady, but the one whose song can cause you to hurl yourself headfirst into the sea. Simon shriveled a little under her rage and hung his head. As it should be.

Shay gave him the finger, and he did the bow thing again. Now I was sure I would kill him. If I did, he'd probably keep doing the bow thing.

I tried to make my way to Shay again, but Malcolm got in the way, saying he wanted to interview Cash and me for the school paper.

"So, Cash, how does it feel to be participating in an innovative art event for Brooklyn Arts, emceed by the famous Simon Ambrogio?" he asked.

"It feels great, Malcolm. There's such a rich history to this sort of action art, Ushio Shinohara and so forth," Cash said.

Malcolm scribbled that down and then turned to me to inquire, "And, um, Dylan, how did you choose that particular outfit to wear?"

I looked down at my simple NYIA sweatshirt and jeans, processing how he'd asked Cash about his art and me about my outfit.

And then I was out of time to talk to Shay. Simon was approaching the mic to announce the festivities, doing the bowing thing yet again.

"Welcome to our art battle extravaganza," he began. "Though our little event today is called a battle, at its core this exercise is meant to be a coming together, not a tearing apart." He looked right at me here. He smiled at me beatifically and continued, "This is what I believe Mr. Edison had in mind when he organized this ritual. A coming together of painted glove and canvas, of violent sport and art, of the artists involved, the emcee, as well as the audience, I would imagine. So, without further ado, let's make something amazing!" His speech was so corny, I was embarrassed for him.

He then took his position off to the side. He put on Wagner's "Ride of the Valkyries." The woman defusing a bomb *needs to take an extra second to clear her mind and be calm or else she'll just blow the whole place up.*

So, I took a moment to clear my mind. As the whole gym waited for us to begin, I just stood there, meditating on this moment in time, all the other moments that had to come before to get to this one, and how they had all stitched together into right now: this art battle. When I turned around, I felt I had become Cash's worst nightmare: a confident woman. I snapped Simon's rubber band and went forth.

Simon said, "Ready, set, go," as if we were two grade school kids in a potato sack race. And the battle began.

Cash was pummeling his canvas and I started out doing the same. Simon looked so proud. But then I reassessed. Was this really how I wanted to do this?

I took a breath, looked at Shay, and remembered what Mom had said at the hospital the night Dad died. She'd said it all came down to love and the little moments. I blew Shay a kiss and calmed myself down.

Next, I dipped my gloves in the paint and spun around, coming at the canvas from different angles. And then something sublime happened. I thought of Dr. Frankenstein's "workshop of filthy creation," and I let it rip, punching harder and faster than I ever thought possible. My limbs changing into pistons, glistening with sweat.

I was stunned at how good it felt to be committing this odd exercise. I threw myself down on the canvas on the floor and started using my whole body as a paintbrush.

Finally, when Simon sounded the bell that indicated we were done, I turned to the audience, in victory mode, prepared to accept my winnings, but the interviewer from NYIA, whom Simon had introduced as Delphine Alderman, was staring with wonder not at my work but at Cash's.

When I stepped back to look at what I'd made, it was a landscape of muddied sameness, a child's paintbox mixed to make brown. It was, in short, the ugliest and most mediocre painting I could have imagined.

Cash's creation, on the other hand, was multidimensional with secrets hidden in every crevice, a whole world come to life. As I peered at the canvas, I could see that, though Cash's movements had looked haphazard, he'd organized his punches in rows so that, with their florid tops and paint dripping down in lovely lines, the punches resembled a garden of exploding flowers.

But as I stepped back, the piece grew into something larger and weightier, a historical commentary on violence that was about more than mere explosive flora. From that vantage point, Cash's work resembled the mushroom cloud over Nagasaki or something, telegraphing the wonder and horror that is any ferocious happening.

This art battle was supposed to be about settling something between Simon and me. I'd barely remembered to think about my actual competitor. Cash was a good artist, and he deserved the win. Simon gave me an unreadable look, almost pitying, before turning to address the crowd. "Well, I think we have a clear winner here, folks," he announced.

"Are you fucking kidding me?" Shay screamed, storming out of the gym.

I ran after her, looking back to see Mom running after me, and Simon running after Mom like some bizarre game of family bumper cars.

We all gathered in the hall outside.

"How can you talk about your own daughter's work like that?" Shay demanded of Simon.

"And how could you assault Shay, you fucker?" I demanded.

"Yeah," Shay said.

"Listen, you're right," Simon said, holding up his hands in surrender, "I should have respected that this was your paramour, Dylan. Not to mention that I took liberties with young Shay, and I sincerely apologize for that. I misread her looking up to me as an artist for sexual interest, and I feel awful about it. I really am a feminist and I truly desire no relation that isn't consensual."

Shay rolled her eyes. "There's nothing more dangerous than the man who thinks he's a nice guy," she said.

Simon ignored this. "I am also sorry if I was rude in the way I announced the winner. And, while I'm handing out apologies, I was profoundly wrong to photograph both your burning works, ladies," he gave Mom and me an imploring look. Mom was looking at me with concern and didn't even seem to register what he was saying. She wasn't going to give him the time of day.

"You're right," I said, "You had no right to destroy my painting."

I very carefully didn't think about how it had actually looked better singed, just in case Simon had secret mind-reading powers. "How could you do that to someone again?" I asked him.

"Again?" He looked puzzled.

"Yes, after you burned Mom's dollhouse," I said.

I looked over at her, expecting an "Amen" from her, but she was looking down. What was going on?

"I never burned her dollhouse. I photographed it once it was burning, which I regret since it hurt her so, but I didn't burn it," he said.

"Well then who did?" I asked.

"I did," Mom said quietly.

"What? All this time that you said my burning my work reminded you of someone, but it was—"

"Yes, it was me," she said.

"But why did you do it?" I asked.

"Well, why do you do it?" she asked.

"I don't know exactly," I said.

"Neither do I," she said. "But, look, regardless of why we do it, I don't want to see you destroying your artwork as I did. I also never want to see you give up on yourself as an artist."

"Mom," I said, feeling the words out carefully, "I would never do that. I may not fully understand why I burn my art but, minus the times I've made something bad and just really wanted to get rid of it, I know I do it to make something new, something different, to transform the material, not destroy it."

She looked thoughtful at that. "For me, it was definitely about destruction. In that moment, I was so full of guilt about what happened with Simon. I felt like I'd torched my own life, and I hated my own art, and myself as an artist. I was punishing myself. Maybe I've been projecting that onto you. I'm glad you believe in yourself, much more than I ever did," she said, proudly petting my head.

Shay turned and walked off while Mom and I were talking, and I felt a sinking feeling.

"Yeah, I do, Mom. Don't sound so surprised. Look, I'll see you at home. I need to take a walk and clear my head," I said.

"Sure, I'll see you at home. I'll go grab your gloves and paints," Mom said.

"Thanks, Mom. I appreciate it," I said.

"Oh, okay, well, keep in touch, ladies," said Simon weakly.

Mom ignored him and walked back into the gym.

"Uh, yeah, whatever," I said, steering toward the door.

That whole time Mom had been making me feel bad about my fires, it was really about her, about how she didn't want my future to look like her present. The whole time she thought she understood me, but she didn't. After my little walk, my head still didn't feel clear.

Whenever I was mad at Mom as a child, I'd threaten to run away. I'd pack a little bag but always stop before I even made it to the door. A few weeks ago, I'd really managed to run away, but I'd ended up somewhere more toxic, and even then I'd felt tethered to Mom, until finally I bounced back. This time, I wasn't running away, I was running toward a new set of plans.

That night I grabbed my backpack, threw in my mini-axe, monster mask, some charcoal and paper just in case the mood struck, and my copy of *Frankenstein*. Then I poured some of the ash from Dad's urn into a Ziploc bag, saying, "Sorry for the baggie, Dad." It upset me that Mom hadn't listened to his final wish to have his ashes scattered in the junkyard he loved, and I was determined to rectify this. At the junkyard, I also planned on starting my real love letter to Shay.

I dialed Wally's number. It rang a bunch of times, and I was worried he wouldn't pick up.

"Hullo?" he said.

"Hi, Wal, it's Dylan. I'm sorry I haven't been in touch since—"

"You broke into my apartment and accused me of being your father?" he asked, but warmly.

"Yeah, that."

"Well, I've missed you, kid. I didn't want to intrude if you needed space, but I'm glad to hear from you. What can I do you for?"

"Can you meet me at the yard tonight with tools? I have a special project in mind."

The reason I loved Wally was that he asked no questions but merely said, "Sure thing. What time?"

But as I left, the errand of delivering Dad to his final resting place was far too depressing. I passed the beautifully tended rose gardens in front of my neighbors' apartments, and then turned onto McDonald Avenue. I walked along the edge of Greenwood Cemetery like one of its spooks. I was mourning not death but life's determination, how it just kept coming at me no matter how many doors I slammed in its face.

"I'm going to get drunk," I said to nobody in particular.

I stopped to stare through the gate of the cemetery that separated me from the dead. A particularly ornate gravestone for "Emily, Cherished Daughter" caught my eye, and I found myself addressing it, at first shyly, and then loudly, like an old friend.

"Help me. Get me through this. What is this? Who am I, and why does it hurt so much to be her? Do other people hurt like this? Is there a cure? I'll figure it out, but first I need a drink."

I had decided for sure to get wrecked. And I knew just the place for it. I dashed toward the subway, pulled my monster mask on, and got on the F train. As I emerged from that shifting netherworld, I shuffled along, feeling myself unraveling onto the sidewalk.

I continued on my way, half out of my mind, to Gorgon, a bar Shay had told me always served without carding. It was a real dive. The second "O" on the sign had fallen below the rest of the letters and nobody had bothered to fix it. Someone must have broken one of its windows at some point because it was now boarded up, with a frayed, yellow paper sign tacked to it reading, "Come in! We're open!"

I'd never gone to a bar by myself. I stood outside for about five minutes, pushing the door open, thinking better of it, retreating, pushing the door open again, retreating. Finally, I went inside.

The black barstools were patched with silver duct tape. There was one guy passed out with his head on the bar with someone's old gum next to him on a napkin.

I sat a few seats down from the drunk guy, just in case he woke up in a fighting mood, and bellowed something from an old-time film, like, "Over here, barkeep," to the bartender who was lingering too long on a blonde lady. The bar stool I'd chosen was greasy and littered with someone else's nut shells, but I didn't bother getting up. I was too busy eating my own bar nuts. Being there was a good thing, I told myself.

When the bartender came over, I tried to think what I'd seen in movies, and said, "Make it a whiskey. Johnny Walker. Double."

I sat holding the drink for what felt like forever. I succumbed. The blazing liquid hitting my lips delivered a rush of pleasure that was almost ghastly. At first, I went slowly, savoring, teasing myself. But then I went faster. I believe I moaned as I guzzled the whiskey. I'd give up everything except this barstool and this glass of liquid fire.

Since I didn't really drink, it didn't take much to get shit-faced. The bartender offered to call me a car twice. The first time was the only one I was clear on.

He stayed out of it after that until I broke my second shot glass. Then he simply said, "Out!" and went back to talking up the blonde.

I teetered off the bar stool because I had to make good on my plan. But then I felt a familiar pair of steadying hands. Shay.

I won't lie. She'd been the one to tell me about the place, and I'd gone there hoping to see her. But it still felt like magic to have her appear right when I needed her most.

"I thought you were mad at me," I slurred.

"I am. That's why I came here to drink, but then there you were, and so pitiful," she said. "But, Dylan, I'm still mad."

"I know. I can't believe I ever thought you would sleep with Simon. I can't tell you how sorry I am." She slung my arm over her shoulder until I figured out how to walk on my own, and then by mutual silent agreement we headed toward the river where we'd first kissed. It was only a few blocks away.

"I'm sorry enough to do anything. Let me prove it," I said.

"Anything?" she asked. "Just how sorry are you?"

"Anything. The sorriest," I said.

"Sorry enough to jump in the river?"

"Not this again. Are you serious?"

"I am," she said.

"Okay. I'll do it. I'll do anything," I said.

We arrived at the same place as last time, and I attempted to climb up onto the rail, but just fell to the ground with a gross sound.

"Wait, Dylan. Are you kidding me? I was just fucking with you. Oh God, are you okay?" she asked, helping me up.

I was so relieved. "Phew. Dodged a bullet there. I'm fine. That was just my brains coming out, ha-ha," I said.

She looked concerned. "You were going to do it though, weren't you?"

"I was."

"Aww," she said. Then she kissed me, right where I could see both bridges.

"Are you still mad at me?" I asked.

"Yeah, but it means something to see that you were willing to do that for me. It helps," she said.

"I have a plan to win you back," I said.

"Your breath smells terrible, Dylan. It's like something died in there. Go home and take a break," she said.

"Okay, but does this mean I still have a shot with you?" I asked.

"Yes, as long as you stop breathing in my face, good God, woman," she said.

"Ha-ha, okay," I said, still planning a comeback.

Chapter Twenty-Three

Shay had told me to go home and take a break, and that was probably a good idea, but I was determined to complete my junkyard odyssey, and Wally would be waiting. The yard where my father used to take me was in Gowanus. It wasn't close, but I figured the half-hour walk would help sober me up a little. As I passed the Gowanus Canal, I saluted its filth, which, along with my shaky footwork, was just one more indication that I was still sauced.

But when I got there and took out my Ziploc baggie with Dad inside, I lost my nerve. I wasn't ready to let him go. I took out my copy of *Frankenstein* and placed the baggie at the end of the book for safekeeping. I couldn't imagine a better place for Dad.

It was the edition Mom had read to me from as a kid, and the same one I'd toted to Darby's lectures. It was the one Bernie Wrightson had illustrated. On its cover it featured the angry creature—at once veiny and skeletal—confronting his maker in the infamous lab.

Dr. Frankenstein looks strangely resigned, calm even, as his creation grabs him. Dr. Frankenstein's hand on the arm of the furious monster he's created appears almost like a caress, or the way you might hold a child who's having a tantrum.

I still felt drunk, yes, but also ready to make something. The impulse reminded me of something I'd underlined in the book when I read it for class. I read aloud to all those wrecked vehicles in the scrapyard: *Then a resistless, and almost frantic, impulse, urged me forward; I seemed to have lost all soul or sensation but for this one pursuit.... I collected bones from charnel-houses and disturbed, with profane fingers, the tremendous secrets of the human frame.... I kept my workshop of filthy creation.*

I had longed for that untamed space of ultimate generation, that *workshop of filthy creation*, for as long as I could remember. Now, shitfaced in this junkyard, it was time to bring it to earth. I attempted to get to work, awestruck by Mary Shelley's ravishing act of putting into words the savage exuberance of artmaking in *Frankenstein*. But I was too shaky on my feet to make much of anything.

As I was swaying near a carburetor and trying to figure out what to do next, someone tapped me on the shoulder. I was sure the ghost of my father had finally worked up the courage to become real. I spun around, yelling, "Papa!"

Instead, I found myself face-to-face with Wally.

"Dylan," he said, looking surprised to find me babbling to myself, clearly inebriated. Luckily, Wally was a supremely kind man and didn't say anything about it.

Instead, he merely asked, "How have you and your mom been holding up?" while patting me on the shoulder with his bear paw of a hand, his deep, sunken eyes set on me. I felt more healed by his ministering than I had by all the psychologists Mom had sent me to over the years. I felt sorry that I'd been avoiding him, but it was hard to come back from being caught holding a man's boxers.

"We're doing great," I said. It sounded so phony and ridiculous given the state in which he'd found me. "But we've missed you terribly," I added, hugging him.

But, see, this man understood what I really needed, and so he stopped the hug abruptly and said, "I got your tools in the truck."

"Yes, thank you. I'll be needing those," I said.

He stopped making eye contact for the next part, "But you're not touching the tools until you've had a nap and some strong coffee from my thermos. Sober you right up," he said, and I agreed, following him to his truck to lie down in the back.

Once I'd rested up and had some coffee, I got my cutting torch and welding mask, and went to work. Wally had made fun of my dad for wearing this mask, which I always pointed out made him look like Hephaestus or something, instead of the goggles most of the guys wore when they used the torch. Dad was never supposed to let me use the torches, but he always did. It was our secret. I loved the sparks best.

"You sure you're good to work that thing now?" Wally asked.

"I'm good, Wally," I said, convincing neither of us.

"Cause your mom will kill me if I let you barbeque yourself."

"Yeah, yeah, I know."

The best possible monument to Shay, to Mom, to my father—who was more of an artist than Simon would ever be—would be made in this junkyard, not in some studio featured in art history textbooks. I was my father's child in ways that went beyond blood.

I stayed up all night, with Wally's help—his soft spot for my father, his brawn, his skill, his lanterns, his thermos of coffee. I started to build, shakily, drunkenly, my own large-scale Bride of Frankenstein out of discarded auto parts in the car graveyard my dad had so loved.

When I got home that morning, Mom was sitting at the kitchen table, looking piping mad.

"I was worried out of my mind. I was this close to calling the cops but then Wally texted me," she said, pounding her fist on the table.

"I'm so sorry, Mom. I wasn't thinking. But I can't even tell you what a breakthrough I've had. We're working on a Bride of Frankenstein piece, and I've never felt more alive," I said, hung over, sleepless, soon to crash, but still high on the whole thing.

I could see her visibly soften as she took in my elation.

"I am happy to hear that, but you give me a call next time, young lady, do you hear me?"

"Yes, ma'am," I said.

"Now, when can I see this Bride?" she asked, and I knew she was sold.

I took Mom to see what I'd been up to the next afternoon after classes ended.

When we got there, she circled the piece like a shark. Her face so full of emotion I couldn't read that I became worried she hated it.

Then all she said was, "May I tell Mr. Edison about this?"

I took the fact that she wanted to show it to anyone as a good sign.

"I guess," I said, not sure why she'd want to talk to him about me at this point. After the public humiliation of the art battle, I'd been keeping my head down at school as much as I could.

Mr. Edison actually came by the junkyard the very next day after class. He was wearing something that looked like a top hat and had brought a walking stick with an eagle's head knob. "Greetings, young Dylan. What have we here?" he asked. When he saw me looking at his stick, he said, "I wasn't sure how rough this terrain would be."

He circled my near-finished assemblage for a full ten minutes. Then he asked only, "You will still be here later this afternoon and into the evening?"

"Yeah. Why?" I asked.

"I'll return. Don't, under any circumstances, leave," was all he said.

"Uh, sure," I said, thinking he'd lost his mind. Or never really had it to begin with.

He came back with the same woman who'd come for the battle. He said, "You remember Delphine Alderman? She's an old friend who, as you know, performs interviews for the Clay scholarship and is on the committee. Would it be okay if she took a look around?"

I was floored. "Yes, of course," I said. "But I don't want any favors, Mr. Edison. Cash earned his win fair and square."

"It's not a matter of taking away. It's a matter of adding," said Ms. Alderman.

"Yes, I called Delphine right away because she'd mentioned there might be extra money this year from a new donor. I told her she had to speak to the Clay Committee about adding a second scholarship. They haven't done so since 2010, but I told her I was sure that once they saw this work, they would consider doing so again."

"Look at these chances you took, Dylan. It's haunting stuff," said Ms. Alderman.

A week later, I tried to talk to Shay, but she was still stiff with me; neither of us really knowing how to talk to each other since that night by the river. But she'd agreed to give me a chance to win her back, and the previous afternoon I'd finally finished my grand gesture in the hopes of doing just that.

I wrote the Gowanus address on a slip of paper and passed it to her during English class. It said, "Meet me here at 5. You won't be sorry."

After school I went home to change before, hopefully, seeing Shay. I prayed she would come. When I opened the door, Mom was standing there with a letter in her hand, a big one. We ripped it open, and I read it out loud: "Dear Dylan Ann Cyllene, we are delighted to inform you that you have been accepted into the Marissa M. Clay Scholarship Program for the New York Institute of the Arts. You will be provided with housing and a meal plan should you opt in. We look forward to seeing you soon for our Meet and Greet on August 20. Welcome to the Clay family." And just like that, my long-held wish was granted, at the last minute, as an add-on, ungracefully, as most miracles happen.

I saw Shay from afar as I was adding a few last flourishes to the piece, which I must admit I was pretty happy with. She walked up slowly with her hand over her mouth, looking very emotional. Then she squealed.

At first, I was worried I'd upset her, but when she took her hand away, I could see she had a huge smile on her face.

"The Bride! Alive! I love her so much," she said, running to give me a hug that almost toppled me.

"It's a love letter for you," I said.

"It's amazing," she said.

"So … am I forgiven?" I asked sheepishly.

"Look, Dylan, there's a lot to talk about, and I'm guessing you feel the same way."

"Oh, yeah, okay," I said.

She was being nice about it, but she was still breaking up with me.

But then she surprised me by saying, "But I'm here for it. I'm willing to do the work."

"So am I. I really am. You have no idea how ready I am," I said, thrilled.

"So, yes, there is all that, and it will happen, and we will have to wade through the different stages of reconciliation," she said, looking a bit weary.

"Yes to all of that, but is there any way I could kiss you right now? Even if you never want to talk to me ever again?" I asked, kicking some scrap metal out of the way so I could inch closer to her.

She moved close enough that I could see those freckles of hers, and said, "I think that can be arranged, on a purely trial basis."

She kissed me with too much tongue, and I took that as a very good sign of things to come.

As it got dark, she pulled me into a totaled car, and we made up ghost stories together. We returned to that wonder-filled space of childhood. At one point, she said, "Turn over," and I obeyed, expecting something kinky. But, instead, she pulled up my shirt and then fluttered her fingers over my back, roaring softly and saying, "Nobody will ever hurt you, Dylan, not with all these tiny monsters here to protect you."

We made a fire in the pit Wally and I had set up, theoretically so we could grill stuff on nights we worked late, but mostly because he knew how much I loved a good conflagration. Shay and I roasted the marshmallows I'd brought with this moment in mind, pulling out the hot gooey centers, crunching on the black roasted outsides.

The Bride may have been ugly to most, but Shay and I thought she was the most ravishing thing we'd ever seen. She had huge metallic hubcap eyes, battery cable Medusa hair, and a taillight heart that Mom and I had rigged up to shine at night when we clicked it on.

But, and this most of all, I'd made it so the Bride was an artist herself—creator, not merely created. In fact, she was in the process of sculpting a smaller version of a new woman monster, also out of car parts. This was the part of the artwork that, to me, felt immense. Our Bride was a fucking art monster.

As I had worked on the Bride, I'd tried to construct an image that would correct her story from *Frankenstein*. The finished piece was a tableau of power in which the female monster breaks through her chains, smashes all enclosures.

I thought of all the girls who live their whole lives trapped inside pretty little boxes. I imagined picking them up, taking them out, freeing them to run beyond enclosure or definition, to create, to explore their own wild spaces.

Shay squeezed my hand as we clicked on the Bride's taillight heart. It illuminated our watching faces. She took out her camera and shot the Bride from all angles, with a look of amazement.

She said, "This is the best present I've ever gotten in my life." And it wasn't just a present for Shay. It was a present for me, for Dad, for Mom.

While Shay took photos, I held the Bride's windshield wiper hand. I rolled a joint, passed it to Shay, took it back, and then placed it in the Bride's fuel filter mouth, holding it there so she had time to take her own puff but not too close to start an actual fire. The Bride had always drawn the short stick and I wanted to correct for that, spoil her real good.

Mom finally arrived, hugging Shay and me, having some marshmallows, declining the weed with a prim look.

The time finally seemed right.

"I'm ready," I said.

Shay and Mom put their arms around me as I took the small plastic bag filled with Dad's ashes out from the last page of *Frankenstein*. I hadn't taken it out of my backpack since the night I started making my Bride.

I recited that astonishing quote from Mary Oliver, as Mom had the night Dad died: "To live in this world you must be able to do three things: to love what is mortal; to hold it against your bones knowing your own life depends on it; and, when the time comes to let it go, to let it go."

It was hard to hear those words without getting misty-eyed, and we all stood there for a moment just feeling our feelings.

Then I opened the bag carefully into the earth right in front of the Bride. I smiled, feeling this was the right place for Dad. I imagined the Bride liked having him there too, that if she could smile or laugh, right now she would.

As I smoked, Dad floated in the plumes, and though I knew he was present only in my imagining, a product of my own wild longing, I was so glad to see that he finally looked at peace.

That day was the last time I saw his ghost. I was glad I got the chance to introduce the Bride to my dad before he left for the final time. I reached out to embrace the puffs of smoke that configured him, but he was already gone.

I said to the Bride, my *filthy creation*, "I'll always take care of you," and Shay and Mom laughed, but I was dead serious. I intended to love the Bride the way Dr. Frankenstein never did in the book. This Bride had been stifled long enough, destroyed and abandoned by her past maker, and that's something that really sticks with a girl.

I told the Bride, "You are wanted, and you are loved. You are my greatest creation." And I did love her, so very much. She was my tribute to Dad, and my love letter to Shay, Darby, Mom, and to all the girls and women who had ever been told they were too much.

Acknowledgments

I want to thank my brilliant editor, Marc Vincenz, and Mad Hat Press for making this book possible. Thanks to Al Zuckerman, Kate McKean, and Nora Long for providing their literary wisdom. Thanks to James Tate Hill, Sharon Mesmer, Erika Wurth, and Melissa Ostrom for reading and supporting early versions of this book. Thanks to my friends, parents, and in-laws for reading early versions of this book, loving it, and still loving me. Thanks to Adriel, Max, and Layla for their love and support, and to Max for being my writing buddy as I wrote this book. Thanks to all my beloved art monsters.

About the Author

CAROLINE HAGOOD is an Assistant Professor of Literature, Writing and Publishing and Director of Undergraduate Writing at St. Francis College in Brooklyn. She is the author of two poetry books, the novel *Ghosts of America*, and the book-length essays *Ways of Looking at a Woman* and *Weird Girls: Writing the Art Monster*.

CPSIA information can be obtained
at www.ICGtesting.com
Printed in the USA
JSHW020846020423
39770JS00003B/13